TANGLED WEBS
VALERIAN'S COVE
BOOK V

H.C. DE COSSY

SpiritThroughout Publishing and Artistry

S hari-Beth Meyer-Casey closed her book with a sigh. She couldn't focus, which was disappointing because she'd been looking forward to this latest installment of her current favorite detective series. But after re-reading the same page twice and still not absorbing what she'd read, it was time to quit. For now.

It was a sunny day in Valerian's Cove in mid-July. Shari-Beth and her friends, Josh, Emma, and Aidan, were all going to be seniors at the Academy this year. With the Academy expanding to the University level, they wouldn't have to leave home to continue their studies unless they wanted to. Shari-Beth loved to travel—she'd spent the first month out of school in France at her grandfather Luc Benoit's Familiar Center and loved every minute of it. Maybe it was being a Falcon Shifter, but Shari-Beth always had the urge to spread her wings and fly. She knew her parents, Celine and Brendan Casey, supported her, whatever she chose.

Shari-Beth had been curled up on the window seat in her room instead of outdoors, enjoying the sunshine. She had wanted to hide away and read for a while. Sometimes, some alone time was a good thing. She glanced out the window at the clear blue sky spreading over the Casey's land and the paranormal town of Valerian's Cove. A cool breeze off the ocean wafted in through the window, stirring the delicate white curtains. Shari-Beth could smell the salt on the breeze.

Setting the book on the window seat, Shari-Beth stood and stretched. She was working at her sister Malia's shop, Wonder, for the rest of the summer. Today was her day off. Maybe she'd go down to the Cove and see if any of the Sea Fae were around. There was one, Alan, that was kind of cute. Of course, a relationship with a Sea Fae would never work out. As a Falcon Shifter, Shari would have to live on land. And no Sea Fae could stay out of the water for long. There were some who had managed, living close to the water so they could go in whenever they wanted, but it was hard on their mates, who couldn't experience that part of their lives. Magic could make it possible to go under for a short time, but land-dwellers couldn't live there. It would take a very special land-dweller to be a mate to a Sea Fae and make the relationship work. The person would have to enjoy being on their own for long periods at a time.

Shari shook her head again. Even if she couldn't have an actual relationship with Alan, he was nice to look at and a good person, too. The Sea Fae at the Academy all were. They were there to support Sinéad, the next Seer. Most were training as Guards to protect her. Jed's mate, Claire, from Fairweather Falls in Maine, was training as the group's Healer. She would be attending her senior year of high school at the new Academy in Fairweather Falls before joining the rest of the Sea Fae here in Valerian's Cove for University. Claire would be studying in the new joint program with the San Francisco Healer's College. Claire was only a quarter Sea Fae. The rest of her heritage was powerful Earth Witch. Claire's mother had bound her Sea Fae side to protect her when Claire was young, and Claire was only now discovering what she could do. She could breathe underwater and survive deep within the depths of the sea. Claire wasn't able to shift into Merfolk form, though. At least, she hadn't, yet.

Shari-Beth's best friend, Emma, a Swan Maiden, was away for the summer, visiting her family in Sweden. Aidan, a Sparrow Shifter, was in town but spent most of his time training with Declan, the Fight Instructor at the Academy. Luc Benoit had told the tiny teen that he would make a fabulous spy and assassin because no one would suspect him. At barely five feet tall and slender, most people mistook him for a child. It helped that Aiden was as mischievous as a Pixie, with an enthusiasm for life that many saw as being childish as well. Aidan had taken Guardian Benoit's words to heart and had begged Declan to give him extra training. The Dragon had readily agreed.

Shari-Beth ran down the stairs to the kitchen, finding Celine preparing food for lunch. Shari-Beth sniffed appreciatively. Mmmm, sugar cookies. The twins must be coming over.

"Mom, I'm going into town. I can't seem to focus on my book. I want to see if the Sea Fae are around. I'll be home for dinner, ok?"

Celine looked up from the fresh bread she was slicing for sandwiches. She smiled at her youngest daughter.

"That's fine, sweetheart. When does Emma come home again?"

"Next week. And Kelly, too. She and Christopher went home to see their friends."

"And Aidan's still obsessed with becoming a fine-tuned weapon, I suppose." Celine sighed, her breath lifting the stray curl that had fallen across her face from the formerly neat chignon at the back of her head. Sometimes, she thought it had not been wise of her grandfather to tell the boy that he would make a good spy one day. The young man now thought of nothing else.

"Have fun, sweetheart. Bring the kids home for dinner if you find them. Josh should be getting off work at five. Bring him too. It's been at least a week since he's been here. He must need fattening up." Celine smiled again.

Shari-Beth grinned back, then waved as she flew out the door, still in human form. Running down the front porch steps, she stopped for a moment, deciding between getting her bike out of the shed or flying. She shrugged, and suddenly, a beautiful Peregrin falcon was soaring up into the sky.

🐉

REBECCA CASEY WAS TWENTY-ONE, OWNED HER OWN HIGHLY successful jewelry design business, played a mean fiddle, and was an accomplished Witch. She was a Fire Mage with a robust second Gift in

Earth. The Fire magic was from her mother's family. Rebecca barely remembered her mother. She had passed away when Rebecca was very young. Her father, Tom Casey, had raised her while running the Seattle branch of Casey Nurseries after taking over from his parents when they had left to go home to Ireland.

Rebecca sat at her work table in her studio at the back of the house, working on a new necklace design. Only, the design wasn't cooperating. She could visualize it, but it didn't look right when she tried to commit it to paper. Rebecca had tried everything she could think of—different scrollwork, knotwork, jewels. Nothing looked right. Usually, when she had a piece in mind, getting the design on paper was easy. This one just refused to cooperate.

Rebecca dropped her pencil on the table and ran her hands through her long, curly brown hair.

That's it. I give up for today, Rebecca thought to herself. She was feeling frustrated and out-of-sorts. Maybe working in the greenhouse with her father for a bit would help.

Rebecca locked the door to her studio and reset the wards on the room. She used precious metals and gems in her work, so she always protected the room with the most potent wards she could make. So far, they'd worked beautifully.

When Rebecca arrived, Tom Casey was in the shop at the Seattle branch of Casey Nurseries.

"All right, love?" He asked as his daughter entered the shop. He'd seen that mulish, frustrated expression on her face quite often lately. He suspected it had less to do with unfinished designs and more to do with a certain Dragon prince who just happened to be his daughter's fated mate. The young Dragon was determined to stay away until Rebecca was 'old enough.' To be sure, Rebecca had only been eighteen when they'd met. Way too young to complete the bond, in Tom's opinion. Even so, staying away from her completely wasn't helping matters any, either.

"I'm fine, Da. I just can't seem to get this new design to work, and I need to bring Malia more stuff by the end of this week. She's selling through my pieces faster than I can even believe."

"Well, that's good, though, isn't it?" Tom asked his daughter.

"Of course it is, but it means I have to work hard to keep making enough pieces to supply Wonder and here. And this new piece refuses to come together."

"Maybe give it a rest for a while, and try something new?"

"That's why I'm here. I thought maybe working here with you for a while would help and take my mind off it for a bit, doing something completely different."

"You're welcome, of course, Sweetheart," Tom said. His daughter's Earth Gifts extended more to metals than to plants.

"Would you maybe think of designing a few more pot holders and window box holders for the new Fae plants, instead, for a while? For here? Maybe Brendan could sell them in Valerian's Cove as well. Those have always gone over well."

"I guess I could do that. I still have to come up with the jewelry for Malia, though. But I guess I could make a few pot holders for you first."

"That would be lovely. Thanks, love," Tom replied. He could see Becca's mind already turning over new designs.

"Listen, love; I was thinking we'd go to the Cove this weekend for dinner one night, anyway. What do you say we go down Friday and stay a few days? You could spend some more time with your cousins. We could come home on Sunday night. What do you say?"

"Sure, Da, that would be fun. It's been a while since I've seen Shari —she just got back from France. I want to hear about her time at the Familiar Center there. I know she's looking forward to establishing one in Valerian's Cove."

"Good. I'll let Brendan and Celine know then. Now, come on. I've got some starts that need repotting in the back. You can help me with that until you're ready to get started on the stands for the pots."

2

Sean Drake grunted as he landed on his back.

"What's wrong with you, cousin? You just got taken out by a Sparrow Shifter. Are you feeling ok?" Declan Muiran, Fight Instructor for the Valerian's Cove Academy, Dragon Guard of the Fire Mountain Clan, asked.

The Dragon prince lay on his back, staring up at the sky. He should have been mad at himself for allowing Aidan to get the best of him, but he wasn't. Sean was actually proud of the spunky young man. Aidan didn't let the fact that he was essentially a prey species get in the way of his fighting skills. The young man in question stood off to the side, looking very pleased with himself.

"Aidan, you did well, friend," Sean said. "I apologize. I'm having a hard time focusing today."

"Are you thinking about Rebecca again?" Aidan asked. Aidan being one of Shari-Beth's best friends, he was, of course, aware of all the family's secrets. And everyone now knew that Rebecca was Sean's fated mate.

Sean looked over at the Sparrow Shifter, glaring at him. He didn't deny it, though. It was getting harder and harder to stay away from Rebecca. He had taken assignments for the Guardians that kept him out of Valerian's Cove—even off the West Coast, as much as possible and thrown himself into his job as assistant Fight Instructor. Nothing helped.

"Cousin, you have to sort this out. I know she's young, but you're about the same age in Dragon years. You're fated mates. It's not like she needs to date around, then choose you. It's the same for her, now, you know. She knows who you are. She won't even be able to seriously look at another person as a potential date. She knows she'll have to come back to you, eventually. She's smart and beautiful and an amazing artist. What are you waiting for?"

Sean hefted himself to his feet, glaring at both Aidan and his older cousin.

"Look, it's not the right time yet, ok? We both need more life experience before we settle down."

Declan took a good, hard look at his cousin.

"Sean, you are the prince of the Fire Mountain Clan. You are a full-on, fully-trained Dragon Guard. You have a good job here at the Academy. You have a family and friends who love you. Anyone would be happy to have you. And Fate chose for you two to be together. You don't have to prove anything to her. Or are you trying to prove something to yourself?"

Sean rubbed his hands over his hair in frustration.

"Look, Dex. You're the head instructor here. You're a Dragon Guard and well-respected in your own right. You earned it; you weren't born to it. I haven't done anything to get where I am besides being born a prince. I just feel like I have to do something, earn my place in the world. I have to make something of myself, so she'll be proud of me. So *I* can be proud of myself."

"Sean, you have earned your place here. I wouldn't have kept you as my assistant if you hadn't. I had to argue with Aunt Aldona for you to stay, you know. She wanted to bring you home, assign you somewhere closer. She knew Devra would stay here as long as Donnie was teaching at the Academy and wanted at least one of her children to be based closer to home. Teaching these kids is an important job. I would never have argued to keep you if you hadn't earned it."

"Thanks, I guess, Dex. I don't know. I just don't feel like I've found myself yet. I don't know what I have to offer her, or anyone, really."

Declan looked hard at his younger cousin again, then shook his head. "Well, I'm certainly not going to be able to convince you otherwise. Still, I think you need to get to know Rebecca better. You're going to come together, eventually. She has family here. Maybe she can come to stay for a while, and you two can spend some time together. You never know; maybe she can help you figure out what you want to do with your life."

Sean shrugged and drained a bottle of water.

"So, are we done here for today? I'm getting hungry. I was thinking of heading over to Celine's for dinner. It's been a few days since we've eaten there, and I miss her cooking."

Declan grinned. "My plans exactly. Coming, Aidan?"

The Sparrow Shifter agreed enthusiastically as the three picked up their gear and went to store it in the changing room. Everyone loved Celine's cooking. The old arrangement of the Dragons supplementing her grocery bill in return for the Kitchen Witch feeding them several times a week still stood. And no one turned down a meal made in Celine's kitchen. No one.

༻❁༺

SHARI-BETH HAD FOUND THE SEA FAE PLAYING IN THE HARBOR AND brought them home for dinner. They'd stopped by Pack lands and picked up Josh on the way.

"Malia, Marissa, and everyone else are coming too, Mom. Mariah and Anne got back today, and Malia's had a hard day with Aoife and Eve. She was already planning on bringing everyone over so she didn't have to cook. Do you need any help making more food?"

Celine counted in her head. Herself, Brendan, Shari-Beth, seven Sea Fae, Josh, so probably Ralph and Liz and her kids, maybe Frankie and hers... "Shari-Beth. How many Wolves are coming for dinner?"

Shari-Beth shrugged. "I only told Josh and Malia, and she called Marissa, and I think Suzette, so her and Remy, who probably told Frankie, who—you know, Mom, I think I'd better call Malia."

Shari-Beth grabbed the phone and dialed as Declan, Sean, and Aidan came through the back door.

"Mom, we're home!" Aidan sang out.

Celine laughed and swatted him with a dishtowel.

"And how many Dragons are coming for dinner, Dex?"

"Just us, I think. I haven't seen Her Royal Pain in the Tucas today."

"What did you call me, Declan?" Devra griped, coming down the stairs from her room on the second floor of the Casey home.

"How do you know I was talking about you? And where did you come from? Why aren't you on campus with Donnie?"

"I just got back from visiting Mom, and I came here first because I missed Celine's cooking. You know how much I hate state dinners. And Donnie is home visiting his Clan. His whole family is. I stayed with them for a bit but decided it was time to come back here." Devra, otherwise known as the bottomless pit, grabbed a carrot stick off the platter Celine was preparing and shoved it into her mouth.

"So, three Dragons, who knows how many Wolf Shifters, a bunch of Witches, a bunch of Sea Fae, several Aes Sídhe.... This is turning into a regular party," Celine mumbled to herself. She ran through the food she had on hand. She could do it if she used her magic to multiply a few things.

"Shari-Beth, call Mollie and invite her and her family as well. Please ask them to bring dessert. And call Suzette and see what she has in her garden, please. Maybe she can make a salad?"

Shari-Beth, who had just put down the phone, picked it back up again.

"Boys, please go out to the shed and get the meat out of the deep freeze. We'll fire up the grills, and you can start cooking. You lot," Celine pointed her spoon at the Sea Fae, "can start shucking the corn and wrapping it in foil to go on the grill."

Celine turned around and stirred the soup she had going on the stove. Then she turned around again as Star-Beth put down the phone for the second time.

"Suzette's bringing the salad, and Malia said Frankie, her kids, Jaimie, Remi and Suzette, Malia's family, and Marissa's family. I think that's it. Oh, and probably Ralph and Liz and her kids."

Yep, this was a full-on party. It would be a miracle if the rest of the town didn't show up, too.

3

Mollie brought Nils Cooke, the grandson of the kindly old Bear Shifter who owned Cooke's Market, with her. Nils had finally asked her out. They had been dating for two months now. And everyone could see they were madly in love. Betsy Gianetti-Reilly and her mate Jason turned up, too. Ralph had called his sister and invited them.

Celine's Kitchen Witch Gift was extremely useful in such situations. She could cook a dish, then use her magic to duplicate it as many times as she needed. So they had plenty of food. Mollie brought several coolers of her ice cream, and Rachel and Declan Murphy brought chocolate cake and sea-salt caramel brownies. Dessert was enjoyed by all.

"Girls, your Uncle Tom and cousin Rebecca will be here Friday," Brendan told his daughters as they sat around the patio after dinner, enjoying the fullness of excellent food and equally excellent company. The younger kids were off in the field, showing off. Milena had cast an illusion of fireworks shaped like the kids' Shifted forms, and sparkly Wolves, Dragons, and Phoenyxes danced across the sky. Sabine and Sarah had Shifted and were snapping at the sparks as they fell through the air. Lucian was talking to Josh, Mariah, and Anne.

The young Wolf had come a long way since becoming a part of the Valerian's Cove Pack. Having a good Alpha made all the difference. Lucian, Mariah, and Anne were juniors this year at the Academy, along with their friend Kelly, who was the first mundane to study there.

Sean, who had been lying on the ground just outside the patio, staring up at the stars, suddenly tensed. Rebecca was coming to Valerian's Cove.

"Oh, good. Rebecca was supposed to bring me more stock this week, anyway," Malia said. "How long are they staying?"

"Through Sunday, I think, if that's ok, Celine?"

"Of course."

Inwardly, Sean groaned. Three days of avoiding his destiny. Maybe he could go home and visit his parents. Or get assigned somewhere far away for the weekend.

"Sean and I were talking about Rebecca today," Declan said, from where he, too, was stretched out on the ground. "I told him it was about time he and Rebecca started spending more time together and got to know each other better. Don't you think?"

"I think that's a fabulous idea," Celine said. "Sean, you'll come over for dinner Friday night. And don't think you can get out of it, either. I'm inviting your mother."

Sean growled loudly enough that everyone on the patio heard it. Suddenly, everyone was laughing as Sean covered his eyes with his arms and hid from the world.

FRIDAY MORNING, REBECCA RACED AROUND, FINDING THE LAST FEW things to put into her overnight bag. It was amazing how everything seemed to go missing at the last moment. She rechecked her studio, making sure that she'd packed all the pieces she was taking to Malia, as well as her tablet for more designs and her spare work kit in case of flashes of Divine inspiration.

"Bex, love, you've got it covered," her father, Tom, told her as he leaned against the door frame, watching her race back and forth. "If you forget anything, you can portal right back here. You can get that young Dragon to bring you."

Rebecca froze. Then she started moving again, slinging her bag over one shoulder as she hefted her box of tools.

"I'm sure Sean has much better things to do than ferry me around," she stated.

"Bex, the man's your fated mate. We all know it. He'll do anything for you."

"Da, we've talked about this. I'm too young for a fated mate."

"Obviously not. And now that you know Sean, would you really want anyone else? The Goddess doesn't make mistakes, a *cailín*."

"*Da....*"

"Rebecca. You're my daughter, and I love you. I'm just saying. You've been blessed with something most people only dream of. The one person who will love you, and only you, for the rest of their extremely, very long lives. Once you're bonded, your lifespan will match his. Think of everything you'll be able to create! The man'll do anything for you, bring you the stars and the moon, the tiniest gemstone in the sea. He'll love you, protect you, and support you in whatever you choose to do. He'll make sure you never want for anything, ever. And he's Dragon Royalty! And a remarkably good fighter. He'll be able to keep you safe. Plus, he loves your music. Why not get to know the lad better? You don't have to finish the bond immediately. He's waited two years now. I'm sure he'll continue to be patient until you're ready. But keeping away from him like this serves no purpose other than to drive both of you crazy."

"Can we talk about this later, Da? Aunt Celine is waiting for us. We should go."

Tom rolled his eyes and followed his daughter out of the house.

THEY ARRIVED IN FRONT OF THE CASEY HOUSE IN VALERIAN'S COVE, all bags intact, to find Celine waiting for them on the porch.

"Good! You've arrived. We're having a dinner party this evening, so I hope you brought your fiddle, Rebecca! It'll be informal, so lots of good food and music—just a few friends. Anyway, come in. Would you like a snack? I've got fresh croissants—Aldona picked them up in Paris from Luna for me this morning."

Rebecca tensed. Aldona. The Crown Princess of the Drake Clan. Sean's mother. Aldona was here. Which meant Sean would be over for dinner tonight.

She paused before heading up the steps.

"Come on, Rebecca. Would you like a hand with your bags?" Celine encouraged.

"No, thank you, Aunt Celine. I'm coming."

Celine told them to dump their bags in the hallway.

"They'll make their own way to your rooms."

Then she led them into the kitchen, where Aldona was seated at the island, eating a croissant with cream and strawberry jam and drinking a cup of mint tea.

"Thomas! And Rebecca. How lovely to see you." Aldona stood from her seat to greet them. She was dressed simply, in jeans and a pink tee-shirt, with only one pearly comb holding the French twist in her hair in place.

The Crown Princess hugged Tom and Rebecca, then held on to Rebecca's hands, looking at her.

"Rebecca, it's been two years since you met my Sean. I know you were young when you met, but do you think you might spare some time to spend with him and get to know him better now? He can't seem to concentrate-he's losing focus in everything he does because the longer he spends away from you, the more he thinks about you, and he can't seem to think about anything else. Please, please have mercy on the poor boy, and spare him some time?"

Rebecca blushed.

"We were telling Sean the other day it was time for the two of you to get to know each other better," Celine agreed, placing a new platter of croissants fresh from the oven on the island, followed by a pot of tea and two mugs. "He'll be here for dinner, of course. I was thinking, Tom, wouldn't it be a good idea for Rebecca to spend some time here in Valerian's Cove for a while? She can stay here with us, of course. Rebecca, you are supplying Malia's store almost exclusively, except for the shop in Seattle, correct? And a few special pieces? You can do your work here, can't you? We can set you up with your own studio here—you might even be able to use Malia's. She mostly works in the studio Tony built for her at their place now. When she paints at all. She's so busy with the children and the shop now. Think about it, why don't you both?"

Rebecca felt her face flush and was sure she looked red as a poppy. Her chest tightened as her breath became shallow. Everyone seemed to know what she should do except Rebecca herself. It wasn't that she didn't want to spend time with Sean. It was just that she wasn't sure she was ready to settle down and start a family yet, either. She was only twenty-one! And her business was really starting to take off. She was getting commissions for jewelry from important people in the paranormal world, and her pieces at Wonder were selling almost the moment they were in the door. And look at Malia—she was so busy she barely had time to paint anymore. Rebecca didn't want to give up her crafting—it kept her sane and truly brought her joy.

Tom saw his daughter's fear and stepped up.

"We'll think about it, Celine. There's no need to decide just yet. It's not like they need to get married and start a family right away, even if they did complete the bond. There's plenty of time."

"You're right, of course, Tom," Aldona said. "Devra and Donnie have been mated for a while now and have agreed to put off having children for a few more years. It's not like it's a rule that you have to have children right away when you become bonded. And I'm sure Sean would always support Rebecca in whatever she wanted to do."

Rebecca's breathing slowed as her heart rate dropped again. The flush slowly faded from her face.

"Well, whatever you decide, we'd love to have you stay for a while, Rebecca," Celine said with a smile. "Come, tell me what you've been up to lately. Do you have any new designs to show me?"

4

Shari-Beth was working in Wonder Friday morning. Malia was at home, working in her studio for once. She was working on a series of paintings she was planning to sell in the store. Prints would be available on the website. They featured the mythic creatures that filled Valerian's Cove in beautiful natural settings and in heroic, mythic settings as well. With so many Dragons, Phoenyxes, and Fae of all kinds around, she had a lot of material to draw from.

Liz came out from the back room where she'd been doing some ordering. These days, most of the details of running the shop were left to Liz. Malia had more than enough on her plate with three sets of twins, from infant to teenager, to deal with. Plus, being the Alpha's mate.

Fortunately, Liz had discovered that she had an excellent head for running a business and actually enjoyed it. Wonder was thriving under her management.

"Hey, Shari. Let's get lunch from Thai Star today. Does that sound good? I'm craving green curry again."

Shari looked at Liz with a grin.

"Are you sure, absolutely sure, you're not pregnant again?"

"Bite your tongue. I already have three kids. That's more than enough. I love them, but boy, are kids a lot of work. So, Thai?"

"Sure. Thai is always good with me."

"Will you go pick it up? I'll stay here and mind the store. Rebecca is supposed to bring in some new stock today."

"Ok. Do you want me to go now?"

"Sure, why not? It's almost lunchtime."

Shari-Beth grinned and headed out. Thai Star was only a few doors down, so it didn't take very long to reach the restaurant. Ben Ma greeted her as she walked in.

"Hello, Shari-Beth! Come for lunch? Liz or Malia today?"

"Liz, please, Ben Ma. She's craving green curry again."

"That girl is pregnant again; you mark my words. Two pups, this time. You'll see. Pad Thai or Pad See Yew for you today, Shari-Beth?"

"Pad See Yew, please, and fresh spring rolls. And maybe chicken satay, too."

"You got it. Chanthira! Shari-Beth is here for lunch. She's feeding Liz again. Extra curry! That Wolf is going to have twins this time, I feel it."

Shari-Beth grinned. There had been a lot of twins recently. The thought of Liz and Ralph having a set of their own was highly amusing. With Ralph's son Josh and Liz's three, Sarah, Carl, and Michelle, who was only five, they already had four kids between them. Josh was one of Shari-Beth's best friends. Sarah was only just thirteen. Carl was 10. Oh, well. At least Liz would be in good company with young twins. Malia and Marissa both had a set, Siofra had one baby, Dervla Eimear, and Suzette and Remy had just announced they were expecting twins as well. Lots and lots of babies. They were fun. It was even better to play with them for a bit and then give them back. Shari-Beth had found herself babysitting for her sisters and Siofra more than once.

"Ben Ma, I'm going down to the harbor for a moment. I'll be right back for the food," Shari-Beth called.

Ben Ma waved a hand at her.

"Ten minutes!"

Shari-Beth nodded and waved back.

She waved at Mr. Cooke, who was sweeping the sidewalk in front of his store, and kept going. At the harbor, she leaned on the sea wall and looked out across the water. A tail flipped above the waves in the middle of the harbor. Then a small head appeared for a moment before diving again. Shari-Beth looked again. That wasn't a Sea Fae. Had a sea lion come in to play? It happened in this part of California. Otters, too. Shari-Beth loved the otters. They looked so sweet, though she'd been told they could be absolutely vicious.

Someone leaned up against the wall next to her, arms crossed on top of the stone. They stood that way for a moment before speaking.

"You in town today, Shari-Beth?"

"I'm working at Wonder. I'm supposed to be picking up lunch from Ben Ma." Shari turned her head and looked at Alan. He was staring out across the water, watching where the sea lion and the Sea Fae tail had been.

"I'm going to have to go home for a while. I'm going to miss it here. Training to be one of Sinéad's guards is perfect for me. I hope they'll let me continue when I come back."

"What? Why are you leaving?"

"I got a message from my mother. My father was injured protecting Sionna—Sinéad's mother, the current Seer—he's one of her guards. I have to go help take care of the family."

"But surely your training here is important? Why would they tell you to come home? As Sionna's guard, I'm sure your dad's being well looked after."

"He is. It's just, they're not sure he's going to make it. It was a terrible attack. He saved Sionna's life and took a hit meant to kill her. They want me to take a Dragon portal to Nova Scotia and swim from there. I'm leaving in twenty minutes. I just wanted to look at the bay here one more time."

"Why did someone attack Sionna?"

"I don't know. She's an incredibly powerful Seer. I'm more worried about how they snuck up on her. And how we can stop it happening again."

"Wouldn't Sinéad have Seen her mother being attacked? Couldn't she get word to her in time?"

"I don't know, Shari-Beth. I do know they talked before it

happened. Maybe they did know. I'm not sure what's happening. I just know I have to go home."

Shari-Beth turned to face him fully, then pulled the tall Sea Fae into a hug.

"I'm really sorry about your father, Alan. I hope he gets better quickly."

"Thanks, Shari-Beth. Me too."

Shari-Beth watched as the young man turned and headed up the hill to the Dragon portal. Her heart felt weighted down in her chest. It was never easy to lose a parent. Maybe his father would pull through.

Shari-Beth turned back towards the water. There were several Sea Fae in the harbor, and now there appeared to be several seals or sea lions too. From here, Shari-Beth couldn't tell which they were. They didn't seem to be playing anymore. They were all gathered in a knot. Maybe they were Selkies?

Suddenly, the group in the water turned and started swimming towards the docks. Jed pulled himself out of the water, climbing the ladder and stepping onto the walkway. He waved at Shari-Beth.

"Hey, Shari-Beth. I'm glad you're here. We just got word of something I think the Council should know about. Would you please call your father and let him know we need to see him?"

Shari nodded and took out her phone.

BRENDAN CASEY WAS IN THE GREENHOUSE WITH HIS BUSINESS partner, Siofra, and niece, Suzette, who had the day off from the Healer's Clinic. They were working on a new Fae-Earth hybrid. So far, it was coming along swimmingly.

They had music on and were deeply engrossed in the plants they were observing. None of them heard the greenhouse phone ring. Suddenly, Brendan's personal cell phone buzzed in his back pocket. Celine had declared that as the head of the Council, he needed to have one and made sure he took it with him every morning.

He slapped his pocket, then took out the phone.

"Shari-Beth? Is everything ok?"

"Hi, Dad. The Sea Fae need to talk to you. They just got some news they think the Council should know. Can they come up?"

"The Council, or the Alliance Council?"

"Both, maybe?"

Brendan frowned.

"Of course, send them up. Thank you, sweetheart. I'll see you at dinner."

Brendan put the phone back in his pocket, still frowning.

"What's up?" Siofra asked. She and Suzette were staring at him, heads cocked to the side.

"Shari-Beth says the Sea Fae have had news that the Council should know. They're coming up."

"Then you'd better wash up and look all official, Uncle," Suzette said with a grin. Brendan had a streak of dirt across his face, and his hair was standing on end. It could probably do with a wash as well. He'd run his dirty hands through it several times.

"You're right. Keep on, ladies. I'll be back."

Brendan headed up to the house, going in through the back door into the kitchen. No one was there. Celine must be at the garden center.

Brendan was heading back down, all tidied up, just as the doorbell rang.

He opened the door to find Jed and a young lady he didn't know on the porch. The young woman had long, dark brown hair and large, liquid brown eyes. She was dressed in a suede leather top and leggings. Brendan's eyebrows rose.

"Hello, Jed."

Brendan turned to the young woman and bowed, keeping his eyes on her face.

"It is an honor to have one of the Selkie come to my door. Please, come in. I am Brendan Casey, Earth Witch and head of the Alliance Council. Be welcome in my home."

The Selkie inclined her head, eyes on his.

"I am Moraya, of the Hidden Tides Clan. Thank you for your welcome." She followed him into the house, Jed a step behind.

Brendan sat them in the sitting room and offered them snacks. Both declined.

"Shari-Beth tells me there's something we need to know?"

Moraya nodded.

"Our Clan stays mostly to itself. We have our own territory on an island made unplottable and unchartable. The island is inhabited solely by Sea Shifters. It's the only island in its area. Normally, we stay away from other people. Sometimes, boats pass by. Recently, there has been a large boat moored about a mile from us. They do not seem to be aware of us. Because they are so close to our home, they are considered a threat, and we have been watching them. There is a darkness on that boat, Witch Casey. The energy feels dark and heavy. And yesterday, a body was dumped overboard. We recovered it without being seen and before anything else could get to it. We examined it in the water, and it was... tainted... with the same dark energy as the boat. I'm not sure what this means. Our Seer says this is the start of something, but she cannot see clearly, only that you needed to know. So, here I am. My brothers wait for me in the Cove."

"I see. Thank you, Moraya. I appreciate you coming to tell me. I release you. Safe journey home."

Moraya stood and bowed again. This time, she smiled a little before turning and heading out the door. Jed followed.

"Jed, please ask Sinéad if she's able to get a better reading on this," Brendan called after the young man.

"Yes, Sir. She's rather caught up in the attack on her mother yesterday, at the moment, but I can ask both of them to check."

"Sionna was attacked? Why didn't anyone tell me?"

"I thought you knew? Didn't Moira tell you?"

"Is Sionna ok?"

"Yes, one of her guards took the blow meant for her. She's shaken but fine. She told Sinéad to stay here. They've been communicating almost constantly since yesterday."

"Is Sionna still at home in the Atlantic?"

"Yes, I believe so. She and her guards were traveling when they were attacked. Close to the coast of France, I believe."

"How would someone have known where they were?"

"They were coming from a meeting with another Clan. Someone could have let it slip. The other Clan had asked for her help. She gave them what they needed, then left."

"Thank you, lad. I'll call her and check in after I speak with the Council. Thank you for bringing this to my attention."

5

B rendan contacted the other members of the Alliance Council through the mirror.

"Well, that's just brilliant," Declan said, running his fingers through his hair. "Is it Demons, do you think, Brendan?"

"I don't know, Dec. I also don't know who attacked Sionna. I don't know what's on that boat. And Moira, why didn't you tell us about the attack on your mother?"

"I'm sorry, Brendan. I was going to tell you today. I've been in almost constant contact with her since it happened and trying to keep Sinéad from running home to make sure Mom is ok. As a Seer, she knows Mom's ok. As a daughter, she wants to hug her mother."

"I understand. Does Sionna know who attacked her?"

"No. Whoever it was used magic from a distance. Mom and Sinéad both knew Mom was in danger, but not more than that. Mom's guards were extra vigilant, which is how one of them was able to stop the bolt from hitting Mom. He's badly injured. Sinéad's guard, Alan, is his son. He's been called home, just in case."

"Declan, keep an extra eye on Sinéad, please. I know she has adult guards as well until hers are fully trained, but she is still one down.

Assign someone to take over from Alan until he comes back, or another Sea Fae can be found to replace him, please."

Declan nodded.

"Brendan, on another note, you are aware that there are Starborn in Fairweather Falls? One of the descendants has been awakened as the next Starborn Oracle. She's super powerful. And she's only ten. They're bringing in a special teacher and guards for her. They've requested that the Seers here form a Seers College with her so that all the Seers and Oracles can be in touch with and learn from each other. Lily has agreed. Moira, Sinéad, and Sionna will be invited as well. As will Fionnuala and Milena, Brendan."

"Another super-powered child. The Goddess isn't pulling any punches. How many is that, now, Brendan?" Lady Caoimhe asked.

"Four here, and two now, in Fairweather Falls. Is that right?" Brendan looked at the others in the mirror, which currently looked like a video conference call, each member in their own little square on the mirror.

Declan nodded.

"I've been in fairly constant touch with Robin George there, helping her set up the Fight Course at the new Academy and helping her find an instructor. I also sent her a Fire Mage teacher, as approved by Luc Benoit. She keeps me informed about what is happening there. Honestly, most of the Starborn descendants are pretty strong in their magic. Several were already Mages. Their Starborn DNA is giving them an added dimension to their Gifts. And from what she's said, not all the Starborn descendants have arrived for training yet. There could be more super-powered children coming."

Brendan rubbed his eyes, then rocked back on his heels.

"All right, well, everyone, keep your eyes and ears open. Let me know of any more attacks or strange happenings right away. And that goes doubly so for finding any more super-powered children."

REBECCA BROUGHT HER WORK INTO WONDER AFTER LUNCH. SHE had spent the morning showing her Aunt Celine the pieces she had brought, as well as her ideas for new ones. Celine had a keen eye for detail and enjoyed looking over the designs with her super-creative niece.

The bell over the door to Wonder chimed as Rebecca carried the box of jewelry into the shop. Shari-Beth was helping a customer at the register, but she looked up and waved at her cousin.

"Hi, Rebecca! I'll be with you in just a sec, ok?"

Rebecca returned the wave and headed into the back room, where she took out the pieces she had brought with her and laid them out on the desk Liz used for doing the books and the ordering.

Shari-Beth came in a moment later.

"Oh, these are gorgeous!" The Falcon Shifter lifted a pendant made to look like a dragon, set with tiny emeralds, and worked in both silver and gold. The piece appeared to glow with its own light. The dragon's eyes were blue topaz. It was a Chinese Water Dragon, wrapped in swirls made to resemble streams of water, with tiny koi swimming around it. Cherry blossoms floated by on the waves. The piece was stunning.

Rebecca blushed.

"Thank you," she brushed her hair back behind her ear. Rebecca knew people found her work beautiful, but she still had difficulty accepting compliments on it. To her, the work was something she did to stay sane. It was as if she had to create, or she would get crazy depressed. Ideas for new pieces filled her mind constantly. Once, when she was fifteen, she had given in to the depression and stopped creating. It had felt as if a deep fog had covered her mind. It had been the worst time of her life. Thankfully, her father had pulled her out of it by insisting she make a birthday present for her best friend, Shannon. Shannon was human and had gone away to college on the East Coast when they graduated from high school. Rebecca had elected to stay home and work on her art. By then, her pieces were already selling well, and she saw no need to leave her family for an academic education that she had no interest in. Tom supported his daughter's decision, knowing how much her work meant to her. And, around that time, she had met Sean. Tom knew that if ever her pieces stopped selling, Sean would take care of her if Rebecca allowed him to. Rebecca was Sean's mate and, therefore, a princess among the Dragons, whether or not she wanted to admit it to herself.

"Here, I thought this piece would look good on you," Rebecca said, handing her cousin another pendant. This one was a hawk in flight with citrine eyes. Every detail was meticulously carved into the metal. There were larger citrines where the tips of the wings connected to the chain supporting it.

"I thought you might wear it in the shop to show off the work. People could get a better idea of what the pieces look like on someone, rather than just in a case."

"That's a wonderful idea! I love it. Thank you. Liz always makes more sales when she wears the pieces you gave her. People do like seeing the pieces worn."

The girls talked about the pieces for a few minutes before arranging them in their display. Liz, who had stepped out for a moment, came back in, carrying a box from The Baker's Delight across the street.

"Rebecca! Oh good, you brought the new stuff. Thank you! Malia was looking forward to getting them in." She placed the box on the counter by the register and headed over to check the new display out.

"Oh, wow, these are stunning. Your work just keeps getting better and better, Bex. And I already thought it was gorgeous, to begin with."

Rebecca blushed again.

"Well, this should hold us over for a little while, at least. Thank you for bringing so many pieces," Liz said as she stepped back to the counter and opened the bakery box.

"Here, I got enough for everyone. I couldn't decide what I wanted."

Inside the box were fruit tarts, a slice of German chocolate cake, an eclair, a piece of rugelach, a chocolate cupcake filled with cream with strawberry frosting, and a chocolate croissant.

"Oooh, yum," Shari-Beth said, grabbing the cupcake and taking a huge bite. She got frosting on her nose. Liz laughed and wiped it off. Shari-Beth grinned and took another bite.

Rebecca reached into the box and took out one of the fruit tarts. Rachel's baking wasn't something to be missed.

"So, how long are you staying, Bex?" Shari-Beth asked her cousin.

Rebecca shrugged.

"I was only planning on staying the weekend, but now Auntie Celine and Aldona want me to set up a workspace here and get to know Sean better. Aunt Celine wants me to stay with you, Shari."

"That would be awesome! You should totally do it. It would be great having you around more," Shari-Beth encouraged.

"It really would," Liz said. "You could take a shift in the shop, too. I'd greatly appreciate it. We're losing two of our after-school employees, as they're going off to university at other Academies. I could really use the help. And having the artist in residence would be a great way to increase visibility on your jewelry and the store. We could even do social media promotions, maybe videos of you working on your pieces or modeling them? I mean, I know you have your own social media already, but I think that would be great for you and the store."

"I hardly ever use my social media account," Rebecca said. "I usually just sell through the nursery and here. And I get a few commissions through word-of-mouth. I don't remember the last time I posted something."

"Oh, you really need to work on that," Shari-Beth said. "I run the social media for the shop—I can help you get it going. Liz is right; pictures of you working on your pieces and wearing them would be great. Maybe a few other people wearing them. Time-lapse videos of you making them. You could do so much with this. People love to see artists at work. I guarantee you will sell even more pieces. Do you have a website?"

Rebecca shook her head.

"Rebecca. Really. You need your own website. I can help you get that set up, too."

"I would have to work even harder to make enough to sell that way, though. It would take up a lot of my time," Rebecca said.

"You could feature the pieces you make for the nursery and the shop and offer to take commissions," Liz said. "Make sure you charge enough to make the time spent on them worth it for you. You could charge a much higher price point on those pieces that way. It makes your work more exclusive. The pieces you sell at the shop would be the lower price-point. We're working on getting our website up to scratch, too, so we'll be selling the shop pieces there, as well. You're going to have to make more, anyway."

"Is there anyone who could help you make pieces?" Shari-Beth asked.

Rebecca shook her head.

"I haven't really thought about hiring anyone. I mean, the person would have to be a Fire Mage, to do what I do. And they would have to be willing to work for me on my pieces until they were skilled enough to make their own.

"Like an apprentice. That would be cool," Shari-Beth said. "I'm sure we can find someone. I'll ask around. Maybe, if you really are into this expansion, we should advertise for an apprentice?"

"That's a good idea. We can advertise at the Academy, maybe at all the Academies. Find a nice, eager young student who's a Fire Mage and extremely creative, with a Gift in Metals. Let's do that," Liz said. "If it's ok with you, of course, Rebecca."

Rebecca's head was spinning again. It seemed as if fate was conspiring to keep her here in Valerian's Cove. Things were moving so quickly! She took a deep breath.

"I suppose we can try it. Do you really think we can find someone?"

"I do," Liz answered. "I think we should look for someone who already lives here first. That would make housing easier. Traditionally, an apprentice lived with their master. But since Bex herself is staying at your place, Shari-Beth, maybe that wouldn't work."

"Who are you kidding? My mother would love someone else to feed. Let's not worry about that until we have to, ok? Let's focus on finding the absolute best person to apprentice with Rebecca, regardless of where they come from."

6

Sean arrived for dinner that night with a bouquet of flowers in his hand. Sunflowers, cornflowers, echinacea, and poppies had been filled in with some pretty green leaves to create contrast. He figured that since everyone was determined to get himself and Rebecca together, he might as well start courting her. Not that he didn't want to—he did. Very much. But Rebecca had seemed determined to stay as far away from him as possible, and he hadn't wanted to rush her. Still, it was only polite to bring your mate something pretty, right? And the flowers really were pretty. He had bought the bunch from Cooke's store, only realizing afterward that they had probably come from the Casey Nursery, to begin with. Oh, well.

He climbed the front stairs, paused at the top, and took a deep breath. Having his mother and Rebecca's whole family there cheering them on was *not* how Sean had planned to get to know his mate.

He raised his hand to knock, only to have the door open under his hand.

"Hey, Sean. Mom says come in." Shari-Beth led the Dragon through the kitchen and out to the patio. Not quite the whole town seemed to be there. Ralph and Declan were minding the grill, three picnic tables were weighted down with food, and the younger members of the gathering were playing soccer in the field. Several instrument cases were piled by the circle of stairs around the fire pit.

"Sean! About time," Aldona exclaimed, rising from her chair. She hugged her youngest child, then looked into his eyes.

"I know this isn't probably how you wanted to begin wooing your mate, son, but it was taking too long. You've known each other for two years now. You need to have at least *some* interaction with each other."

"I know, Mom. But I don't think Rebecca wants to."

Aldona sighed and hugged him again.

"Go give her those pretty flowers, sweetheart. It will all work out. You'll see. It took Malia and Tony years to get together. Celine and I aren't willing to wait that long again. And you shouldn't be, either. Talk to her. Find out what she's thinking. Work it out." Aldona turned and pushed him in the direction of Rebecca, who had her back to him as she very determinedly talked to her two younger cousins in front of her. Mariah and Anne were both grinning, looking over Rebecca's shoulders at Sean. Rebecca's shoulders were tense, her stance rigid.

"Mom, I wish you wouldn't push this," Sean whispered. "Look at her. She's not happy. She doesn't want me here."

"Rebecca is your Fated Mate, Sean. Go talk to the girl. Work it out." Aldona shoved him again.

Sean sighed and headed over to his mate. He walked up beside her, carefully, staying just out of reach. Just in case. Rebecca had more than a little red in her brown hair. He had no desire to be on the receiving end of her temper.

"Hi, ladies," Sean said to the twins. They grinned at him. As usual, they had dressed very differently, Mariah in more punk goth, while Anne was in more preppy clothes. Mariah had one of her hand-designed tee shirts on. It was purple, with black writing on it that said 'who's your dragon?', underneath the silhouette of a dragon in flight. Sean was sure that shirt was aimed at Rebecca and him.

"Hi, Rebecca," Sean said more softly. He held out the flowers. "These are for you."

Rebecca finally looked over at him.

"Thank you. You didn't have to do that."

"I wanted to. I know this is kind of overwhelming, with our families pushing us to get together, but I honestly do want to get to know you more," Sean replied.

Mariah grabbed Anne's arm and pulled her away. The girls kept glancing back over their shoulders, grinning.

Rebecca looked down at the flowers, then lowered her nose to smell the sunflowers. She loved their warm, honey smell. She tucked the flowers into the crook of her arm.

"I should go put these in water," she said, turning to go inside.

"I'll do that. Nice choice, Sean," Celine said, hurrying over to them. "Why don't the two of you go for a walk? There's still time before the food's ready. The grill's only just getting hot enough."

Celine smiled at them, then walked away towards the kitchen with the flowers.

Sean ran his hands through his hair.

"We'd probably better humor them, or we're never going to hear the end of it," he told Rebecca.

She nodded and started walking off down the field, keeping out of the way of the young teens, who had given up playing soccer and were watching Milena make illusions instead. There seemed to be an awful lot of younger people in the group. It definitely wasn't just the Caseys.

"The twins brought friends," Rebecca said as they walked. "Malachi and Amie, Siobhan, Bethie, and of course Liz and Frankie's kids." Rebecca did her best to make small talk, so she wouldn't feel so awkward. It didn't work.

They reached the training ground that Devra Drake had created for practicing their magical Gifts. The large oval area was heavily shielded, so no Fire magic could escape and cause damage to the Casey's property. With Fire Mages, Dragons, and Phoenyxes all practicing together, that had been a very good choice.

Sean reached out and put his hand on Rebecca's arm.

"Rebecca, wait. Listen, I know you're not exactly overjoyed about this, about being my mate. I understand that you need more time. You're still very young, by Dragon and Witch standards. I get that. But we are Fated Mates. The Goddess doesn't make mistakes in these things. I would really like to get to know you better. We can take as long as you like. It's not like I expect anything from you. I don't expect you to complete the bond and start having kids right away. We can take as long as you want to complete the bond. And kids are totally up to you. I know you have your own business, and that's important to you. I want you to do whatever is important to you. I just would hope that maybe I could become important to you, too."

Rebecca looked up at Sean. He was a full head taller than she was, plus some. The Dragon had hit the nail right on the head. She honestly wasn't sure what she wanted yet. Malia and Marissa hadn't settled down with their mates until they were nearly forty. Though, there were extenuating circumstances in both cases. Suzette was in her mid-twenties when she completed the mate-bond with Remy. Suzette had kept her job as a Healer. Liz and Malia still worked at the store, and Malia still painted, even with the baby twins. She had her family to help her with the kids. Which, Rebecca knew, she would, too, if she ever decided to have any. Which wouldn't be for quite some time, if she had anything to say about it.

"Thank you. Your mother and my aunt want me to stay in Valerian's Cove so we can get to know each other better. Shari-Beth and Liz want me to help at the store and take on an apprentice to help with my jewelry, because Shari-Beth is sure she can boost my sales through social media and a website. They've got it all planned out."

"What do *you* want, Rebecca?" Sean reached out and softly brushed her long hair back behind her ear again.

Rebecca looked out over the field.

"It would be nice to be with my cousins again. I've been feeling a little stagnant in Seattle for a while. A change might be a good thing."

She looked up at Sean again.

"I want to take this super slowly, Sean. Especially if I am taking on an apprentice and setting up a new workplace here. I'll be extremely busy making jewelry if Shari-Beth has anything to say about it. It's not that I don't want to get to know you. I'm just not ready to settle down, yet."

"Then we take it slow. I'm ok with that. Just please let me be a part of your life? I'll try not to push. I promise." Sean smiled down at her. She really was beautiful, he thought to himself. Beautiful, talented, creative. And a good person. All the Caseys were. Sean felt incredibly blessed that the Goddess had chosen to put him and Rebecca together.

Rebecca watched him for a moment, then nodded.

Sean reached out, and slowly, Rebecca took his hand.

☙❧

SHARI-BETH WAS OVER THE MOON THAT REBECCA HAD DECIDED TO stay in Valerian's Cove. She got right on advertising for an apprentice through the Academy system and started building Rebecca a website and social media platform. By Monday morning, she had sent the ad to Maria Hemenway, Head of the Valerian's Cove Academy. Maria had agreed to forward the ad to the rest of the Academy campuses. By Wednesday, replies had started to drift in. By Friday, twenty people had applied.

Rebecca looked at all the applications Shari-Beth had printed out in astonishment. "There are that many Fire Mages who want to make jewelry?" she asked.

Shari-Beth shook her head.

"No. Some of the applicants are other kinds of Witches. I think there are a few other races in there, too. Maybe they can still learn from you, even without controlling Fire?"

"What I do requires the control over fire of a Fire Mage or a Dragon," Rebecca replied.

"What about a Phoenyx or a Dwarf?"

"I don't know if a Phoenyx could use their flame the way I do. And a Dwarf would have to find a way to make a hot enough sustained flame to do things the way I do. I mean, I guess it's possible. But the Dwarves are already Master Crafters. Why would a Dwarf want to work with me? They would have plenty of their own people to study with, and aren't they very reclusive? I thought they didn't leave their people often."

"They don't, but we have one application from a young Dwarven woman. She's just finished school at an Academy in Sweden. I think her parents were the Ambassadors for her people there, so her upbringing was a little different. Her parents aren't able to train her–

they're politicians. And she wants to see more of the world. I guess her parents are encouraging her in the hope that she'll be the next ambassador after them."

"Huh. Ok. Well, I'll look over her application. What's her name?"

"Flora Unfrid. Her last name means 'the one who brings peace.' Perfect name for an ambassador."

Rebecca smiled and looked down at the pile of papers in her hands. She had been in Valerian's Cove for a week now. Malia had been happy to have her take over the studio on the Casey property. It was all set up for her jewelry business, now, and Rebecca had begun working in it yesterday. The large windows let in plenty of light, making it a pleasant place to work.

Shari-Beth grinned back, then left for her afternoon shift at Wonder. Rebecca placed the pile of applications on the table in front of her. She had been working on another pendant, just beginning it, really, when Shari-Beth had walked in. Rebecca started looking through the applications in front of her.

There were several from people who wanted to learn to work metals into jewelry but who were obviously not familiar with her work and what it entailed. Several hadn't read the application all the way through, or had ignored the part about requiring extreme control over Fire magic.

Rebecca found Flora's application and set it aside to read in more detail. The Fire Mage found four other possibilities in the pile—two young Witch Fire Mages, one Aes Sídhe Fire Mage, and a young Dragon studying at the Academy before Guardian training. As she looked over them, Rebecca began to consider the possibility of taking on more than one apprentice. Three applications stood out to her: Flora; the Aes Sídhe, a young man named Daniel; and one of the Witch Fire Mages, another young man named Simon. All three had applications that sounded excellent on paper. Rebecca was still concerned that Flora wouldn't have the required control over Fire, but maybe there was a way to compensate? Dwarven metalsmithing was famous for good reason.

Rebecca grabbed her tablet and emailed back the three applicants that seemed the most promising. Then she emailed the other seventeen to thank them for applying and let them know that she had chosen other applicants to move forward with.

Five minutes later, she heard back from Flora, who was eager to start immediately. Rebecca replied that she wanted to meet in person to get a feel for if they could work well together and to discuss how Flora could handle the extreme Fire needed for the work. They set up a time to meet on Monday morning. By the time she finished with Flora, she had emails back from the other two applicants. She made appointments to see them after Flora on Monday.

An almost giddy, lightheaded sensation flowed through Rebecca after she finished the last email. She was really going through with this. Holy snapdragons. She grinned as she got back to work.

$\begin{array}{ccc} \text{❦} & 7 & \text{❦} \end{array}$

Shari-Beth's friend Emma came home on Saturday. Shari-Beth was thrilled to have her bestie back. Of course, it meant that school would start again soon, but since learning at the Academy was actually fun, returning to school had become something to look forward to. Plus, fight training with more than just the usual group of family and friends. Shari-Beth loved fight training. And she was in excellent shape because of it.

Emma threw open her home's front door and flew down the steps, shrieking, when Shari-Beth arrived. Emma was a few inches taller than Shari-Beth's five-foot-six, so if it hadn't been for Shari's fight training, the Swan Maiden would have knocked the Falcon Shifter on her butt. The two girls hugged each other, dancing around the front yard.

"How was France? Was that cute guy you met before there? Did you have fun? How was it staying with your grandparents? What Familiars are at the Center now? Anything unusual?" Emma's words flowed from her without pause for air.

"It was great. No, he was away on a trip with friends. There was this one other cute guy, though—I'll tell you about him later. I love staying with Grandpa Luc and Grandma Marthe. The Familiars are awesome. Nothing really unusual this time. Though, there is a Firebird, like Siofra's Familiar. It's a male, though. His name is Vion, and he's gorgeous. Whoever ends up with him as a Familiar will be immensely powerful." She stopped for a breath, then continued.

"How was Sweden? How's your family? What did you do? Did you meet anyone? What's the most exciting thing you did? Did you take pictures?"

"Sooo many pictures! Come inside; my phone's in the house. I dropped it when I saw you coming up the path."

Emma led Shari-Beth into the house, grabbing her phone from the small table in the hallway. The two girls flung themselves onto the couch in the living room, leaning against each other, heads together as they looked at the photos on Emma's phone.

Emma's mother looked in on them from the doorway. She smiled. Though she didn't think either girl was aware of it yet, Hanna was pretty sure that Shari-Beth and Emma were fated mates. There was just something about how close the two girls were that sang to her. She made up a tray of sweet anise-flavored cookies and two glasses of milk. The girls looked up as she entered the room.

"Oooh, thank you, Mrs. Nilsson! I love those!" Shari-Beth exclaimed, reaching for a cookie as soon as the tray hit the coffee table in front of them.

Emma grabbed two.

"Drink your milk, girls. It's good to see you, Shari-Beth. Emma missed you while we were away."

"I missed her too. France was fun, but I have so much more fun when Emma's around!"

Hanna smiled at the girls and left them to it.

"Next year, you'll have to come to France with me again," Shari-Beth told her friend.

"And you'll have to come to Sweden with me afterward," Emma agreed.

⚜

AFTER LOOKING THROUGH ALL THE SUMMER PICTURES ON BOTH their phones—Emma was enraptured by the video Shari-Beth had taken of Vion, the firebird—the girls decided to walk into town. Emma's family lived on one of the roads that curved off from the town around the right side of the harbor if you were looking at it from land. The girls walked into town with their arms around each other. They met Josh Merrit, Ralph's son, cousin to the Valerian's Cove Pack Alpha, outside Cooke's market.

"Hey, guys. Glad you're both back now. Shari was miserable without you, Emma. Barely wanted to do anything at all."

Shari-Beth swatted at the Wolf Shifter.

"That's not true! I've been working at Wonder a lot and helping Rebecca get her business moving. Besides, you're working at the auto shop all the time now. I never see you anymore unless we have a party." Shari-Beth pouted at her other best friend.

Josh grinned.

"We've both been working a lot. I have today off, though. What do you want to do?"

"Let's grab Aidan and force him to take a break from training for a change. Maybe find Kelly, if she's back, and Mariah and Anne. Maybe the Sea Fae, too. I'm sure we can think of something to do if we all get together," Shari-Beth said.

"Is Aidan still training every day?" Emma asked.

Josh nodded.

"He's obsessed. I didn't think it would last this long, honestly. I'm beginning to think it's not healthy. I might ask Declan to speak to him, actually. Aidan hasn't taken a break at all, all summer."

"Let's find him, then, and make him take one," Emma said determinedly. "Where does he usually practice?"

"The Academy."

AIDEN WAS, INDEED, AT THE ACADEMY. HE WAS SPARRING WITH Sean when the three friends walked onto the practice field. Sean called a halt and waved at them when he saw them.

"Hey, guys. Did you come to practice, too? You're probably really out of shape, Emma, since you've been gone all summer," Aidan grinned at them as he wiped the sweat off his face.

"I practiced while I was away, doofus," Emma retorted.

"Anyway, we're not here to practice. I'll join the regular Casey practice sessions, as usual, starting tomorrow. We're here to steal you away, actually. Josh says you haven't taken a break all summer. I've decided you need an intervention, so we're kidnapping you and forcing you to have some fun today."

"That sounds like a great idea," Sean broke in. "Aidan, take a break. We've already practiced for an hour—you need a break, anyway. You've come a long way this summer; you can afford to take an afternoon off. It's good to relax a little and let your body rest. I'll see you tomorrow, ok?" Sean said goodbye and headed inside to get cleaned up.

"Guys, I really need to practice if I have a chance of getting into the Guardian training," Aidan said. He was frowning as he watched Sean walk away.

"Aid, you know all the Guardians are Dragon-Kin. Guardian Benoit was talking about getting you in with special forces or something like my dad was. You know that, right?" Josh said.

"I know, but I can train with the Guardians if I can prove I'm good enough. It would really help my skills a lot. I need to be the best I can be if I want anyone to take me seriously," the diminutive Sparrow Shifter said.

"I get that, dude, but you need to relax and have fun, too. Come on; we're going to look for Kelly and the twins. Kelly got home last night. Christopher has a major job to work on, so they came home a few days early."

Kelly and the twins were a year younger than Shari-Beth's friends. That didn't stop the girls, and Lucian, another Wolf Shifter, from being a part of the group, though. Lucian was working at the Pack auto shop, too. The young man had come a long way since his family fled their abusive Pack in Canada. That Pack had been completely restructured under a new Alpha and was well on its way to healing and becoming the family it should be. Lucian's family, however, had stayed in Valerian's Cove. Everyone was much happier here.

"Lu is working today until three," Josh said. "We can swing by the

Pack and grab him and the twins together. I think the girls are working on new designs for their shirts today."

"It's almost three now. Why don't we all shift and meet there?" Shari-Beth suggested.

The others agreed, and soon three birds and a wolf were heading toward Pack lands to find their friends.

SEAN RUBBED A TOWEL OVER HIS HEAD TO DRY HIS HAIR AS HE CAME out of the Academy changing rooms. He threw the towel in the laundry basket and headed to Declan's office.

"Hey, cousin, got a minute?" He asked as he stuck his head around the door.

Declan looked up.

"For you, of course. Just don't ask me to spar right now. I've got to finish this training schedule for the Sea Fae today and run it past their Fight Master. He's expecting me to call." Declan was working with the head of Sionna's Guards to ensure that the Sea Fae got adequate training while at the Academy. Since he couldn't train them in underwater tactics, one of the adult guards sent to watch over Sinéad was in charge of that aspect of their training. The other two participated in the training as sparring partners. Even Sinéad took part, as it was thought wise that she should be able to defend herself if necessary. The Seer was learning to use her Sight in battle to predict what her opponent might do. It was rather hit-or-miss at this point, but she was improving.

"I was just sparring with Aidan. Josh and the girls came to get him. Josh said that Aidan hadn't taken a break from training all summer. When I thought about it, I realized it was true. He's here every day, isn't he? I hadn't realized how... dedicated he's become."

Declan frowned.

"I told him to take the day off today. I didn't realize he'd asked you to spar." Declan sat back in his chair.

"Aidan has been hard at it all summer. He's come a long way. But you're saying his friends think he hasn't taken a break at all? That's too much. Everyone needs a break every now and again. I wonder why he's pushing himself so hard?"

"Maybe he feels like he has something to prove since he is, in effect, a prey species, fighting with the more dominant Shifters?" Sean suggested.

"Maybe. But still. I'll have a talk with him. Did you make him take the rest of the day off?"

Sean nodded.

"I sent him off with Josh, Shari-Beth, and Emma."

"Good. They'll keep him busy for the rest of the day. I'll have a talk with him, and we should both keep an eye on him. Maybe Luc can speak to him next time he's in town."

8

S ean left Declan's office and decided to see what Rebecca was up to. She had said she would be working on new designs this weekend. Sean was happy that they were at least talking now. Maybe he could get his mate to take a break and go into town for ice cream at The Sweet Delight Ice Cream Shoppe.

REBECCA WAS IN HER STUDIO, WORKING ON A NEW DESIGN. SHE HAD sketched it out and was now fine-tuning all the little nuances of it. Something wasn't coming together just right, and it was incredibly frustrating. This had been happening more and more often lately. She blew the hair off her face with a sigh. It was also boiling out today, much hotter than usual. Sweat ran down her back, even with the windows and door open.

Rebecca stood up and pulled the elastic out of her hair, rewinding the long wavy mass into a knot on top of her head. Fixing it with the elastic again, she walked over to the counter to get a drink of water. She kept a pitcher of lemon and mint-flavored ice water with her as she worked in the studio these days. Today's pitcher had cucumber in it as well. She leaned against the counter as she sipped, looking up as a knock came on the door frame.

Sean stood in the doorway, admiring the view. Rebecca had hole-y jeans on, with a Kelly-green tank top. Her feet were bare, and a few tendrils of hair had escaped the knot on the top of her head and spiraled down the back of her neck. Her face was flushed from the heat.

"Hey, beautiful. It's scorching today. Want to take a break and get some ice cream with me?"

"Oh, yes, please. That sounds like bliss. Mollie enchants the shop and the patio, so it's always cool inside. In winter, it's always warm, and she enchants the coolers, so the treats stay fresh."

Rebecca locked up the studio and followed Sean out. She looked around.

"How did you get here? I don't see a bike or a car. Did you fly? I'm telling you right now, I am not walking to town in this heat."

"No, I teleported. Come on, I'll take us." Grasping her hand, he did, depositing them right in front of the ice cream shop. Rebecca grinned. Having access to Dragon transport was so cool. Some powerful Witches, like Celine's mother, Rosalie, could teleport, too, but it wasn't a skill she'd mastered. Not yet, anyway. If there were any way she could learn it, she would. Or she could just have Sean ferry her around. He was supposed to keep her happy, right? She grinned at herself. She'd never abuse the mate-bond by making him her personal transportation service... would she? Mayyyybe. Hey, it was hot. Teleporting was by far the best way to travel.

Mollie Murphy greeted them as they entered the shop. Rebecca had been right—it was blissfully cool inside. They made their way towards the counter, behind a family that seemed to be having difficulty deciding what they wanted.

After a few minutes, the family had made their choices, and Rebecca and Sean stepped up to the counter.

"Hey, guys! Glad to see you," Mollie said. "What can I get for you today? Cones, sundae? Milkshake?"

"It's too hot for a sundae," Rebecca groaned. "I love hot fudge; you know that, but today, ew. Now, whipped cream on top of my ice cream cone, that I could do."

Mollie laughed.

"You got it, Bex. I have a new cinnamon toffee crunch ice cream. Wanna try that?"

"Oooh, yes, please! With whipped cream. And chocolate sprinkles. In a waffle cone, please!"

"You got it. Sean? What can I get for you?"

Sean looked at the tubs of homemade ice cream in the case. Every single one was guaranteed to be amazing. It made it very hard to choose.

"One scoop of rocky road, one scoop of moose tracks, please. Also with chocolate sprinkles in a waffle cone, please. Hold the whipped cream on mine, though. Thanks, Mollie."

"You got it."

Mollie quickly made up their cones and handed them over. Sean and Rebecca thanked her, paid, and headed back outside to the magically cooled patio. They found a table and sat, enjoying their treats.

"So, what's new with you?" Sean asked between licks of his ice cream.

"I'm interviewing three possible apprentices on Monday," Rebecca told him. "I'm so scared and so excited! I mean, I'm really young to take on apprentices. There were over twenty applications! That means that my work is well respected. I feel excited and humbled, and I really don't want to screw this up!"

"You won't. And your work is amazing. Of course, you have people wanting to learn from you. Do you know which application you like the most?"

"The three I've chosen all seem promising. One is a Dwarf, and I'm not sure how she'll be able to handle the Fire necessary to do the work I do. The other two are Fire Mages, a Witch, and an Aes Sídhe."

They talked for a few more minutes about the applicants and about Sean's job at the Academy as Declan's assistant. By the end of their ice cream, both were very pleased with how the impromptu date had gone.

"This was nice. Thank you for dragging me out of my studio today, Sean," Rebecca said, smiling at him.

Sean grinned back at her.

"Any time, beautiful. Would you like to get dinner sometime soon? We could stay in town, or go somewhere else. Anywhere you want."

"Anywhere? Be careful, Sean. I might abuse that teleporting ability to go to Europe every week or something." Rebecca grinned at him.

"Whenever you want. Just let me know. In fact, do you want to have dinner in Paris?"

Rebecca blinked. Paris. She was on the verge of saying yes, then she remembered. Rosalie.

"If we go to Paris, and Rosalie finds out, she'll either crash our date, or get mad we didn't visit her. How about Milan? Oh, or Venice! I've never been to Venice. The pictures all look so beautiful. Can we go to Venice?"

"Of course. Dinner in Venice. How does Wednesday sound?"

"Sounds good to me. Thank you, Sean."

"Any time, sweetheart. Any time."

◈

ON MONDAY, FLORA TURNED UP RIGHT ON TIME. IN FACT, SHE WAS early and hung around the garden center until it was time for her interview. Rebecca greeted her with a smile.

"Come in, Flora. It's nice to meet you," Rebecca said, showing the young woman into the studio. Flora looked around, noticing the bins holding the precious metals and jewels.

"This is nice. I like your space. It's very well organized and tidy. My uncle Gordon says that's very important in a workspace."

"Is your uncle a smith too?"

"Yeah, he's a silversmith. Makes jewelry and other fancy things for rich people, mostly the Fae. He's very well respected for his work."

"Out of curiosity, why haven't you apprenticed with him?"

"Uncle Gordon is an excellent silversmith, but he believes females should stay home and leave the smithing to the males. He won't even look at my designs."

Rebecca rolled her eyes.

"I get it. Why don't you show me your designs? Did you bring a portfolio?"

Flora took out her tablet and showed Rebecca her designs and some of her pieces. They were very good.

"I think you're well on the way to being an exceptional crafter, Flora. Why do you want to apprentice with me?" Rebecca asked.

"Your work has something, a luster, that makes the pieces look almost alive," Flora said. "There's something about them that sings to me. I want to learn how to do that in my own pieces. I'm hoping you can teach me."

Rebecca smiled.

"Thank you," she acknowledged the compliment. "I'll be honest with you, Flora. I like you, and I think your work has real potential. I'm just not sure how to show you what I do since I use my Fire Gift to do it, and as far as I know, other than their affinities for metal and stone, Dwarves don't have magic, do they?"

Flora shook her head. "No, but I've been thinking about that. I think I can build a torch hot enough to echo your flame, and if you tell me what you feel as you're working, if I can get myself into the same space, I think it could work."

Rebecca considered it.

"Maybe we can get a Techno-Mage to help build the torch? If we can, there might be a market for them. We could make money off the patent, as well. That would benefit both of us."

Flora blinked. "Could a Techno-Mage somehow harness a Fire Mage's Gift and use it to power the torch?"

"I'm not sure that would be the way to go about it, but they could copy it, enchant it to replicate it, maybe? Or to replicate Dragon Fire? I think we should bring in a Techno-Mage and a Dragon. Thankfully, I have access to both, though my Techno-Mage is only thirteen. Or, almost. Still, he's very powerful and incredibly smart. He loves projects like this. Why don't I talk to them and set up a time to meet? If they can put this together, I would love to work with you, Flora. I'm curious to see if I can teach you what I do. And I like you. I would like us to be friends."

Flora grinned. "Me too. Thank you, Rebecca."

"No problem. Give me a moment, and I'll see when we can set up a meeting with the Mage and the Dragon. I have two more potential apprentices to interview today, but maybe tomorrow? Are you staying in town? Or can you come back?"

"I'm staying in town for a few days. I wanted a bit of a vacation from my family, and I've heard wonderful things about Valerian's Cove, especially since the Academy has expanded. Tomorrow would be great."

Rebecca called Sean and Ian Casey, her cousin Malia's son. Both were able to meet the following day.

"Thanks, Bex. This will be great," Ian said. "I just finished my last project and was getting bored. This project ought to keep me busy for a while. I'm sure we can figure it out, though. I wonder if anyone else has ever tried this before? I mean, to be able to harness Dragon Fire, or a Fire Gift. Surely someone has tried this already."

"Maybe, but not for this application. It needs to be very precise and able to respond to thought, almost. That's where the Techno-interface comes in."

"Ok. I'll do some research and see if anyone has managed it before. See you tomorrow!"

Ian rang off, sounding excited. Rebecca smiled. She adored her younger cousins. It would be fun to work on this with Ian.

REBECCA MET WITH THE AES SÍDHE FIRE MAGE, DANIEL, JUST AFTER lunch. He smiled at her as he introduced himself.

"Daniel ap Ioan, at your service."

"Thank you. Rebecca Casey. Earth and Fire Mage. I have an affinity for metals, which is how I create my work."

"Your work is stunning. You're already making a name for yourself in Faerie. Expect to see more requests for commissioned pieces from that realm," Daniel told her.

Rebecca blinked.

"That's very kind of you to say," she replied. "Why are you interested in working with me?"

They talked about Daniel's experience, his interests, and what his long-term plans were.

"I want to study outside Faery for a while," he told her. "My family are cousins to the MacNamaras, and Siofra suggested I speak to you. I would have looked you up even if you hadn't posted the advert for an apprentice."

Rebecca nodded. Daniel had brought a few examples of his work to show her. It was pretty enough, with a more classical Fae flavor. Swirling vines and flowers, inset with gems. Pretty enough, but not, to Rebecca's eyes, spectacular. And she had a feeling that Daniel wanted his work to be spectacular. Hence his desire to learn how she created her pieces.

"Where do you live at the moment? Would you commute, or are you planning to move to Valerian's Cove?" Rebecca asked the young Fae.

"I had planned to commute, but there are definitely some very attractive incentives to moving to Valerian's Cove," Daniel replied, smiling at her.

Inwardly, Rebecca sighed.

"I am only available as a mentor and teacher. I take that role seriously and would consider it a breach of trust to date an apprentice. Also, I have a fated mate. He's a Dragon. He can be rather territorial. And his family is rather well known. I'm surprised Siofra didn't mention that. She knows him very well. He's here all the time—he's the assistant Fight Instructor at the Academy. His cousin is the Lead Fight Instructor, and his sister's mate is the Psychic Studies teacher. You may have heard of his family, the Drakes of the Fire Mountain Clan? Sean is the youngest child of Crown Princess Aldona."

Daniel blinked and turned rather pale. "Sometimes, I hate my cousins," he said. He shook his head, smiling wryly. "Siofra has always liked to try to trip me up. She says I need taking down a peg or three. She told me you were a fabulous creator and quite beautiful besides. She neglected to mention you had a fated mate."

"Will that affect your application to be my apprentice? Will you be able to work with me and take directions from me, knowing there will never be any hope of a relationship beyond Master and apprentice and possibly friends?"

"It makes it easier, actually. I would like to learn from you. And there is the added benefit of getting to know a lot of very influential people while I'm here. That's always a good thing."

"As long as you are straight with them, and they like you. We have a large group of psychics and Seers around here, as well as two Fae Illusionists who have a direct line to the Goddess. It would be foolish to be anything less than that. It won't be tolerated," Rebecca warned.

Daniel nodded. "I appreciate that. In Faery, it is all about who you know and who you can call for help. Making strong connections is important, and connections through friends are much stronger than those made through obligation. I would hope that I would be able to make friends here."

This time, Rebecca nodded. "Ok then. I think your work has potential. I would be happy to take you on for an introductory period of three months to see if we can work well together. At the end of that time, we can re-evaluate. If either of us is displeased, we will end the apprenticeship there. Otherwise, we can continue to work together for as long as I feel is needed to bring your work to the best it can be under my teaching. Eventually, you will have to take what you learn here and make it your own, changing and developing it as you see fit to create your vision of your work."

Rebecca stood and held out her hand.

"I have one more person to interview. If he works out, I will have three apprentices. Would you be able to start a week from today? Will that give you enough time to sort out your living situation?"

"Yes, thank you. I appreciate the opportunity, Ms. Casey. I look forward to beginning my apprenticeship with you."

They shook hands, and Daniel left. Rebecca sat down again with a sigh. She hoped the next young man didn't try to hit on her, too.

9

Simon, the young Fire Mage, arrived just minutes after Daniel had left. Rebecca stood to shake his hand. He held her hand a minute too long, staring intently at her. It wasn't an attraction, Rebecca felt. There was something else going on there.

"Please have a seat," she invited.

Simon sat at the table across from her.

"Your application was very thorough," Rebecca began. "Your photos of your pieces showed potential. Did you bring any pieces with you to show me?"

Simon brought out a small box, from which he took a pendant and several brooches. They were not as impressive as Daniel's work but showed a sense of design and the promise of something more. Simon's work used more common gemstones rather than expensive ones. His pieces were set with hematite, snowflake obsidian, carnelian, and garnet. The pieces themselves were a little heavier than Rebecca liked. She had the feeling that Simon hadn't been working as a metalsmith for very long.

"How long have you been making your jewelry?" She asked the young man.

"Three years. I got started as a way to keep myself busy after school. I finished early and didn't know what I wanted to do. I've always drawn, and someone said I should try metalwork. A community college nearby had a jewelry-making class, so I gave it a shot. I really enjoy it, especially the precision work. I know mine isn't up to your standards, but that's why I'm here, right? To learn."

"So you live in the mundane world?"

"My father is a mundane, and my mother settled with him. He's a mechanic. He taught me how to work on cars, and I figured out how to use my Gifts to help him in the shop. Safer than a blowtorch. I started welding some of the scrap metal into statues and things in my spare time, which is why my friend thought I might enjoy making jewelry. She was right."

"Do you still make sculptures?" Rebecca asked.

"Yes, sometimes. I've been mostly focused on the jewelry for a while now, but sometimes the urge to make something bigger comes over me, and I take a break to work on it."

"While you're working with me, you'll be expected to put all of your time into your jewelry design and creation. Are you ok with that?"

Simon nodded. "Of course. I'm looking forward to it."

"And you won't have any problem learning from someone younger than you?"

Simon was a year older than Rebecca.

"No, of course not. It's about the level of skill, isn't it, not the age of the instructor?"

Rebecca looked at him for a moment, then down at the pieces on the table in front of her. There was something about this young man that unsettled her a bit. She couldn't put her finger directly on it—there was just... something. Still, she had an idea that it would be good to keep this young man close by, to keep an eye on him. And his work did show potential.

"All right, Simon. We can give this a try for three months. If, at the end of that time, the arrangement isn't working for either of us, we'll end it. Are you considering moving to Valerian's Cove for the duration of the apprenticeship?"

Simon blinked.

"I suppose so. I hadn't thought much about it. It would make more sense than trying to drive all the way here every day. I'm from up past Novato. I suppose I should see if there are any short-term rentals available."

"I'm sure there are. We have people come to visit the Academy all the time. Families, guest teachers. I'm sure there's something. You can ask at the realty office in town. You can't miss it; there's only one. The Cove is a great place to stay. I think you'll like it."

"Thank you, Ms. Casey. I appreciate you giving me a chance."

"Thank you for making the trip down, Simon. Are you able to start a week from today? Will that give you enough time?"

"Yeah, that's great. Thank you. I'd better go find somewhere to stay."

Simon rose and held out his hand. Rebecca shook it, then walked behind him to the door, watching him go. The car he got into was old but well-cared-for. It started right up, the engine purring quietly. Simon waved as he drove away.

"Well? How did it go?" Celine asked her niece as she approached from the garden center building.

"I'm taking on all three of them," Rebecca said. "I'm giving them each a three-month trial. I like Flora, the Dwarven woman, a lot. I think we'd work really well together. And I might be able to get materials through her family, which would be great. Daniel is a bit of a rake, but he's Siofra's cousin, and I told him about Sean. If he forgets and tries anything, I'll sic Siofra on him."

She paused.

"Simon is another thing. I don't know about him, Aunt Celine. There's something about him that sets off my warning bells, but I don't know what it is. He seems eager to learn and has some potential. Not as much as Daniel, I'd say, but he should be able to make a living off his work. It's heavier and clunkier than I'd like. I just get the feeling that we should keep him close and keep an eye on him."

"Then that's what we'll do," Celine said. "Do they all live nearby?"

"No, Flora is from Sweden, Daniel from Faery, and Simon from somewhere around Novato. They'll all have to find places to stay around here."

"We can ask Granny Niamh to make them rooms here," Celine offered.

Rebecca shook her head.

"Flora, I would be happy with. But not the other two. And I don't want to show favoritism."

"Whatever you think is best, sweetheart." Celine smiled at her niece. "So, how does it feel to have your own apprentices, niece of mine?"

"Oh my gods and little fishes, Aunt Celine! I can't believe it!"

◈

REBECCA SPENT THE REST OF THE DAY WORKING ON HER OWN designs. Shari-Beth was working at Wonder until three, then hanging out with Josh on Pack lands. Lucian joined them after he got off of work at five.

"I like working on cars," Lucian said as he came out onto the back patio at Josh's house to join them, "but I don't think this is what I want to do for the rest of my life."

"It's good to have a skill, though," Josh said, standing up and slapping the younger boy on the back. Shari-Beth smiled up at them.

"Oh, I get it. I just think this will be more of a hobby for me. I'm not sure what I want to do instead, though. I was thinking about joining the military, in one of the supernatural branches, like Tony and your dad, Josh."

Tony, the Pack Alpha, and Ralph, Josh's father, had both been Special Forces in elite branches made up of Shifters and other supernatural beings.

"Don't get killed. We'd miss you," Shari-Beth said.

Lucian shrugged.

"Why don't you see if you can do more Guardian training?" Josh suggested. "That would look good to the military if you're really thinking about applying."

"You and Aidan could train together," Shari-Beth said. "He's mad into it. We have to drag him away from training and force him to have fun."

"I'll ask," Lucian said.

"Ask Declan and Sean what they think," Josh said.

Lucian nodded.

"So, what are we up to this evening?"

"I don't know," Shari-Beth started.

Both boys suddenly froze, then sprinted towards the center of Pack lands. Shari-Beth ran after them.

"What's going on?" She called. Both Wolves could run faster than she could. Neither of them answered.

They arrived in front of the Pack Meeting House along with most of the Pack. Tony Gianetti, the Alpha, was facing off against a shorter, older man. A man that no one in the Pack had ever thought they would see again.

Caleb Gianetti, Tony's uncle and the father of his Third, Remy, stood in front of Tony, his hands clenched at his sides. Caleb looked rough, as though he had been living wild. He was by himself. Shari-Beth and Josh looked around.

"Where's Aldo?" Josh whispered, wondering about Caleb's older son. When Caleb and Aldo had left, Aldo had promised to keep his father in check. Caleb had been the previous Alpha of the Valerian's Cove Pack. Tony had Challenged his uncle and beaten him formally in a fight. Caleb had chosen exile over submitting to the new rules that Tony was imposing—rules that made the Pack much more the family it was supposed to be rather than the abusive mess it had been under his grandfather, father, and uncle.

Remy ran up, slowing as he reached Josh and his friends. His face hardened as he took in his father standing on Pack lands, where no one had ever expected to see him again. Remy walked up to stand next to Ralph, just behind Tony.

Caleb looked at his younger son, then back at the Alpha. Remy stared impassively ahead.

"Look, boy, I know we parted on bad terms, but you have to help me! My son is missing. He's been gone for three weeks, and the police are no help. He just vanished. There's no sign of him anywhere. You have to help me find him!"

Remy looked troubled.

"Where did you last see Aldo?" Tony asked.

Caleb took a breath, his shoulders shuddering.

"I last saw him in San Diego three weeks ago. We were granted admission to join the Pack down there on probation. Aldo was working his way up to being an enforcer in the Pack. We've been there for almost a year now. He headed to work one day and never came home. His boss at the shop says he never made it in."

"Are you sure Aldo didn't just decide to move on, go somewhere else?" Tony asked. If it had been him, he would have ditched Caleb as soon as he was sure the man was in a Pack where he'd be safe and kept under watch. Caleb wasn't exactly the sanest of Wolves. And he had a vast superiority complex, one that wasn't backed up by anything in the world of reality. It had to be exhausting, being around that all the time.

"No, I'm telling you. No one's seen him. Our Alpha put calls in to all the other Packs in the area. No one knows where he is."

"This is the first I've heard of it," Tony stated.

Caleb shrugged.

"I may have told him not to bother with you. Aldo would never come back here after the way you stole what should have been his birthright."

"I beat you in formal Challenge, Caleb. As was my right. Aldo could have Challenged me after that. He didn't. He chose to leave, with you. That's not the point. Why wouldn't Aldo come back here? He's welcome, as long as he follows our laws. He left when you did to keep an eye on you."

Caleb growled, his eyes flashing. Then he seemed to regain control of himself.

"So why have you come here if you hate us so much?" Remy asked, breaking protocol. Technically, only the Alpha was supposed to talk in situations like this. Still, Caleb was his father, as horrible as he had been.

Tony raised an eyebrow at Caleb. He was curious to know the answer, too.

"Because everyone knows how connected you are," Caleb ground out. "If I had any other choice, I wouldn't be here. You know Dragons and Witches and all sorts of people. Surely one of them can find Aldo."

Tony looked at Remy.

"Would Aldo take off like this, do you think?"

"I don't know," Remy shook his head. "Aldo always did what Father wanted. I don't think he would, but who knows? Maybe once he saw how other Packs lived, he got tired of my father's messed up way of thinking and decided to leave?"

"Aldo would never leave me!" Caleb spluttered.

Tony and Remy ignored him.

Do you want me to look into this? Tony asked his cousin through the Pack bond.

Remy hesitated for a minute, then shrugged.

"I think we have to," he said out loud.

Tony turned back to Caleb.

"I'll see what I can find out. You are welcome to stay with us while I do if you swear to abide by our rules. If not, you can find somewhere else. I'll have someone keep in touch."

Caleb glared, then lowered his eyes.

"I'll behave," he grumbled. He had never been comfortable around other paranormals. The last thing he wanted to do was to stay in town.

"Ok. You can stay in the bunks at the meeting house. You will be watched at all times. If you act in any way at odds with our laws, you will be escorted from Pack lands, and I will ask a Witch to ban you permanently. You will never be allowed to come here again. Is that understood?

Caleb nodded.

Tony called over one of his Peacekeepers.

"Will, I'm sorry to ask you, but will you please keep an eye on my uncle, so Remy and I can focus on finding my cousin and the other things we need to do? I'd feel much better knowing you were watching him."

Will nodded.

"Thank you," Tony said. He turned back to Caleb.

"This is Will. He'll help you get settled. He's new to the Pack since you left and completely loyal. You won't be able to convince him to act against us in any way. He will stay with you while you are on Pack lands."

Tony waited for Caleb to nod his agreement, then turned. Ralph and Remy followed their Alpha into the Meeting House and his office.

Tony sat behind his desk and motioned for his Beta and Third to sit.

"What do you make of this?" Tony asked them.

"Is he for real, or is this a way to work his way back in and try to stab you in the back so he can take over again?" Ralph asked.

"I don't think he's that clever," Remy shook his head. "If he was going to do something like that, he would have done it by now, and it would have been more of a frontal attack. Backed up by whatever dregs of society he could have gotten to help him. My guess is that Aldo kept him from doing that before now."

"Well, we'll take this as a real missing-persons case for now," Tony, a detective with the Valerian's Cove police force, told them. Both men nodded.

"Remy, are you going to be ok with having Caleb around? I can put him somewhere else."

Remy shook his head.

"I'll be ok. I'd rather have him where I can see him while he's in the area. And Will can manage him. He'd just better stay away from Suzette, or I won't be responsible for my actions."

"Do you think he's a threat to your family?"

"Not really. Suzette is a powerful Witch. I know her Gift is mainly Healing, but the other side of healing is destruction. She can be terrifying when she wants to be."

"And Malia and Marissa will help her, and believe me, you do *not* want to go up against those two when they're angry and defending someone they love," Tony said. "Ok, I'll start making some calls. I'll call the Alpha of the Pack they joined and the police down there, make sure everything is as he said. Then I'll call Peter Chizinsky on the Council. Make sure Aldo didn't run away to join the Army or something. We'll figure this out."

"Thank you, Tony. I appreciate it. Aldo's not the best brother, but I want to know what happened to him. Then we can decide what to do next."

Tony nodded.

"You haven't heard from him at all since he left?"

"No. Not once."

"Ok, then. Back to work, Remy. Ralph, stay a minute."

Tony waited until Remy was out of the building.

"Something about this feels off. I don't think Aldo would just ditch his father without telling anyone. He would have made sure someone was keeping Caleb in line. I think he really might be missing."

"I'll reach out to some of my friends, too," Ralph said. Ralph was a former undercover officer, in addition to being former Special Forces. He had connections like Tony did, as well as some in darker places. Between the two of them, they should be able to figure this out. For Remy's sake. Goodness knew they weren't doing it for Caleb.

10

Tuesday afternoon, Rebecca met with Flora, Ian, and Sean about the magic-powered torch they wanted to create for Flora.

"So, I did some research," Ian started. "Turns out there is a tool something like what you want to make that they're already developing for medical use, in micro-surgeries and stuff. It's not as powerful as you want, only about the power of a mid-grade Fire Witch. Siobhan could do better—much better. Anyway, I emailed the Techno-Mage in charge and explained what we wanted to do. He could see even more applications for it and wanted to know if he could get in on the action. For a part of the royalties from the patent, of course. He thinks we can make a mint off it." Ian grinned.

"Is he trustworthy, do you think?" Sean asked.

Ian nodded.

"I can have mother's lawyer work up a contract for all parties involved. That's probably the best thing to do," Sean thought out loud.

"That's a good idea," Flora agreed. "It's always important to have these things in writing."

She looked around at everyone else, who was staring at her.

"What, daughter of politicians, here. You learn a lot."

"Will he share the design of his current tool?" Rebecca asked.

Ian nodded again.

"Yeah. He thinks we can modify it. We might need stronger metal to build it out of, though. His is currently enchanted steel or something."

"I can get us star metal," Flora offered.

"Really? I would love to play with that!" Rebecca and Ian exclaimed together.

Flora grinned.

"I think we should meet this other Techno-Mage, and look over his designs to see if they're workable. Also, to figure out whether we can work with him before we make any agreements," Sean said. Everyone else nodded.

"Ian, can you email him back? Where is he? Can he come here? Or can we do a video call?" Rebecca asked.

"He's here in California. In San Jose. I don't know if he can teleport or if he's near a portal. I can ask."

Ian brought out his tablet from his backpack and sent a quick email. A moment later, they had an answer.

"Jordan says he can come here. He lives near a portal."

"Cool. That works out nicely. Thanks, Ian," Rebecca said. "When can we expect him?"

"He says half an hour? Maybe more, depending on how busy the portal is. He says he should be able to get through fairly quickly. It's a large portal facility."

"Yeah, with all the tech business in Silicon Valley, it made sense for their facility to be large and very well monitored. There is a permanent attachment of Dragon Guards and Guardians at that facility to keep track of everything," Sean said.

About forty-five minutes later, Jordan knocked on the door.

"Come in!" Rebecca and Ian called.

A young man with tossled dark hair and bright blue eyes walked in. He appeared to be around Rebecca's age. He grinned at everyone as he came in.

"Hey, guys. Thanks for inviting me. This project is going to be really fun."

Ian grinned back.

Rebecca studied the young man. She had a good feeling about him. Rebecca's intuition was usually spot-on, and she had learned to trust it. She smiled back.

"Thank you for coming. I'm Rebecca Casey. This is my apprentice, Flora, my cousin, Ian, who's also a Techno-Mage, and my mate, Sean Drake of the Fire Mountain Dragon Clan. It's nice to meet you."

"Jordan Smith. Glad to be here. It's nice to meet you all. Why don't you tell me what you want to use the tool for, and then I can show you my current designs?"

"Let's get to know each other a bit. I want to make sure we can work together and that we are all on the same page about any revenue from this project," Sean said.

"Sure. That's cool. I'm an open book. What do you want to know?"

"First off, would you be willing to sign a contract as to how the revenue will be distributed among the people here? And what the tool can be used for?"

Jordan blinked.

"Of course. I would prefer it, actually. It keeps everything so much cleaner."

"Excellent. If you will excuse me for a moment, I need to make a call."

Sean stepped out of the studio and called his mother's lawyer, Lord Kylan.

"He's emailing a basic contract right now. He had one on file from another project. He says we can refine it as we get further into the work. At the moment, it says that we, the five of us, will receive equal portions of any and all revenue from the creation and sales of the tool and that none of us will share the design with anyone else without the permission of the group as a whole. There will be further terms for licensing the plans, etc. We should have it in just a minute."

There was a knock on the door. Everyone turned toward it.

A tall Dragon was standing there, holding a briefcase. Behind him stood Princess Aldona.

"Hi, Mom," Sean said. "I didn't expect you today."

"I overheard what you were discussing with Kylan here and decided to see what you all were up to. It was a good idea to get this in writing at the start. I approve."

"Jordan, this is my mother, Her Royal Highness Aldona Drake, Crown Princess of the Fire Mountain Dragon Clan, and her lawyer, Lord Kylan. Mother, Lord Kylan, Jordan Smith, Techno-Mage."

Jordan's eyes had widened at Aldona's formal title. He bowed.

"Your Highness. It's a pleasure to meet you."

"My son didn't tell you who he was, did he?" Aldona asked with a smile.

"He gave me his name and Clan name, but I wasn't sure if he was the Prince. I am honored to be working with him."

Aldona smiled. Sean blushed.

Jordan grinned at his discomfort.

"Before I knew I was a Techno-Mage, I was an engineering student. I have low levels of Earth Gifts. Metals, of course. I'm also a card-carrying geek. I LARP and read fantasy novels. I am definitely up on at least the basics of the royal families of most of the currently known races. I just didn't expect to find the Prince of the Fire Mountain Clan here working on a project like anyone else. Though I suppose I should have figured it out. I mean, I knew you lived here. I wondered, but I wasn't sure."

"I try not to abuse my title," Sean said. "It's my sister, Devra, who will be Crown Princess after my mother. Thank goodness. I am much more suited to civilian life."

"You are an excellent Guard and Guardian and an excellent teacher," Aldona declared. "You should be proud of yourself, Sean. Your father and I are, as are your grandparents."

Sean blushed again.

"And we are also all very proud of Rebecca," Aldona said with a grin.

Rebecca felt her face flame almost as red as her Fire Gift. She had no idea the Drakes were keeping tabs on her. Though, of course, they were. She was the mate of their son and Prince.

"Thank you, Princess Aldona," Rebecca managed to get out.

"Just call me Aldona, or Mom, Bex," Aldona said. "Surely we know each other enough for that by now." Aldona smiled at the young Mage. Rebecca had lost her mother at an early age, and Aldona was determined to fill the spot as much as possible. She sincerely liked the young woman the Goddess had chosen for her son. Princess Aldona was very fond of the entire Casey Clan as a whole.

Kylan cleared his throat, pulling six copies of the contract out of his case.

"Here, read it, and have your own attorneys look it over. If you have any questions or suggestions, call me. When you are satisfied, sign it. Sean, you keep two copies and send one of them back to me when it's signed. I'll keep a copy on file."

"Thank you, Lord Kylan. I appreciate it," Sean said.

The attorney nodded.

"Well, that's sorted. Now, Ky. Since we're here, let's drop in on Celine. You haven't lived until you've tasted her food. We have an arrangement where we pay her grocery bills in return for being fed when we drop in. The woman is the most talented Kitchen Witch I have ever met. And her sister Luna is the most amazing baker. I think I gave you one of her pastries once, didn't I?" Aldona took her attorney by the arm and pulled him out of the studio, heading towards the house. Dragons were always hungry and loved to eat. The lawyer went willingly, following the Crown Princess without argument.

"Well, what should we do now?" Flora asked. "I suppose we should wait to go any further until the contract is signed? Are we sure we can all work together?"

Rebecca looked around the room.

"Let's take a break and go into town. Jordan, I don't know if you've ever been here before, but Ian's mother's best friend owns the ice cream store in town. She makes the absolute best ice cream you've ever had in your life."

Jordan's eyes lit up.

"Oh, by all means. We can talk, and all get to know each other as we go. Great idea."

They walked into town, talking as they went. Jordan and Ian talked about projects they had worked on. Flora, Rebecca, and Sean talked about places they'd been, what Flora's plans were long-term, Sean's position at the Academy, and Rebecca's plans for her studio. Ian and Jordan joined back in on the conversation, adding their own plans for the future.

"I mean, as a Techno-Mage, I can pretty much write my own ticket," Ian said. "I know I'm young, but I'm smart. And with all our contacts, I can go anywhere. I think I want to keep inventing things. I really enjoy having the challenge and figuring stuff out."

"Remember, we're counting on you to keep Allie grounded, too," Rebecca told the young Mage.

Ian groaned.

Jordan looked curiously at Rebecca.

"Ian's twin, Alison, is the Wielder of the Sword of Fire. She and Ian are part Witch, part Dragon, and Part Phoenyx. I mean, obviously, since Ian is a Techno-Mage. Ian is the strongest Techno-Mage discovered yet. Allie is also über-powerful. She can shift into both Dragon and Phoenyx forms and use both Fires. As well as being a Fire Mage in her own right. She can be rather scary. She is also impetuous and has an enormous sense of justice that you really don't want to get on the wrong side of. She took on a full-grown hybrid like herself last year, with a little help, and won. And that crazy pants guy was several hundred years old."

Jordan looked at Ian in amazement.

"*How* old are you?"

Ian grinned. "We'll be thirteen in November," he replied.

Jordan stared.

"My cousins Mikey and Milena are super powerful too," Ian said. "They are Fae-Dragon-Phoenyx hybrids. Mikey's an Earth Mage, and Milena is a Fae Illusionist with a direct line to the Goddess."

Jordan blinked.

Ian grinned and kept going.

"My baby sisters are all that, plus being half-Shifter Wolves as well. They can both shift already, and they're not even two yet. We're all taking bets on what magic Gifts they'll have and when they'll show. My cousins Mariah and Anne are Witch-Pixie hybrids."

Jordan just looked stunned.

"There has been a surprising number of super-powered young people turning up lately," Sean told the Techno-Mage. "Both here and in other places. Our friend in Fairweather Falls, in Maine, is part Star-born, and her children are super-powered too. Especially her daughter, and she's only eight. The Goddess seems to be preparing for something huge. We figure we have some time since most of the super-powered are still quite young. But, just to be safe, if you see anything out of the ordinary, anything wrong, or that feels strange, please, let me know. There have already been incidents."

Jordan blinked again, then nodded.

"Yeah, of course. I mean, I figured something was going on, what with Dragons and Phoenyxes coming back into the world and a whole new class of Mage being discovered." He stared at Ian again for a moment. "Are there really that many super-powered kids?"

"That's just some of them. We also have three super-charged Seers, all from different races. And we've been told that not all of the super-powered have shown up yet. Life is going to get very interesting soon," Rebecca said.

Jordan winced.

Sean grinned at Rebecca.

"Donnie would say you just jinxed us, Bex."

"It's not anything everyone else isn't thinking, anyway," she retorted.

Sean grinned and put his arm around her.

Shari-Beth was working in Wonder Tuesday afternoon when a young Aes Sídhe walked in. He smiled at her as he began looking around.

"Welcome to Wonder. Please let me know if you have any questions," she told him as he wandered through the store. He paused at each jewelry display, paying particular attention to Rebecca's.

The bell over the door chimed again as the young man was looking at the display of Dragon metalwork. Another young man entered, this one appearing to be more human.

"Welcome to Wonder," Shari-Beth said again.

The new young man nodded to her. He, too, looked around, focusing on the jewelry displays. He paused by the case holding Rebecca's work.

The Aes Sídhe moved over to join him.

"Those pieces are exquisite, aren't they?" Daniel asked. "They're the work of a very talented Fire Mage. I'm starting an apprenticeship with her next week."

The other man looked up.

"So am I," he said.

Daniel grinned at him.

"Excellent! Well met. Daniel ap Ioan, of Faery, at your service," he bowed.

"Simon Rawlings. I guess you're a Fire Mage too?"

"That's correct," Daniel answered. "I'm extremely excited to be working with Rebecca. Will you be living here or commuting?"

"Living here. My family is further up the state."

"Do you have a place in mind yet? I'm looking for a place for myself. If you like, we could look together. It may be easier to find a place we can rent as roommates."

Simon stared at him for a moment, then nodded.

"That would be great. I wasn't sure I was going to be able to find something on my own. And since we'll be going to the same place every day, it makes sense." He grinned suddenly. "I'll warn you now, I'm a terrible cook, though."

Daniel grinned back.

"That's ok. I can cook. Our housekeeper at home taught me. I'll cook if you clean?"

"Sure, that sounds good," Simon agreed.

The two young men talked for a while longer, then waved at Shari-Beth as they left together, heading off to the Valerian's Cove Real Estate office a few doors down.

Liz came out from the back room as the door closed behind them.

"I thought I heard the bell. Everything ok?"

"Fine. Two of Rebecca's apprentices just came in and met each other. They're going to look for a house together."

"What did you think of them?"

"One of them seems really friendly. The other one, I'm not so sure about. He seems much more quiet and reserved. I get kind of a weird feeling from him, to be honest. Not sure why."

"Hm," Liz said as she sniffed the air. "There's definitely something there I don't recognize. He's a Fire Mage, right?"

Shari-Beth nodded.

"Well, I guess we'll just keep an eye on him and see how it goes," Liz smiled. "Now, how about some desert from The Baker's Delight? I'm craving chocolate and cherries for some reason."

"How far along are you, again?" Shari-Beth asked, then ducked as Liz swatted at her.

"Bite your tongue!" The Wolf Shifter exclaimed, heading out the door.

TONY WAS TROUBLED. HE WAS MORE WITHDRAWN THAN USUAL AT dinner Tuesday night, and Malia noticed.

"Hey, you. What's going on? Are you still thinking about Caleb turning up?"

"Yeah, I guess. I called the San Diego Pack Alpha. He has a large territory, but he knew right away who I was asking about. He told me that Aldo truly seemed to be working hard to overcome his prejudices and was becoming a helpful member of the Pack. Caleb still has difficulty, but the Alpha says he seems to be trying. Especially when Aldo is around to keep him in line. He was worried about Aldo, too. There's been no sign of him, just like Caleb said."

Malia frowned as she lifted her youngest daughter, Eve, from her high chair. Eve's twin, Aoife (and yes, Malia realized the irony of giving the twins the same name in different languages. That's why she'd done it), had already fallen asleep in her chair. There was a smear of pasta sauce across the sleeping toddler's cheek.

Tony stood and took Eve while Malia worked Aoife out of her chair and wiped her face. The infant girl slept through it all, curled up in her mother's arms.

Malia's older twins, Ian and Allison, were in the sitting room, playing a board game with their cousins, Malia and Tony's foster-daughters, twins Mariah and Anne. Ian had told them all about the new tool he was going to be developing with Rebecca and her crew. He was extremely excited about it, and had only good things to say about Jordan, the other Techno-Mage involved. Malia was happy to see her son so excited. There had been a time, after Allie came into her powers and before Ian had, when they had all been worried about Ian. Now, no one was. For one thing, Ian and Allie would both have extended lifespans, even beyond their Witch lifespans, which were already longer than human, thanks to their Mythic Shifter genetics. And they were both immensely powerful. They both had their interests and talents, along with their Gifts. Malia smiled as she heard a shriek from the sitting room. Someone must have won a game against Allie. 'Quiet' was definitely a term that absolutely no one would use to describe Malia's most fiery child. Thankfully, the infant twins were used to their sister and could sleep straight through her outbursts.

"What did the police say?"

Tony shrugged.

"They have no leads either. It's like he really did just vanish into thin air."

"And we're sure this isn't some sort of weird plan to come back here, get you to trust them, then take over again?" Malia asked.

"I mean, as sure as I can be. It doesn't feel that way. Caleb is really very worried, scared almost, for Aldo. I could smell it on him."

Malia and Tony carried Aoife and Eve up the stairs to their room and got them cleaned up and ready for bed. Aoife stayed asleep through the entire experience. The tiny twins had only recently transitioned into sleeping in their own crib. It was a double-sized crib that Tony and Remy had built for them, so the twins could sleep together. Eve's eyelids drifted closed as soon as she was laid in the crib next to her sister. She rolled over and put her arm around her twin.

Malia and Tony stood with their arms around each other, looking down at their youngest children.

"We really are blessed, aren't we?" Malia said.

"We really are," Tony agreed.

BACK DOWN IN THE KITCHEN, TONY FINISHED CLEANING UP FROM dinner while Malia sat, a cup of tea and a cookie in front of her.

"Ralph heard back from his friends. No one in the military has heard from Aldo. He hasn't joined up, as far as anyone can tell. My sources say the same."

"How can anyone just disappear from Pack lands?" Malia asked. "Surely, if anything had happened, or if anyone strange had come in and done something to him or carried him off, there would be signs? The other Wolves would be able to smell them? Smell what happened?"

"You would think," Tony said. "Which tells me that either he did leave of his own volition, or this was an inside job, and someone is hiding something. Either way, it will not be pleasant when we figure it out."

"If he did leave on his own, it really will kill Caleb, I think," Malia said.

"Yeah, I know." Tony agreed. He kissed Malia on top of her head, then finished loading the dishwasher.

❦

CALEB GIANETTI WAS NERVOUS. HE STARTED AT EVERY LITTLE sound. He didn't feel safe here, on the land of the Pack over which he had ruled not so very long ago. He had noticed when he arrived how much better everything looked. The most telling thing had been seeing how the whole Pack had stood in support of Tony, their current Alpha, and the smiles on their faces as they went about their day.

Will had continued to stick to Caleb like glue. His presence made Caleb feel a little safer, but not much. He knew that if anyone here in Valerian's Cove had a grudge against him from the past, it would be easy enough for them to reach him. And yet, coming here had been the only thing the former Alpha could think to do. He had to find his son. Aldo was all he had left. Caleb had no delusions that Remy would ever forgive his father for the death of his mother or the way he had treated Remy for most of his life. To Caleb, Remy was just another member of the Pack. Not his son. But now, having lost one son and everything else he held dear, Caleb was beginning to think that maybe he had been wrong. Seeing how well Remy looked, tall and strong beside his cousin, and how well-respected Remy was in the Pack opened the doors of Caleb's mind to thoughts he'd never had before. Kinder, more accepting thoughts. Seeing that other Packs were now run much the way that Tony was running his after the Council had cracked down on abusive Packs like this one had used to be; having lived in one of the better Packs himself in San Diego, Caleb was questioning his entire way of life, and everything he thought he believed. Caleb and his brother, Clive, had been raised by a sociopathic man who taught them that they were better than everyone else and that everything they wanted was theirs for the taking. They had both run the Pack that way, as their own personal playground and harem. And yet, neither of them had been happy. Caleb hadn't even realized that until he left. Until he was on the road with his older son, looking for a new place to live, a new Pack. They'd stopped in the Silicon Valley Pack, the Bakersfield Pack, and the LA Pack before settling down in San Diego. All Packs that were run with respect for their members, the way they were meant to be. Seeing how happy the other Packs had been had awoken something in Caleb. He felt as if he were being cracked open, and light was streaming in where only darkness had been before.

Someone dropped something out in the hallway, and Caleb jumped. Voices from the common room of the Meeting House burst into laughter. Caleb sat on the edge of his bunk, his face falling into his hands. What was he going to do?

12

By Thursday morning, everyone had had their legal advisors look over the contract, approve it, and had signed. Sean forwarded Lord Kylan a signed copy of each person's contract. The lawyer would keep them on file at the palace.

Ian and Jordan were in their element. The two had started bouncing ideas off each other as soon as the contracts were filed at the palace. Sean and Rebecca had to practically sit on Ian to keep him from contacting Jordan before then. Ian spent the time waiting coming up with his own ideas. So had Jordan. They had a lot to talk about.

By Friday morning, Jordan was ensconced in his own room at Celine and Brendan's house. The older Techno-Mage had decided it would be easier if he and Ian could work directly together, and since Ian was still a young teen, Jordan had come to him. They were using the Techno-Mage classroom at the Academy, with the permission of Headmistress Maria Hemenway, who was very interested to see what the pair came up with.

Flora had returned to Sweden via the portal to pack her things and let her parents know what was going on. Rebecca had decided that even if the Techno-Mages failed and Flora couldn't replicate something close to Rebecca's process, she could still help the young woman with her design skills and basic jewelry smithing. Plus, she found she truly liked Flora. There was the potential for a close friendship there.

Daniel and Simon found an apartment in town, not far from Emma's house, on the right-hand curve of the road above the harbor. The apartment was in an old Victorian house that had been divided into three apartments, one on each floor. They had the one in the middle. It was a two-bedroom, with plenty of light streaming in through the large windows that graced every outside wall. Daniel went home to Faery and returned with furniture and kitchen supplies. All Simon had to pick up were his clothes.

Rebecca looked around her studio. It was a long, two-roomed building. Tony and Brendan had built it for Malia when she was in high school, and Brendan had expanded it to include the second room when she had moved back to the Cove several years before.

I wonder if we'll have enough room in here, Rebecca thought to herself. She liked to spread out as she worked. The work table in the first room was really only big enough for her. And there wasn't enough room to put out a second table. The next room was the same size, maybe a little smaller.

Rebecca headed for the greenhouse housing Brendan and Siofra's Fae hybrid plants. Most of the time, now, if he wasn't teaching at the Academy, that's where Brendan could be found. It was lucky he had hired nursery helpers and had a few apprentices himself now as an Earth Mage. Otherwise, the rest of the nursery would have been severely neglected.

Rebecca ducked as Siofra's firebird Familiar swooped down to land on her shoulder as she entered the greenhouse. Strains of Fae music played softly through the space over the music system Brendan had installed. The pipes and strings sounded as if they were singing a lullaby to the plants inside. Amaia, the firebird, started preening Rebecca's hair. Amaia loved people who had Fire Gifts. She could always tell.

Rebecca scratched Amaia's head, right above the bird's eyes. Amaia trilled happily.

"Let's go find Brendan and Siofra, ok?" Rebecca said to the bird on her shoulder. She walked through the greenhouse, which was filled with so many plants it felt as if she were walking through a jungle. Plants reached out to touch her as she passed. There were plants that sang, plants that chimed like bells, plants that put out the most intoxicating scents you had ever smelled. Bright splashes of color were everywhere. Birds flew overhead, and the chittering of Fae animals sounded on the air. Brendan and Siofra had gotten special permission for the plants, animals, and birds from the mundane government, the Council, and the Fae Council. There were spells on the greenhouse that kept them all inside, safe and protected. The greenhouse was not open to the public.

Rebecca found Brendan and Siofra towards the back, studying a healthy-looking little plant with heart-shaped pale green leaves. It looked like a perfectly normal plant to Rebecca, who knew that none of the plants in the greenhouse were anything that could be called normal by Earth standards.

"Hey, you guys," Rebecca said as she approached.

The others turned towards her, smiling.

"Hey, Bex!" Siofra said.

Brendan hugged his niece.

"What brings you in here, sweetheart?"

"I was wondering if you would have time to look at the studio with me. I'm not sure there's enough room for four people to work there. Do you think we could expand it a bit more?"

Brendan cocked his head to the side, thinking.

"How far are you thinking of taking this apprenticeship thing, Becca?" He asked. "Are you going to continue it on after these three, or is this going to be it? Are you going to seriously consider hiring others to help you with your work?"

"I think I am," Rebecca said. "I'm hoping that at least Flora will stay with me for a while after her apprenticeship. An apprenticeship is three years, so by the end of that, we'll all know each other very well and be able to tell if we would continue to work well together, and if their styles would complement my own and the direction I want to take the studio in at that time."

"You're right; you're going to need a larger space," Brendan said thoughtfully. "A more permanent space, too." He turned to Siofra.

"Siofra, darling. Do you think you could get that nice Fae architect that helped expand the Academy to come out and build Rebecca a permanent studio? We'll have to find the perfect site. We could put it here, down the field closer to the training ground. Or out along the cliffs near the Academy. I'm sure the Dragons would be fine with having it on their land, given Rebecca is Sean's mate. Would that work for you, Bex?" He turned back to Rebecca.

Rebecca blinked. Once again, things were moving much more quickly than she had expected, in new and scary directions. Scary, but exciting. Also, this was looking more and more like her move to Valerian's Cove was going to be permanent. What would her father say?

"Can I talk to my Da about it? I mean, I wasn't planning on staying here forever. Though, I suppose I should have. Sean's work is here, and mine is somewhat portable. Also, most of our family is here. And Da could visit whenever he wants. I just want to make sure he's ok with it." Rebecca thought for a moment. "Do you really think the Dragons would let me build on their land?"

The Dragons had built their own enclave in Valerian's Cove when it became apparent that Devra, Sean, and Declan were making it their home base. The Dragon land was home to Dragons, Guardians, Dragon Guards, and Lily, their oldest and most powerful Seer, who had followed her grandson Donnie when he decided to stay in Valerian's Cove at the Academy with his mate, Princess Devra Drake. Donnie's younger sister, Bethie, was the next Seer. Lily said that Bethie would be even stronger than she was. Bethie was only twelve yet, and already highly accurate in her Visions.

"I'm sure they will. If I know Lily, she's already put aside the perfect place for you," Brendan smiled. Just then, the phone in the greenhouse rang. Siofra got to it on the last ring.

"Hello? Hey, Lily. Yup. We were just talking about it. Brendan said you did. Oh, really? Thank you. We'll head out now. Thank you!"

Siofra hung up, then turned to Rebecca, grinning.

"Lily strikes again. Though, she says Bethie helped. Not only have they picked you the perfect site, they've already started building. She says you'll love the plans."

Rebecca rolled her eyes. Of course, she would. Lily probably picked them right out of Rebecca's own mind. It would have been nice to actually be consulted, but still. Oh, well. She was grateful to the Dragon for getting all of this moving for her.

"Lily says come out now, and she'll show you the plans and what they've done so far."

"Let's go, then," Brendan said. He grinned down at Rebecca, who smiled back. "Let's grab Celine—she'll want to see it too."

Lily had, of course, thought of everything. The new studio was going to be perfect. It was near the Academy, at the edge of the Dragon enclave. You could look out the windows and see the ocean. The plan was for a large, open room on the first floor that would be the workroom, then upstairs would be bedrooms, bathrooms, a sitting room, and a kitchen for the apprentices.

"Of course, you and Sean will eventually have your own house here, too,' Lily said to a slightly bemused Rebecca. "I figure we can get this all finished in a few months, if Siofra here will bring in her Fae friends." Lily raised an eyebrow at Siofra, who grinned and nodded.

"That would be wonderful, Lily. Thank you," Rebecca told the old Dragon. Lily looked like a tiny older grandmother. Looks were deceiving. She was one of the most powerful Dragons alive. Well, she was old. And she was a grandmother. She also possessed a twisted sense of humor and more energy than most beings even a quarter of her age. Lily was training Bethie in mischief-making as well as in the skills of a Seer. Whenever the younger members of the Casey Clan got into trouble, you could bet that Lily and Bethie were right in the middle of it. And they rarely got caught, because, Seers. Unless they wanted to, of course. Sometimes, it was fun to let the others catch them out.

The studio would be built of stone. There would be two full forges, plus workstations for Rebecca and nine other workers.

"Nine? And two full forges? I don't use a forge, really, though, Lily," Rebecca said.

Lily smiled a little sadly.

"Flora will. Her armor will be the strongest and most beautiful the world has ever seen. Her uncle Lars will come and teach her about armor. Your jewelry will become talismans, Rebecca. You will partner with a High Magic Witch, who will become one of your dearest friends, to create pieces enchanted to keep combatants healthy and safe. And to bring them home." Lily's eyes stared off into the distance before she shook her head, then grinned. "You have a little bit of time before Lars moves in. Flora will need to learn everything you can teach her before then. Your Witch will show up soon. You two will need to learn to work together on pieces—they will need to be enchanted as you create them, so the magic is inherent to the piece, a part of its molecular structure. They will be virtually indestructible. Her name is Sarah, by the way. You'll know her when you see her. You two will be great friends. I've Seen it. Sarah's your age. Her life's been very different from yours. Lots of ritual, and... I'll let her tell you. Anyway, have fun!"

Lily left them abruptly, turning to head back towards the Academy, where Bethie, the younger Casey twins, and their friends were attending fight practice. They kept it up all year round. It seemed important, what with everything that was going on.

Rebecca looked at her aunt and uncle, then at Siofra. Then she looked back at the site of her new studio.

"What's wrong, sweetheart?" Brendan asked his niece softly.

Rebecca felt her eyes fill with tears.

"Everything is moving so quickly. I mean, I'm excited about the studio, and my apprentices. It's great to have others to work with." She paused.

"This is about Sean, isn't it?" Siofra asked.

Rebecca nodded, wiping a tear off her face.

"I know we're Fated Mates, and the Goddess is never wrong. And Sean told me he wouldn't stop me from having my business, or insist on making the bonding official soon, or having kids."

"Then what's the problem?"

Brendan put his arm around Rebecca and pulled her in against his chest. She snuggled in, her head against his heart.

"Is this about your mother, Rebecca?" Brendan asked.

Siofra glanced at him sharply.

After a moment, Rebecca nodded. Brendan kissed the top of her head, then looked back at Siofra.

"Rebecca's mother and twin vanished when the girls were two. They were coming home from visiting friends in the San Juan Islands, and the ferry went down. There were no survivors found. My brother has always insisted that his wife was still alive, that he would have known if she was dead. But we haven't heard from her since."

"Were they Fated Mates?"

"Yes."

"Then he's probably right. I wonder why she hasn't been in contact."

"We don't know. We spent years looking for them. Never found a trace. But Tom insists that they are still alive."

"It's why he never dates, and hasn't remarried," Rebecca added, wiping her eyes. She gave her uncle a quick hug, and straightened up again.

"Mom vanishing, being missing for so long, broke Dad's heart," she told the other woman. "He's never given up hope. It's almost like an obsession. Sometimes, when he thinks I'm not looking, he looks so terribly sad. I don't know if I'm strong enough to love someone like that. Or to keep it together if I lost them. I think the pain would kill me."

"Bex, you know what happened with your parents is extremely unusual, right?" Brendan asked. "I mean, look at your Aunt Celine and I. We're as happy as clams. And we're both perfectly fine. We love each other, and take each moment together for the gift that it is. If anything were to happen to Celine, I would be devastated. But I know she would want me to keep living, and I would want the same for her."

"My friend Lori's grandfather died of a broken heart when his wife died. He lived for her. Anything she wanted, even if it wasn't the best for the rest of the family, he gave her."

"That's not love, Bex. That's obsession. The two are very different. When you love someone, you want them to be happy, yes, and you understand that a healthy relationship means both people getting their needs me. If Celine decided to move back to France, and I for some reason needed to stay here, we would still make it work. The point is to talk it out and figure out what both partners really need, really want. It's a partnership. You work together for the wellbeing of both of you, and for any children that might come along. Or anyone else in your family that you feel has a part in the matter."

"I know I'm being ridiculous," Rebecca said, still sniffling a bit.

"You're not being ridiculous, Rebecca. What you're feeling is completely understandable. And, the Goddess knows what she's doing," Siofra told the younger woman. "She put you and Sean together for a reason. She seems to be awfully fond of you Caseys for some reason. I'm sure she wouldn't put you with someone that wouldn't work out. And," Siofra said with a grin, "just because the Dragons are already building you a house, doesn't mean you have to live in it until you're ready. Take your time. As much as you need. You do have a lot going on right now."

"And talk to your father about it, Bex," Brendan told his niece. "I know he only wants you to be happy, whatever that takes. We'll all help you as much as we can, whenever you ask us to. And even sometimes when you wish we wouldn't. It's only because we love you, and we want you to be happy."

Rebecca nodded, looking out over the cliff. Then she turned back to the site of her new studio.

"I guess I'm really doing this. I really need to call my Dad."

"I'll put in the gardens for you, Bex," Siofra said.

"I'll help," Brendan agreed.

13

Shari-Beth looked at her young niece in exasperation.

"Allie, violence is not always the answer. You *know* that."

The younger girl glared back at her.

"But Shari, he's stupid and mean. Can't I just smack him around a *little* bit?"

Allie was less than happy about Caleb being on Pack lands. She knew how much trouble he had caused and how hurt Remy had been when Caleb and Aldo had left. Remy had lost all hope that he would ever reconcile with his father, ever earn his father's love and approval. Even if he knew he didn't want to be the kind of person that would earn Caleb's approval. He had harbored a hidden hope that there was good inside his father, somewhere, and it would come out someday and love him. Having Caleb back again was playing mind games with poor Remy.

Allie was also very aware of the state of the Pack when Tony had taken over and how hard he had worked to change it. She lived on Pack lands as Tony's daughter. There was no way she could miss it. Caleb had said something derogatory in Allie's hearing that morning, and the young teen was still fuming about it. It was lucky Shari-Beth was visiting. She was able to pull her niece away before the young firebrand started something. Allie had literally had steam coming out of her nose. She was seconds away from going full Dragon on the old Wolf.

"No, you can't. But if Caleb does anything that physically hurts someone, then you can. It's much harder to prove mental abuse. For that, you need to get an adult."

Allie continued to glare. Mikey, Milena, and Ian glared too. All four had been together that morning, and all four had heard Caleb's comment.

"Come on, let's find the others and have a water balloon fight," Shari-Beth suggested. "Didn't Liz's daughter Sarah win the last one?"

"I'd rather fry Caleb," Allie grumbled, her arms crossed over her chest.

"Well, you can't. So let's go." Shari-Beth put her arm around the younger girl and led her away.

❦

THEY FOUND LIZ AND FRANKIE'S KIDS, AS WELL AS SOME OF THE other children of the Pack. Mariah and Anne were out on the patio in back of Malia and Tony's house, taking a break from their tee-shirt business. It was a hot day. Both girls had their hair pulled up on top of their heads and cool glasses of lemonade in their hands.

"Hey, you two. We're going to have a water balloon fight. Want to play?" Shari-Beth asked.

"Oh, hells yes," Mariah declared, climbing to her feet. She went inside to grab the balloons. Malia always kept a large box of them under the kitchen sink.

"Did you ask Josh and Lucian?" Anne asked.

"They're at work. They'll have to wait for next time," Shari-Beth said with a shrug.

Anne went in to help Mariah fill the water balloons. For twins that had been raised apart since they were very young, the girls had become extremely close. They were an excellent balance for each other. Anne was loosening up some, and Mariah was learning to think things through before rushing into them. They were good for each other.

"Ready?" Shari-Beth asked. They had broken into two teams. Both sides had a large bucket of water balloons. One member from each team was designated to keep their team supplied with fresh ammunition.

Soon the air was filled with shrieks and colorful balloons. A couple of the Pack kids had brought water guns, too, which only added to the chaos. Malia came home from Wonder and heard the mayhem happening at the back of the house. She looked out the kitchen door, just missing getting hit in the face by a stray red balloon.

"Sorry, Malia!" One of the kids yelled.

She waved back. Malia turned to the two kids at the sink, filling balloons. There was water everywhere.

"You two go outside and join the fun," she told them. "I'll fill the balloons."

The children grabbed their buckets and ran outside. They came back long enough to hand over empty buckets to be filled, then ran outside again.

Malia called Marissa, who had been minding the youngest twins with her own.

"Hey, Sis. There's mayhem happening here. Come over!"

Marissa showed up with four toddlers shortly afterward. She used her Water Gift to dry up the kitchen and help fill the balloons while the babies played on the floor at their feet. Evie Shifted, running around on all fours. Malcolm, Marissa's son, threw a ball of water at her.

Malia stared at Malcolm, then at Marissa.

"When did he start doing that?!?"

"This morning. He was watching me make the water dance for them, and suddenly, he could make water balls."

Malia looked down at the children on the ground, then back up at her sister.

"Riss, you know what this looks like, right?"

Marissa nodded.

"Whatever trouble is coming, it will not be over quickly if the babies are coming out super-powered."

"If the ages of the kids are anything to go by, it could last for at least ten years," Malia said softly. Her chest tightened as she looked at the babies playing together, then out the door at the children in the backyard. The game had ended. Kids were collapsed all over the grass, soaking wet. Allie was in Dragon form. There were several Wolf pups lying around, too. Flowers were popping up around Mikey where he lay, and Milena was idly spinning an illusion as she leaned against a tree.

"I don't want them to grow up and have to fight," Malia said.

"I know. I don't either," Marissa agreed.

The kids were all being trained to fight. Most of them enjoyed it. But they had never seen the horrors of a true battle. Malia and Marissa both hoped that somehow, whatever was coming would be diffused before it got that far.

Please, Goddess, keep them safe, Malia prayed. *If there's any way to avoid it, please don't make them fight.*

✦

TONY WAS IN HIS OFFICE, WORKING ON PAPERWORK FOR THE PACK accountant. His phone buzzed, startling him.

"Hey, Boss," Lexi Trudeau, the Pack Administrative Assistant, said. "Peter Chizinsky from the Council is on the line. Wanna take a break from paperwork and talk to him?" Lexi knew how much Tony despised paperwork.

"Yes, please, Lexi. Please put him through."

"This is Tony," he said as the phone rang again.

"Tony, Peter Chizinsky. I checked our records for your cousin. Just to be sure. The last notations we have were from when he and his father joined the San Diego Pack. Nothing after that. He's definitely not working for us."

Tony sighed. "Thanks, Peter. I appreciate you checking."

"I'm sorry I couldn't be of more help," Peter replied. "Now that I have you on the phone, though, I wanted to tell you. Your cousin isn't the only person vanishing into thin air recently. We've had several reports of people, all different supernatural types, going missing. Not enough from any one area to cause much of a stir, but enough that a pattern is starting to emerge when you look at the country as a whole. I'm not quite sure what it is yet, but it's getting clearer."

This time, Tony frowned.

"How many people?"

"Twenty so far. Two from San Diego, one from San Francisco, and two from Oregon. One from Texas, one from Louisiana. They're from all over. They're all adults, though some are young adults, barely into their twenties. So far, the one thing they all have in common is that they all had ties to someone important in some way and were labeled as discontented with their lives."

"But Aldo wasn't. Caleb says Aldo was doing really well in the San Diego Pack. Their Alpha there agreed. He said Aldo was really making an effort to fit in and was working his way up to enforcer."

"But from the outside, look at his history, and at his father. They were kicked out of their Pack after Caleb lost a Challenge fight. They lived rough, then had to start all over again with a new Pack. Plus, Caleb's no peach, and Aldo was keeping him in line. There's a lot to be unhappy about there, if you're looking for it."

Tony shook his head.

"But if they researched their targets at all, they would know he was turning over a new leaf. He doesn't really fit the profile."

"Maybe they thought he was still close enough to the situation, to losing his birth Pack, to be easily swayed?" Peter suggested.

"I don't know," Tony said. He sighed. "I hope we find him soon. Caleb is pissing people off just by being here. No one from the original Pack is happy he's here. I really want to find Aldo, if only so that he can take his father and go home to San Diego."

Peter chuckled. "For your sake, I hope we find him soon, Tony. I'll keep my ears open. If I hear anything, I'll let you know."

The men said goodbye and hung up. Tony stared at the phone for a moment, then picked it up again. He called the Pack in Canada that Aldo and Remy's mother, Tracie-Marie, had come from.

"Hey, Tony," the Alpha, Jean-Paul, greeted him. "How are Lexi and her family? Everything ok?"

"Yeah, they're great. Everyone is doing really well. Malia thinks Liz is pregnant, but Liz vigorously denies it. I don't think anyone believes her, though."

"The kids are all doing well? Lucian?"

Frankie's son had been troubled when they moved to Valerian's Cove.

"Lucian is great. He's working with Josh at the auto body shop over the summer and continuing to train with us every week. He's got a great group of friends and is really doing well."

"I'm glad to hear it," Jean-Paul said. "So, what can I do for you?"

"I was wondering if you'd heard from my cousin Aldo recently. Caleb turned up here, claiming Aldo was missing. We thought it might be some sort of trick, a way to worm themselves back into the Pack so Caleb could try to take over again, but it seems that Aldo really is missing."

"No, he hasn't been here. We do get people applying to be members of the Pack every now and again, but no one recently. How long has he been missing?"

"About three weeks, I think. Caleb is freaking out, and having him here is causing a very tense situation with the Pack."

"I can imagine," Jean-Paul replied wryly. "I'm honestly surprised the Council didn't lock him away somewhere."

"I think we all were, a bit," Tony replied. "Anyway, if you hear from Aldo, or anything about him, or anyone else going missing, please let me know. My insider on the Council told me just now that around twenty people that they know of, so far, have gone missing recently. Completely vanished."

"Weird. I will, of course, let you know. Please keep me posted as well."

Tony said goodbye and hung up again.

"Where the hell are you, Aldo?"

TONY WAS STILL IN A MOOD WHEN HE GOT HOME THAT EVENING.

"Why don't you ask Lily if she can find Aldo?" Malia asked.

Tony stared at her.

"I didn't even think of that. Thanks, Lia. I think you've just solved our problem."

Tony headed for the mirror over the fireplace in the sitting room. He placed his hand on the frame and called Lily.

"Yes, I know. I've looked. I will use this as a training exercise for the Seers College. I'll call you back when we're done. We're meeting tomorrow in Fairweather Falls. Field trip!" And Lily closed the connection.

Tony sighed and went back to the kitchen to help with dinner.

14

The Monday of the beginning of the apprenticeship dawned bright and beautiful. Birds sang, the sky was a gorgeous, clear blue, and the sun was warm. A gentle, cool breeze brushed against Rebecca's face as she left the house to get the studio ready. Her new space on Dragon lands would take a few weeks—even with magic, it wasn't instantaneous. There were still supplies and equipment to buy and have delivered, everything for two working forges, furniture for the apprentice's rooms upstairs; details. So, for now, they were working in her smaller studio on the Casey property. Rebecca smiled at the space as she opened the door. She leaned against the doorframe as she looked around. It hadn't been her space for very long, but she was rather attached to it already.

I wonder who will use this space next, she thought to herself. *Maybe Suzette will brew potions here.*

At eight a.m. sharp, Flora turned up, an eager smile on her face. Ian and Jordan had created the perfect tool for her, harnessing a combination of Mage and Dragon Fire. There were different settings, magical commands set in gems that she could touch to activate depending on the effect she wanted. Rebecca had explained her process to them, giving them a demonstration as she created several small pieces, charms designed to hang from a bracelet. The bracelet was a gift for Milena for her thirteenth birthday. Rebecca was working on something for each of the twins. Both sets of younger Casey teens had birthdays the first week in November.

Of course, with Ian there, Rebecca had only told them the charms were for a bracelet. She didn't want him telling his sister and cousin what they were getting for their birthdays quite yet. The boys would get charms to go on their key rings.

"You know," Jordan had told her, "if you're not already marketing these as protective amulets, you should. I mean, it seems like most of your pieces are decorative. But there is quite a market for enchanted pieces, too. And if what I've been hearing is true, the market for protection spells is going to explode."

Ian and Rebecca had looked hard at Jordan.

"What do you mean?" Rebecca asked.

"I have connections in a lot of places because of the work I do and the people who use what I design," Jordan said. "I've had a couple of contracts with the defense department. I can't tell you what they were for. But I've heard that there are a lot of strange things happening. More violence than usual in some places. Disappearances that can't be explained. It's getting bad enough that the media is starting to pick up on it, though they haven't connected it yet. They're putting the violence down to gangs fighting since most of it is in rougher areas." He looked at Rebecca and Ian. "The thing is, I've got friends in some of those areas, and they say the people involved are acting out of character. They're picking fights with former allies, starting trouble where before they were working on peace between groups. A lot of effort is being washed away as if it had never happened. The people in the neighborhoods are worried. They don't know what to do. They're sure it's not normal, though, and no one wants to go back to the days of gang wars in the streets."

Rebecca had told Brendan at dinner that night, who had informed Peter Chizinsky at the Council.

Rebecca shook her head, then pushed up from the door. Clearing her thoughts from the dark turn they had taken, she smiled at the light streaming in the windows. Everything was as ready as she could make it be.

She greeted Flora with a smile.

"Are you ready to get started?" She asked her eager apprentice.

"Of course! I'm really excited," Flora replied. "This is going to be so much fun! I can't wait to practice with the Fire tool. We've got to come up with a better name for that, by the way, especially if you're going to market it."

"I know. Dragon Fire precision tool, maybe? Anyway, it's over here."

Rebecca led Flora to the work table, where the tool sat next to a box of metal scraps.

"I thought you could get used to using it at its different settings today. If you make anything salable, great, but don't worry about it. Just focus on learning how the tool works and what you can do with it. Tomorrow, we'll get more into my process and actually creating something."

Flora happily picked up the tool and a visor that would protect her eyes from the light of the flame. She pawed through the box, picking out several pieces of metal to work with. As she got started, Daniel and Simon arrived. Daniel was smiling, of course. Simon just nodded.

Rebecca got them settled as well.

"Flora is working on getting used to the new tool we've created for her," she told the two young men. "For you two, I want to see how you work, especially how you use your Gift to shape metal. Pick yourselves some scraps, and let's get started."

Rebecca watched the two young men as they got ready to work. Daniel went straight for the gold scraps, while Simon chose copper. As expected, Simon's work was much more elementary than Daniel's. His ideas were good, though. Daniel used his Gift with a flourish, while Simon seemed to have some difficulty with focusing his Fire for fine detail work.

Rebecca looked at what the three apprentices had created at the end of the day. Flora's piece was burnished into almost a rainbow sheen. The Dwarven woman had an enormous grin on her face as she turned off the Dragon Fire tool.

"This is amazing! I love this thing!" The young woman exclaimed. "I can see so many possibilities for this! I am totally excited about learning to have more control with it. This is so cool!"

Flora hadn't really focused on detail, as she was just learning to use the tool, but she had still created a beautiful sculpture of a rose. The leaves were gold, the stem steel, while copper wires wrapped around the stem, creating a lacework around the flower. The stem at the bottom curled into a horizontal circle so the flower would be free-standing.

Daniel had made a rose, too. He had used his Fire for soldering pieces together, then creating a fine sheen over the petals.

Simon had made a California poppy out of copper on a silver stem. The stem of his flower also curled to make the flower free-standing.

Rebecca looked over all three pieces.

"Well, thank you, guys. This gives me a much better idea of what you are each capable of and what I can teach each of you." She looked at Simon, who was glaring at Flora's beautiful flower.

"Simon, I know you're not up to the level of the other two yet, but I honestly do see a load of potential in you. I know you're used to creating sculptures more than jewelry. We'll focus on learning detail work for you. With practice, I think you will be an excellent designer and jewelry smith."

"Daniel, you have a certain flair, but I think you need to slow down and really focus your attention on detail. It's not the flashiness of a piece that makes it beautiful. It's the workmanship and the feeling that goes into it. 'Good enough,' isn't good enough. Perfectionism is a good thing here. You're learning to make pieces that will last, that will be treasured, passed down through families over time. Not something that will only last a few years that you can get anywhere. You need to find your own flavor and own it. Really own it. Make it truly your own, so that it shows in your pieces and becomes what they are known for."

She turned to Flora.

"Flora, I can already see how the Dragon Fire tool will enhance your work. I'd like you to spend time getting to know it and working with it. Work up some designs and practice bringing them into reality. See what you can do so you refine your skills with the tool. As you think of new things you can do with it, write them down. We'll go over them together." She looked around. "Ok, everyone. Let's clean up. Today was a short day. Tomorrow, we'll really get into it. Everyone come in with a design you want to work on. Remember, jewelry. Something you would either be proud to wear yourself or to give to a loved one. Something to be treasured. Something that reflects who you are in the piece. I'll see you all in the morning."

The apprentices cleaned their workspaces, then left. Flora and Daniel were talking animatedly together while Simon followed behind them, head down, hands in his pockets, listening.

Rebecca watched them go. There was real potential there, in all three of them. She had the feeling that Simon had never really been encouraged in his creativity. He had some catching up to do. She knew he could do it, though. If she could only convince him of that, they'd really get somewhere.

"How'd your first day go?" Sean asked, appearing in the doorway. Rebecca started. She'd been lost in her own thoughts as she put away her tools and hadn't noticed him arrive. She brushed a strand of hair out of her face, redoing the braid that flowed down her back to her waist.

"It was good. I was right; Flora and I are going to get along great. I'm definitely going to see if I can keep her after the apprenticeship is over. I think we can really make a business together. Daniel needs to dig deeper inside himself for real inspiration, rather than just using what's on the surface, and Simon needs more confidence in himself. They are all at different levels, but that's what makes it so interesting. They can all learn from each other."

"Have you told them about the new building yet?"

"No, I'll surprise them when it's done. The boys have a three-month lease on their place, so there's no rush. We'll have a moving-in ceremony when the three-month trial run is up. If I decide to keep them all, they can move in then."

"That's probably a good idea."

"At least for now. I may change how I do things once I have more experience with this lot," Rebecca smiled at the handsome Dragon.

"Were you visiting for a reason?"

"Do I need a reason to visit the most beautiful Witch on the planet?" Sean asked.

Rebecca blushed and turned back to her table.

"Ok, that was corny. But still, Bex, I just wanted to see you. I figured you might need ice cream, or something else, after the first day. This is a huge step for you. Want to go celebrate?"

"Sure. Why not. Can we get Thai and eat down by the harbor? We can get ice cream afterward."

"Sounds good. Let's go."

CELINE WATCHED THEM GO AS THEY WALKED PAST THE GARDEN center. She smiled after them. Rebecca was a lovely girl who deserved the very best. She was somewhat absent-minded, sometimes, as her mind was constantly lost in designs. Sean would make sure she had everything she needed to be happy. The Dragon was the perfect match for her niece. Plus, Celine really liked his mother, Aldona. She foresaw lots of time spent with the Dragon princess in the future and was very much looking forward to it.

15

Caleb Gianetti stood in the bay doors, watching the mechanics of the Pack work on several vehicles in the Pack shop. The Pack had an auto shop on Pack lands for Pack vehicles and one in town for everyone else. The Pack mechanics were the best around, and a large part of the Pack income came from the auto shop. Caleb had never learned a skill beyond bossing everyone around and demanding things go his way. His father had taught his sons that they were better than everyone else, and everything should be given to them as their due. Consequently, Caleb had no idea how to manage his time when he had nothing else to do and no one to boss around. The women weren't scared into submission anymore and wanted nothing to do with him. The men of the Pack, even the new ones, were wary of him and mostly stayed away. Caleb was bored and feeling rather sorry for himself. He was starting to look for something to do, just to keep himself occupied. Something to take his mind off of his missing son, because if he kept thinking about him, kept going around in circles wondering what could have happened to Aldo, he would go mad.

"Can I help you, Caleb?" Josh Merrit, the son of Tony's Beta, asked. He wiped his hands on a rag as he came out of the shop toward Caleb.

Caleb shook his head.

"I don't think so, son. I'm just looking around."

"Do you have a car for us to work on?"

Caleb shook his head again, pushing himself off the door frame.

Josh stared at the older man for a moment.

"I guess you're probably bored. Is there anything you like to do? What did you do down in San Diego?"

"I didn't really do much. I was still trying to find my place. I guess I don't really have much experience in anything, really. I was taught how to run a Pack, not how to work."

"Do you have any hobbies? Like whittling, or painting, or sports?"

Caleb shook his head.

"I appreciate you trying to help me, son. I guess I'll just have to figure something out."

"You could always learn something new. You might find something you really like."

"I'm old, boy. I can't be learning anything new at this stage."

"You're not dead yet," Josh replied with a grin. "If you're still alive, you can learn. Pick something you want to try. Give it a shot, and if it doesn't work out, try something new."

Caleb looked at the boy. Wise words from someone so young.

"I might do that, son. Thank you for talking to me." Caleb turned and walked away towards the meeting house. Josh watched him go.

"That's one sad and bad old Wolf," Mike, one of the other mechanics, said.

"I know he was horrible," Josh said. "I've heard all about him and his brother. But, you know, he's lost everything, even his sons. Aldo's missing, and Remy will barely talk to him. I guess that's Caleb's fault for never treating Remy right. It must have been tough for Caleb to come back here and ask for help. I mean, he's lucky he wasn't formally banished when he left. I know a lot of people wanted him to be. Everyone hates him. It took a lot of courage to look past that and come back anyway."

"Or desperation," Mike said.

"Yeah, but he still came back. He realized Tony could help him and got past his own issues to ask. Maybe he's changing. Having the Pack taken away from him, and seeing how healthy Packs are run, maybe he's actually learning something new." Josh paused for a moment as Caleb went into the meeting house. "Maybe we should all try to help him find something he likes to do. Something to keep him busy while we search for Aldo. Who knows, maybe he'll actually become a productive member of the Pack?"

The idea stuck in Mike's brain, spinning around and around. Could someone as bad as Caleb had been change? If he could, shouldn't they help him? If they didn't, didn't that make them as bad Caleb himself?

When he left the auto shop that evening, Mike went to find Will, Caleb's shadow. Caleb was still in the meeting house, eating dinner in the cafeteria the single Pack members ate in if they lived in the dorms. Most had their own homes, but some preferred to live communally. Caleb sat off by himself at a table for two in the corner opposite the kitchen. Will sat nearby, at a different table.

"Hey, Mike. How's it going?"

Mike sat down opposite Will, his back to Caleb. There was enough noise in the room that he figured Caleb would have difficulty hearing him, even with enhanced Shifter hearing.

"I was thinking. Josh said something at work earlier today, and it got my mind going. I think the kid might be right."

"About what?"

"Caleb isn't the same Wolf he was when he left. He's not pleasant, but he's not trying to boss everyone around and act like he's in charge. He's not trying to make us all submit to him. Josh thinks that maybe getting kicked out of the Pack and seeing how other Packs are run is starting to open Caleb's eyes and make him learn other ways of living. Josh thinks Caleb is lonely and bored. Maybe we should help Caleb find something healthy to do?'

Will watched Caleb over Mike's shoulder. Caleb was pushing the food around on his plate. He'd only eaten about half. The older man's clothes were loose on his body, the bones in his face prominent.

"He doesn't go out much," Will said musingly. "I mean, at all. I thought he was afraid of being attacked for the things he did as Alpha. But everyone is pretty much ignoring him. He doesn't read, barely watches t.v. He probably is bored. And I guess it can't be good for him to stew over Aldo when there's nothing we can do that isn't already being done. Sitting around moping isn't healthy for anyone." Will stared at Caleb for a moment. "I guess I could try to help him find something to do."

"Thanks, Will. I'll help, too. There has to be something he'd be interested in. Maybe Remy will know," Mike suggested.

"We can ask him. I'm not sure he'll want anything to do with it, though," Will said.

"Can't hurt to ask," Mike replied.

❦

TONY WAS AT THE VALERIAN'S COVE POLICE DEPARTMENT. Technically, he was still the town's detective, though most of his time was spent with the Pack. Being Alpha was a full-time job in itself.

"Tony, come here a minute, will you?" Chief Kenny called from his office next door to Tony's.

Tony stood, stretched, and went next door.

"Yeah, Chief? What's up?"

"Your cousin, Aldo. He doesn't have any military training, right?"

"Yeah, none. Caleb kept him at home, supposedly learning how to run the Pack when Caleb died."

Chief Kenny looked down at his computer again.

"I'm sure you know about the escalating violence that's been happening around the world lately. And how much of it is paranormal-related."

Tony nodded.

"I just got an email from a friend in the SOC's enforcer division. He attached a video of a raid on a bank in Detroit. The men were armed and took no prisoners. Several people were shot, but there were no deaths. They made off with three-quarters of a million dollars. It would have been more, but the armored car delivery was delayed due to traffic. Tony, I'm not really sure what's going on, but one of those gunmen... it looks like Aldo."

Tony blinked.

"You can't be serious. Aldo's not that stupid. And the Alpha in San

Diego said he was fitting in there and training as an enforcer and was happy there. There's no way."

Tony headed around the desk and looked at the image on the Chief's computer.

"Well, shit," Tony said. "What the hell?"

Aldo's face stared back at him, looking directly at the security camera.

⚜

Tony called Remy the minute he arrived back on Pack lands. Remy was home, so Tony went to the house Remy shared with his wife and mate, Suzette. Suzette opened the door when Tony knocked.

"Hey, Tony!" Suzette greeted him. She kissed him on both cheeks. Suzette was French by birth.

"Hey, Suzette. You and Remy should come over to dinner soon. Right now, I really need to speak to Remy. Can I come in?"

"Of course. He's in the kitchen. Come on through."

Remy was chopping up vegetables for a salad. Tony could smell steaks grilling on the back deck.

"Hey, cousin. What's going on?" Remy laid the knife down and wiped his hands on a kitchen towel. He offered Tony a drink. Tony declined.

"Listen, Remy. Did Aldo ever show signs of being criminally stupid? Like, wanting to rob a bank or something?"

Remy stared.

"No, he's not that dumb. Plus, it would be too much work and too dangerous. He might mar his pretty hide. Or go to jail. He wouldn't do anything that could get him caged. Aldo doesn't do well in small spaces."

Tony ran a hand through his head.

"Yeah, that's pretty much what I thought. Here's the thing—Chief Kenny has a friend who's an enforcer for the Supernatural Oversight Council. This friend sent him a video today. It showed Aldo, with a bunch of other men, robbing a bank at gunpoint in Detroit. They got away with three-quarters of a million dollars."

Remy stared at Tony as if he'd never seen him before.

"You can't be serious."

"Unfortunately, I am. I saw the video myself. It's definitely Aldo."

Remy shook his head.

"There's no way. I mean, he's a right ass and a complete jerk, but he's not that stupid. How did the camera catch his face?"

"None of the gunmen were wearing masks."

"What? That doesn't make sense. Why would they risk being identified?"

"I don't know," Tony replied. "I don't understand it either."

"You are both very, very sure that this is not something he would normally do?" Suzette asked.

Both men turned to the pretty Witch.

"Very," they answered together.

Suzette pursed her lips, her brows drawn.

"Is there anything they could hold over him to make him do something like this, whoever's in charge?"

"I can't imagine what," Remy answered. "I mean, they left here with nothing, and they haven't really had the time to build something worth threatening over in San Diego."

"Maybe a girlfriend?"

"I mean, I guess, but we're Shifters. Our women are even more vicious than our men when you get them angry. If someone had tried to threaten anyone in the San Diego Pack, we would have heard about it and about what they did with the idiot's body afterward."

"Could someone have threatened Caleb?"

"Maybe, but I don't think that would be a strong enough threat to make Aldo do something this stupid," Remy argued.

"There are ways to control someone, to make them do things they would rather not do," Suzette mused slowly. "There are potions you could give them to make them more susceptible to suggestion and ways to mess with a mind with magic. A Mind Healer's Gift, if abused, could be used to make someone behave out of character. Are we missing any Mind Healers?"

Tony stared at Suzette for a moment.

"If we take it as gospel that Aldo would not do something like this willingly, then maybe the other men were coerced, somehow, too. I think we need to know who the other men were and where they came from. Suzette, could you get me a list of potions that could control someone like that? I'll ask Marissa about Mind Healers."

Suzette nodded.

"Of course. It's a short list as all of the potions with those effects are either illegal or highly restricted, only used in extreme circumstances. Which means, of course, that they are probably readily available in the right places. I hate it when people use good things for bad purposes." Suzette went to her computer and sat down. She had one of the new computers the Techno-Mages had made that Witches and other Magic users could use. It was the first thing the Techno-Mages had worked on as a group. Sales were huge as many Witches and Mages eagerly bought the life-changing technology.

After several minutes, Suzette handed Tony a list.

"I'll check with the Potions Master at the Academy and my professors at the Healer's College tomorrow," Suzette said. "It is possible there are others I am unaware of. I'll let you know what they say."

"Thank you," Tony replied. He looked at Remy. "I'll keep you in the loop about anything we find out," he said.

Remy nodded. He still looked stunned.

"You're sure it was him?" He asked again.

"It was definitely Aldo," Tony replied. He said goodnight and left them to their dinner.

16

After the first week, Rebecca and her apprentices pretty much had a stable routine down. Flora was becoming more and more comfortable with the Dragon Fire tool and was turning out some pretty decent work. It wasn't quite up to the standard Rebecca believed Flora was capable of yet, but it was a good start.

Daniel had come back after the first day with designs that were pretty but typically Elven. Rebecca sent him home that night with instructions to draw until he came up with something that he felt was uniquely him.

"Don't just draw jewelry," she told her Aes Sídhe apprentice. "Draw whatever comes into your mind. What lights you up? What turns you on? What's your greatest fear? Your greatest love? If you could design anything in the world, what would it be? What would you most like to work on? If you were reading a fantasy novel, what kind would it be? What would the people be doing?"

Daniel looked frustrated, but he took out a sketchpad and started to draw as soon as he got home.

Simon needed experience making more delicate objects and working with richer metals. Rebecca gave him the same instructions to go home and draw, asking him to include as much detail as possible in his sketches.

"Think, if you were making the most delicate piece of jewelry you had ever seen, what would it look like? What would it be made of? How would you make it? What would you include in it?" She asked him. She had to get him thinking beyond heavy sculpture. Yes, his pieces could have elements of sculpture, but they needed to be light enough to wear comfortably. In the studio, she helped Simon work with a hotter Fire, etching simple designs into metal, then learning how to use the Fire to shape and solder. Simon could easily see how these applications could extend to his larger sculptures as well and dove in willingly.

"Everything is going really well, so far," she told her father over the mirror that night.

"And you're happy with the apprentices you've chosen?" He asked her. "Still glad you stayed in Valerian's Cove?"

"Yes, Da. You'll just have to come down here to visit more often."

"I will don't you worry. By the way, darling girl, we need more jewelry up here. A bridal party came in and took most of what you had in the shop."

"Really? That's great! Ok, I'll have some more pieces ready to send you by the end of the week," Rebecca told him. As she ended the call, she was already planning new pieces in her mind.

She wandered into the kitchen, almost walking right into Devra Drake, who was at the house visiting until Donnie returned from visiting those of his family still living in Dragon lands. Devra had just arrived the day before, having been away on Guardian business before that.

"Oops! Sorry, Devra!" Rebecca exclaimed, coming out of her daze.

"No worries. Got pretty things dancing through your head again? Good, I need some more pretties." The Dragon princess grinned at the more petite Witch.

Rebecca grinned back.

"I'll be making some new pieces to send to my father this week," Rebecca told her. "If you see anything you like, you can have it. For a good price, of course."

"Of course! I am very willing to pay full price for excellent crafts-manship, and your pieces are gorgeous."

Rebecca got herself some lemonade. Devra already had a glass and a piece of cake. With ice cream. Rebecca got herself a plate too.

They took their treats out onto the patio, catching up on what they were doing over the summer. Marissa came around the corner of the house, carrying a bag of food. Teddy followed, carrying the twins. Mikey and Milena followed after their father, with their friends Malachai and Amie.

"Are we having a party?" Devra asked.

"Family party, though, who knows who will actually show up," Marissa said with a smile. "Lia should be here soon, too."

Malia, Suzette, and Tony walked around the corner of the house, carrying more food and babies, while several Wolves came from the woods, two Phoenyxes flying overhead.

Ralph, Liz, Frankie, and their children all shifted as they reached the patio. The kids ran off into the field as two Dragons flew overhead and touched down near the training field. Lily and Bethie shifted, Bethie joining the other young teens while Lily made her way to join the adults. She looked at Devra with a twinkle in her eye.

"Better get a nursery set up," she said, causing Devra's eyes to grow wide.

"Oh no, not yet, not on your life," Devra exclaimed. "I have way too much to do with the Guardians for the next hundred years or so."

Lily cackled.

"I don't think so, my dear. The Goddess has other plans for you. Just you wait!" Lily wandered into the house, looking for Celine.

Devra's eyes were wide, her face pale. Marissa, Malia, Suzette, Frankie, and Liz all grinned at her.

"Something you want to tell us, Devra?" Malia asked with a grin.

Devra shook her head rapidly.

"Nope, she's just messing with me. No babies, now way, no how."

"Preach, sister," Liz said. Then she rubbed her stomach, which was looking a little rounder.

Everyone looked at Liz.

"What? It's just indigestion. My stomach's been a little upset lately."

"Liz, come on. This has gone on long enough," Malia told her friend. "Have you been to the Healer? You're definitely pregnant."

Liz glanced nervously over at Ralph.

"Come on, Liz, you can't tell me he hasn't noticed the changes in your body recently. You're starting to show," Marissa said.

"I don't want to talk about it," Liz insisted.

"Liz, what's going on? I'm going to push on this. Denying the obvious isn't going to make it go away," Malia said, sitting down next to Liz. She took the other woman's hand in her own.

Frankie sat on the other side of her sister and put an arm around her.

"In the Pack we were raised in, pregnancy was a scary time," Frankie told them quietly. "The men all wanted sons. You know how they treated their boys, what they made them do, how they taught them to behave. We were terrified to have boys, for that reason, but also terrified to have girls because we knew they would be treated even worse. Having a child was not the joyful experience it is here."

"But you know that would never happen here, right?" Malia looked anxiously at both women.

"We know, but it's still hard to change. All of our other children were born into that environment. It's not something you easily forget."

"Liz, you need to talk to Ralph about this. I guarantee he will be overjoyed. He won't care what gender the baby is, and he would never behave the way the men in your old Pack behaved. Children are welcomed here and given the chance to develop into who they choose to be. Not who we think they should be."

"I know," Liz whispered. "What if Ralph doesn't want another kid? Josh is eighteen—that's a huge age gap."

"Ralph will be thrilled to have a child with you. You're his mate. Never worry about that," Suzette put in. "Come on, talk to him now. We'll all be here for you when you get back."

Liz took a deep breath, then stood. She walked over to Ralph, where he stood with Tony and Teddy, taking her mate's arm and leading him away into the field. The women watched from the patio.

They all smiled when Ralph picked Liz up and spun her around. Setting her down again, he took her face in his hands and kissed her, then got down on his knees and kissed her belly. The kids, who had been watching from across the field, raced over. Josh hugged his dad, then picked Liz up and hugged her too.

The watching women had tears in their eyes.

"See, I told her so," Malia said, wiping a tear away. Allie, Amie, Milena, and the other girls were doing happy dances in the field, running up to Liz and hugging her, then jumping up and down again. Ian, Mikey, and Malachai were standing nearby, smiling. Sarah, Carl, and Michelle, Liz's children, all hugged their mother and joined in the dancing. Sarah hung onto her mother's hand as Ralph wrapped his arm around Liz and led her back to the patio.

"Everyone, we're having a baby!" Ralph called out.

"Woot! Congratulations!" Teddy called back. The men all gathered around, slapping Ralph on the back and hugging Liz, kissing her cheek.

Tony said something to Sarah, who nodded, looking up at him seriously. She smiled at him, then, hugging her mother again, ran off back to the others in the field.

"I guess that went rather well," Marissa said with a grin as the women all joined the group by the grill, hugging the happy expectant parents as they did.

❧

MALIA WAS QUIET AS SHE GOT READY FOR BED THAT EVENING. TONY noticed, coming up behind her and putting his arms around her.

"Hey, what's wrong?" He asked her.

Malia turned to face him, laying her head on his chest for a moment. Then she looked up at him.

"I've been thinking about the children," she told him. "Our lot are all hybrids and tribrids and hugely powerful. Even the new twins. Ours are shifting already, instead of in their early teens, and Marissa's are already using magic, even earlier than their siblings did. I mean, baby Witches able to use their Gifts? What is the Goddess thinking? Ralph and Liz's new child will be pure Shifter, but given the children they will grow up around, you know they'll be something special." She paused for a moment. Tony, sensing there was more, wisely waited.

"When Allie bonded with the Sword of Fire, and we realized we had Dragon and Phoenyx blood, and the children were all so powerful, and then Fae on Teddy's side, we realized the Goddess had plans for us. Then, as we continued to gather allies from so many races, it became obvious that whatever's coming it's going to be huge. I figured we had some time since the twins were still so young. I mean, Allie and Ian are still not thirteen yet. I figured that whatever was coming, we would deal with it, hopefully when the twins were grown. And that would be the end of it. But the babies are coming out supercharged, too, even more than their siblings. It makes me think that whatever's coming, it's not going to be over quickly and could actually get worse if we are going to need children stronger than Allie. I don't want that for our children, Tony. I want them to grow up, have fun, live their lives in safety and enjoy themselves. I don't want them to be in danger. And we can't even run away because the Goddess would always be able to find us. Plus, Allie will never back down from a fight. And now, to think that my precious new babies will have to fight, too, when they're barely two years old...." Malia started crying, working herself into a panic. Her words had gotten louder and louder as she spoke. Her voice was thick with tears.

Tony kissed the top of her head, holding her close.

"Maybe the Goddess is hedging her bets, just in case. Maybe we will be able to handle whatever's coming easily. They may not have to fight at all. Though that would upset Allie—she's dying to use that sword properly on someone," Tony joked, trying to lighten the mood. It didn't work. Malia just cried harder.

There was a knock on the door as Mariah stuck her head around it. Anne was right behind her.

"Is everything ok?"

Tony looked over at his wife's younger cousins.

"Malia is worried about the children having to fight when they get older. They're all so powerful, and the babies are even more so. Malia's worried that whatever's coming will be really bad and last a long time.

She doesn't want any of you hurt. She wants to keep you all safe and happy."

Mariah and Anne stepped fully into the room and put their arms around Malia.

"Lia, the important thing is that whatever's coming, we have time to prepare and to train, and we are always together. No one will be fighting alone," Anne said, stroking her cousin's curly hair. Malia had let it grow long, and it flowed almost to her waist.

"We'll never let the kids fight by themselves," Mariah agreed. "We've been working hard on our Pixie and Witch Gifts, and we have Shari-Beth and Josh and everyone too. We'll help keep the younger kids safe. And they'll help with the babies. Whatever happens, we'll face it together. And you know none of us would like a quiet, boring life. Except maybe Amie, but she's outvoted." Mariah grinned at Malia.

"But I-I-I don't want any of you to have to fight at all!" Malia gasped out.

"Well, it looks like we'll have to, so instead of arguing about it, let's figure out how we can make it work for us," Anne said sternly. Tony looked down at the seventeen-year-old in surprise. That was a very mature way to look at it.

Malia took a minute, then she nodded.

"Ok. What can we do?"

"We let the kids know how much we love and support them," Tony said. "We continue training, all of us. We've gotten a little lax over the summer. We'll start up proper training three times a week or more tomorrow. I'll call Declan tonight. We have everyone train individually and in groups, as we were before, so we all know each other's fighting styles. We all learn to work together. We have Milena, Fionnuala and the Seers try their hardest to get an answer out of the Goddess about what's coming. We take advantage of the Seer's College that's being set up. We strengthen our ties with the member realms of the Alliance Council and with the Supernatural Oversight Council. We work more with our friends in Fairweather Falls and at the other Academies. We all stay in touch and compare notes frequently. When something comes up, we handle it as best we can, learn from it, and move on. We do everything we can to keep everyone safe, happy, and well. We celebrate what we have and keep our focus on the future we hope to see. And we love each other like there's no tomorrow. Got it?"

Malia and the girls nodded. Tony hugged them all, then kissed Malia, wiping the tears from her face.

"I'll go call Declan now. We'll start training tomorrow. I'll have Ralph design a training plan for the Wolves and speak to Chief Kenny about getting the other groups in town to start training as well. We'll have open training sessions everyone can come to. And we'll schedule specific training sessions for certain groups to work together on a rotating basis, so everyone gets to work with everyone else. I'll speak to Maria Hemenway about getting the Witches to strengthen the wards on the town and suggest to Peter Chizinksy that the same be done for all the Havens and supernatural towns. I'll ask the Dragons to ward the portals. You know they're already protecting them, but I will ask Aldona to make sure that they are properly guarded. Luc can talk to the Guardians as well." He kissed Malia again.

"We'll get through this, Lia. Together. All of us. I love you, ok?"

Malia nodded, still wiping tears from her face.

"I'm going to call Declan. Why don't you call Marissa or your mom? Let them know what's going on, ok? I'll be up soon." Kissing the top of her head, he hugged her one more time, then headed downstairs to use the mirror in the sitting room.

Mariah and Anne hugged Malia again, then went back to their own room. Malia and Tony had offered them separate rooms, but the twins had been apart for so long and wanted to stay together.

Anne looked at Mariah once they reached their room and closed the door.

"I think we ought to tell Shari-Beth what's going on. I think our group needs to train extra hard, so we can protect the younger kids. We need to work even harder on learning our Gifts."

"I know," Mariah agreed. "We should call Grandma and Grandpa Beaulieu in the morning and tell them, too. I want to double down on our Pixie training."

Anne nodded. The girls had a mirror in their room and used it to call Shari-Beth, filling her in.

"I think we should ask Bethie and Sinéad to See for us," she said after a moment.

"Tony said he was going to speak to the Seer's College," Anne replied.

"I know, but there could be different answers depending on who's asking and how it's asked," Shari-Beth said.

"Then maybe we should all take turns asking," Mariah said.

"Maybe we should. We'll start tomorrow," Shari-Beth said. "It's too late to ask Bethie right now, and Sinéad was going to spend tonight in the water. We'll catch them both in the morning. And we'll start extra training. The teachers will all be back from vacation soon. We'll ask them as soon as they get back. We'll talk to Josh, Kelly, and Lucian in the morning, too. And Emma and Aidan." Shari-Beth smiled. "At least Aidan is ready to go. He never stopped training. He can probably fight rings around the rest of us by now."

17

Daily fight practices were reinstated. The Seers were tasked with bugging the Goddess for answers as much as possible. The Goddess was being very circumspect with her replies.

"Bah!" Lily exclaimed one day after a fruitless session. "These brief glimpses we keep getting are useless. We still don't know when, why, or how things are going to go to hell in a handbasket, only that they are. Tony will be injured but survive. Josh will lose a leg, though we can't tell him that. He'll end up Alpha and training other young Wolves to support the Witches and Fae. Kelly won't make it, nor will Christopher, but we can't see how they die. Lucian will go feral at the loss of his mate and have to be put down. My Bethie will be hurt but come out stronger than ever. The Sea Fae will fight a huge battle, losing many of their people, but survive. And all of this could come to pass, or something could change, and none of it will. We can only See what might come to pass if things continue as they are now. Yet hundreds of little changes are made each day that could affect what we have Seen, changing everything. And we still can't See anything around the special supercharged children, except for Bethie and Sinéad, and why that's so, I don't know. Why are we not able to get a clear vision on this?" It took a lot to frustrate Lily, who was thousands of years old and had seen it all. Yet, the Goddess had managed it. Everyone else was feeling it. A frustrated Lily was not pleasant to be around.

Allie was thrilled that there were more fight practices now.

"I wish we could just fight instead of going to school," she said to Milena as they took a break for water during practice one day. She brushed a reddish-brown curl out of her face.

Milena, whose own blond locks were slowly darkening to a golden brown, took a drink of lemon water, then set the glass down on the table beside her.

"We need to learn to use our Gifts in other ways, too. You know that, Allie. The more control we have, the more ways we have to use them, the better off we are." Milena's Familiar, the unicorn Nimuë, stuck her head over Milena's shoulder and huffed in her ear. Milena reached up and scratched the unicorn's face between the eyes. Nimuë's eyes closed in bliss.

Allie's fire lizard Familiars, Queenie and Grunt, flew down, Queenie landing on Allie's shoulder, wrapping her tail around the girl's neck for balance, and Grunt on the table, where he immediately stuck his snout into the pitcher of water, then sniffed around for a cookie. Allie reached up and stroked Queenie's scales.

"I know. I don't have to like it, though. I'd rather be fighting."

Ian and Amie walked up to get some water.

"Don't drink that one; Grunt's had his nose in it," Milena said, grabbing the pitcher before Ian could get to it. He reached for another one instead, pouring a glass for Amie, then himself. Ian had been drawn to Amie from the first moment he saw her. Her parents, figuring that the two might be fated mates, treated Ian like their own son and included him in everything. Amie was shy, and Ian supported her and stuck up for her when necessary. He knew when to encourage her and let her step up for herself, something quite astute for someone so young.

"Let me guess, Allie is griping about having to do anything else but fight practice," Ian said with a grin.

"Yup," Milena agreed.

Amie smiled.

"Come on, Allie. You know you like our magic classes. And you and

Vannie have fun showing off in class all the time. When is she coming back, anyway?"

Allie's best friend, Siobhan, had gone home to her family's farm in Ireland for the summer.

"Tomorrow. I know she wanted to see her family, but I'll be so happy she's back!" Siobhan and Allie had started out in competition with each other, both being powerful Fire Mages. After a moment in their classroom on the first day of school in sixth grade—a moment when the teacher thought she was going to have an explosion on her hands and started to worry—the two had joined forces and become inseparable. Vannie had been to France with Allie, and Vannie's grandfather had come to Valerian's Cove to see them train together. He had become great friends with Luc Benoit, Allie's great-grandfather and the Guardian in charge of their training program in battle magic and fight practice. Allie and Siobhan were terrifying when they fought together, and they were still only twelve.

"Oy, you lot!" Declan called them from the training circle. "We're not done yet. Get back here."

෬෬෬

"STILL NOTHING?" SHARI-BETH ASKED SINÉAD AS SHE WATCHED HER friend come out of her trance.

Sinéad shook her head. Her guards were standing around, trying to blend into the furniture.

"It's really frustrating. I'm not used to not Seeing at least *something*. All I'm getting are tiny pieces, little flashes that I can't even make out."

"Maybe something is supposed to happen that hasn't happened yet, that will bring everything into focus?" Jed, one of Sinéad's guards, suggested. Jed was from Fairweather Falls, where his newly discovered fated mate, Claire, still lived.

"It's possible, I guess. Bethie hasn't Seen anything either. Not even my mom or Lily can get anything. I can See regular stuff, like, day-to-day stuff, and anything not directly affecting anyone involved here. I've even tried scrying on the powered-up kids in Fairweather Falls. Nothing. I can't See anything on anyone with superpowers or anyone directly connected to them."

"What about the people only indirectly connected to them?" Shari-Beth suggested.

Sinéad cocked her head to the side as she thought about it. "Maybe," she said. "Let me give it a try."

She closed her eyes and took a deep breath. Under her eyelids, her eyes moved quickly about.

Shari-Beth looked at Emma, who was standing next to her. Emma shrugged.

After several moments, Sinéad opened her eyes. She was grinning.

"I think we've got it, folks. I scryed on Liz. Ralph's too close; got nothing on him. But I could see Liz and the baby. Who will be fine, by the way. The baby is a girl whose name will be Rochelle. She'll be a guard for Evie and Aoife, then retire to be Beta for Suzette and Remy's daughter Laurieanna. Laurie will be the first female Alpha, and she'll take the position fairly young, like Tony did."

Shari-Beth looked shocked.

"Not the same way, don't worry. And not the Valerian's Cove Pack. They'll start their own Pack, and it won't be just Wolf Shifters. Informally, it will be called the Mutt Pack, but its real name will be the Alliance Pack. They will be guards, answering to the Alliance Council. They'll all train with the Guardians. Shari-Beth, you and your friends will be advisors to them."

"So, this roundabout way works."

"Yes. I'll tell Lily, and we'll start working this way when we meet tomorrow."

Sinéad's mirror chimed. One of her guards answered.

"I need to talk to Sinéad! I figured it out!" Bethie's excited voice sounded from the mirror.

Sinéad grinned. "That girl is too smart for her own good," she said with a smile. She stood, then moved to stand in front of the mirror.

"Hi, Beth. I figured it out too. What was your solution?"

"Scry the people around the superpowered ones! I was trying Allie again and couldn't see anything, like usual, but then I saw a flash of Amie, so I tried to scry her, and it worked. She and Ian are fated mates, by the way. I'm going to have fun teasing them about that for, like, ever."

Sinéad smiled at the younger Seer.

"That was my answer, as well. I scryed Liz. It worked. I'll let everyone else know. Tomorrow, we'll get to work. We'll have my scribe write everything down."

"I think we need at least two more scribes," Lily said, peeking over Bethie's shoulder. "We should each have our own, anyway. Before, those who asked me a question were responsible for recording the answer themselves. Now, I think this is too important. We need dedicated scribes for each of us."

"Can they use recording devices instead of writing things down? Wouldn't that be more accurate?" Shari-Beth asked.

"Yes, it would. They can transcribe it later."

Lily paused for a moment, thinking.

"These scribes should be people we trust implicitly, people who will stay with us for the long hall. It makes sense that they should be people of our own races or of races that live as long as each of us does. I'll talk to the Princess. I have one or two people in mind for myself and for Bethie."

"Grandma, I don't want an adult. I want someone who can grow with me," Bethie insisted.

"We'll work it out. The young one can train with the person I choose for myself," Lily said. "As it is, Bethie, you will have your own guard unit. You know that. In fact, I believe the Guardians already have some candidates in training. You will meet them when they transfer to the Academy this Fall."

"Maybe there will be a scribe with them," Bethie said.

Lily shrugged. She looked very smug about something.

"What, Grandma? What are you hiding?"

Lily shook her head, smiling.

"Come on! That's not fair! Please tell me!"

Lily smiled, waved, and closed the mirror as she turned away, Bethie following along behind her, still begging.

SHARI-BETH AND EMMA LEFT SOON AFTER, LEAVING SINÉAD ALONE with her guards.

"So, what didn't you tell Shari and Emma, Nadie?" Jed asked her. He had known Sinéad most of his life and knew when she was hiding something.

"Shari-Beth will be the one to start the Alliance Pack. She'll be its first Alpha, not Laurieanna. Laurianna will be its most famous, but Shari-Beth is the first. Emma and Aidan will be part of it. Many people will. Not just Shifters, either. And Jed, she's starting it by the end of this school year. I think the fighting is closer to starting than we thought."

18

By mid-August, Rebecca's new studio was finished. She took her apprentices over one Wednesday morning to show them the new space.

"Wow!" Flora said as she looked around. "This is amazing. And what a gorgeous view!"

"Are we really on Dragon land here?" Simon asked. He was starting to come out of his shell more as his work improved and he was praised for it rather than ignored or shot down.

"Yes. Sean and I will have a house not far from here. Lily insisted. It will be ready by Samhain. We'll have a dedication and move-in party, both here and at the house, if we decide we're ready to move into it by then."

"But we get to work here before then, right?" Flora asked. "I mean, there's so much more space here! And a full forge! Two full forges! I can't wait to try them!"

"Why do we need a forge, Rebecca?" Daniel asked. He had been looking around quietly as the others talked.

Rebecca debated on how much to tell them.

"Lily, the Dragon Seer, has Seen a few things. She thought it was necessary."

Daniel looked hard at her for a moment, then apparently decided to let it go. For now.

"What's upstairs?" Flora asked.

"Bedrooms, a kitchen, and a common area," Rebecca replied. "In mid-October, when your three-month trial is up, if you choose to stay for the full three years, you will get a rent-free room here."

All three apprentices turned to stare at her.

"Really?" Simon asked, his eyes wide.

Rebecca nodded.

"Yep. I thought it made more sense. It will bring us all closer, too, and if you get an inspired idea in the middle of the night, you'll be able to work on it right away rather than waiting until morning."

"Wow, Rebecca! Thank you!" Flora gushed, rushing over to hug her mentor. Daniel bowed, and Simon thanked her, too.

"This is really huge for me. Thank you," he said.

Rebecca smiled at him, knowing that he was the most financially challenged of her apprentices so far.

"How many bedrooms are there?" Flora asked.

"Nine. Plus one on the other side. There will be another Master Smith coming to work with us. We may have visiting teachers too, every once in a while."

"Are you taking on more apprentices, then?" Daniel asked.

"We'll see how it goes. The plan is to take on three more every year, with the senior apprentices taking on some teaching duties in their areas of experience and interest," Rebecca replied.

"Wow," Flora whispered. "This is so much more than I ever thought. This is wonderful."

"What kinds of visiting teachers will we have?" Simon asked.

"We'll see," Rebecca replied. She wasn't quite ready to tell them just yet. Rebecca was already talking to Flora's uncle Lars about coming to do a short tutorial on armor. She was looking for a Master Smith who focused on sculpture, too, for Simon, and a Fae Master Jewelry Smith for Daniel. Maybe a Dragon Master Smith, too. She wanted her apprentices to get as much experience as possible, especially since it appeared that they would need skills beyond jewelry smithing. Though everything she taught them could be applied to more significant works. But still, it was good to introduce them to other applications. They would all learn from each Master who visited. The spare bedroom would house each visiting Master Smith until Lars moved in permanently the following year. According to Lily, at least.

They looked around for a while longer, poking around upstairs and inspecting the workspaces. They walked around outside, too, where Marissa, Suzette, Siofra, and Malia had begun putting in gardens around the patio overlooking the ocean. It would be a beautiful place to take a break from working. Rebecca took them back further into the property and showed them where her new house was under construction.

"This will be done before Samhain, surely," Daniel stated as he watched the Fae architect and Shifter crew work.

"It will, but I thought it would be a nice way to celebrate Samhain, with a move-in party and new home. Maybe. Until then, we'll be painting and decorating."

It was a lovely afternoon, and Rebecca was pleased that her apprentices were so happy with their new workspace and eventual home. If all three of them decided to stay, that was. So far, Rebecca thought they would. Everything was going well, and they all worked well together so far.

So far, so good, she thought to herself as she said goodbye to her apprentices in town and headed home to the Casey house.

༻⚜༺

SHARI-BETH RAN THE BRUSH THROUGH HER HAIR ONE FINAL TIME, then set it on the vanity. A pretty young woman with hazel eyes looked back at her from the mirror. To look at her, you'd never know that she was anything other than human or that she was one of the best-trained fighters in the country. You'd just see a pretty high schooler getting ready for the first day of her senior year.

Shari-Beth stood up and headed for the door. She could smell breakfast from here, two floors up. Celine was making waffles. And bacon, and sausages. Probably fruit salad, too. She always made a fancy breakfast on the first day of school.

"Good morning, Sweetheart!" Celine smiled at her as she opened the waffle iron and removed a perfectly golden masterpiece of deliciousness.

"Morning, Mom," Shari-Beth said. She'd been with the Caseys for two years now. They were her family. Shari-Beth couldn't remember much about her birth family, anyway. They'd died when she was young, and she'd spent several years in the foster care system before getting kidnapped, rescued, and adopted by the Caseys. The men that had abducted her were long gone, their organization in the U.S. brought down. Shari-Beth rarely even thought about it anymore. There hadn't been any sign of the drug they'd been developing to use on Shifters for over a year now.

"Ready for school?" Celine asked.

"Yep. It's weird—it's like the summer never happened, and at the same time, it feels like forever since the end of last year," Shari-Beth said as she grabbed a plate from the pile on the table and sat down.

Brendan made his way into the kitchen, followed by a yawning Devra. Rebecca was a few steps behind.

"Something smells so good it woke me up," Devra yawned again, heading for Celine. She gave the Kitchen Witch a hug, then stole a piece of bacon from the pan. Celine swatted at her. Devra grinned and grabbed a plate.

Brendan kissed the top of Shari-Beth's head as he got himself a plate from the pile. "Good morning, sweetheart. All set?"

"Yup. All ready."

Brendan was the Professor of Supernatural History at the Academy. He would drive in with Shari-Beth that morning for the assembly always held at the start of the school year.

Rebecca sat down, grabbing the carafe of coffee as she did so. She filled her mug, then grabbed the pitcher of fresh-squeezed orange juice. The oranges were from the Casey's orchard. She took a sip.

"It seems like forever, but then only yesterday, that I was in school," she said with a smile. It'd been two years since she'd finished with her Academy training.

"I was just saying that!" Shari-Beth exclaimed. "It seems like forever since last year, but no time at all."

The family ate their breakfast while talking about their plans for the day and reminiscing about other school days. Finally, Brendan stood.

"Well, my dear, let's go. Maria will have my hide if we're late for the assembly." He kissed Celine and smiled at Rebecca and Devra.

Shari-Beth took her plate to the sink, stacking it on top of her Da's. She kissed Celine, then ran up to her room to grab her bag.

◈✦◈

THE ASSEMBLY WAS NOISY AND LONG, AS THEY ALWAYS WERE. Students at the Academy generally loved going to school—what wasn't to love, learning about magic, paranormal history, and for Shifters, how to use their Shifter senses and work with their other half? Then there was fight practice. Shari-Beth loved fight practice at school because she got to work with many more supernaturals than she got to work with over the summer when many of the students had gone home.

At lunch, she sat with Emma, Aidan, and Josh. Mariah and Anne joined them, followed by Kelly and Lucian. The younger four were talking about their classes and the stories their classmates had brought back from over the summer.

"Selena got into trouble for setting a fire by accident," Mariah told everyone. "She says two human boys were bothering her and her friends at the beach one day. She was with a human friend. The boys didn't know Selena was a Witch. They were tourists. She lives in a beach town down the coast. The boys were being mean, and she got angry. She set a nearby garbage can on fire. The boys didn't know it was her, but her friends did. And the lifeguard saw the fire and called the fire department. Her parents were furious at her lack of control. They grounded her for the rest of the summer."

"Why did she lose control?" Shari-Beth asked. "I mean, she's been practicing her Gifts for at least three years now, right? She should be able to keep them under control."

"Well, she is a Fire Witch, and we all know how volatile they are," Anne said. Everyone who spent any time around Vannie and Allie knew that.

"Yeah, but still," Shari-Beth said.

"Selena said she got really angry, like, more than usual. The boys were following them around and wouldn't leave them alone. Normally, they would have just reported the boys to the lifeguard or moved their blanket somewhere else. Selena said she didn't think it was fair that they should be the ones to move when they were already in their favorite spot on the beach, and it was the boys who were being dicks. She started to yell at them, and then the garbage caught fire. The girls left after that. Her friends were worried they wouldn't be able to get her calmed down and something worse would happen. She said even her friends were scared. She'd never felt so angry."

Lucian cocked his head to one side.

"I heard a similar story," he said. "Roger, a bear shifter in my class, comes from down south a ways too. He said he was out with a group from his sleuth over the summer, and they got harassed by a group of tourist kids too. He said that two of his group, who had both been shifting for several years and had great control, were provoked into shifting to protect the group. The tourist kids ran, and the cops showed up. The bear guys were ok once they calmed down, and the cops were cool about it. Apparently, there've been a few incidents like this all summer. Tourists provoking local kids. The cops think it's stupid human kids trying to get supernaturals to show themselves, like some kind of dare or hazing or something."

"Did Roger say that either of the boys who shifted were unusually angry, like Selena?" Shari-Beth asked.

Lucian shook his head.

"No, but he was surprised they had lost control and shifted. The other bear-kin didn't, though everyone was upset by what the tourist kids were saying. If the guys hadn't shifted, there probably would have been a fight."

Shari-Beth frowned.

"That's really weird," she said. It could be coincidence, but Shari-Beth wasn't in the habit of believing in coincidence.

"Does Roger live near Selena?"

"Roger lives in Pacifica," Lucian said.

"So does Selena," Mariah said. She looked at Shari-Beth. "What are you thinking?"

"It seems strange that three people lost their cool and their control of their Gifts and in similar situations," Shari-Beth said slowly. "And in the same town, too." She paused for a moment. "Listen, guys. Can you all find out if anyone else has had similar experiences this summer? Please?"

"Do you think there's something wrong?" Kelly asked.

"I don't know. But I'd rather figure it out now if there is."

SHARI-BETH WAS STILL THINKING ABOUT THE CONVERSATION WHEN she got to Wonder that afternoon for her shift. During the school year, Shari worked three hours a day after school. Wonder closed at six on weeknights during the school year, as both Liz and Malia had school-aged children. They took turns staying to close so that each woman could spend time with her family.

Liz noticed that Shari-Beth was somewhat preoccupied and called her on it.

"Everything go ok at school today?" Liz asked.

"Yeah, it was fine. It's good to see everyone again, and my classes are going to be really great this year," Shari-Beth replied.

Liz waited.

"Several kids had trouble over the summer," Shari-Beth said. She finished straightening the books she was putting away, then turned to Liz.

"What kind of trouble?" Liz asked.

"They all had trouble with a group of tourist kids in the town they live in, and several of them, or their friends, lost control of their Gifts. One Fire Witch set a garbage can on fire, two Bear Shifters shifted suddenly, and a Water Witch caused a small storm."

"Really? That's strange. Did all of this happen in the same town?"

"Yeah, Pacifica. South of here."

"And what are you worried about, specifically?" Liz asked.

Shari-Beth shook her head.

"I'm not sure, exactly. It's just, they shouldn't have lost control. All of them were old enough that they'd been using their Gifts for several years. None of them were immensely strong in their Gifts—even the Shifters were pretty low down in the Pack in terms of the strength of their Bears. But still, it's weird. And the circumstances were way too similar." She paused briefly, fussing with the business card holder on the counter. "I was wondering if maybe there's another drug out there, targeting supernaturals, that makes it harder to control our Gifts."

"Did these kids all eat or drink the same thing? Were any of them using drugs, to begin with?" Liz asked. It was very unusual that a drug would affect Shifters. Their metabolisms were just too fast.

Shari-Beth shook her head. "I don't know. I know they wouldn't have been doing drugs. What's the point? They wouldn't work. And the Witches are both girls who would never. One of them is friends with Mariah and Anne, and the other is friends with Kelly. They all swear that these kids would never use drugs."

"Sometimes, things like that can be hidden for a while until it gets too bad," Liz said.

Shari-Beth shook her head. "I know, but I really doubt it," she replied.

"Well, if you're really worried about it, tell your dad when you get home tonight," Liz told her.

"I will," Shari-Beth agreed as she looked up to greet a customer as they entered the store.

◈

BRENDAN TOOK WHAT SHARI-BETH HAD TO SAY SERIOUSLY. HE called Maria Hemenway on the mirror after dinner.

"You're not going to tell me we have to expand the school again, are you?" the Headmistress asked as she answered.

"No, but I think we need to be on our guard," Brendan replied seriously.

Maria looked at him sharply.

"What's going on?"

Brendan relayed what Shari-Beth had told him.

Maria looked thoughtful.

"I think she's right. I'll look into this more. I'll check with the families of the children involved and see what they know. Thank you for bringing this to my attention, Brendan. With everything else that's been going on, the escalating violence in the cities, the Veils thinning, everything, I think we do need to be very vigilant. Though, if these kids were in groups, why were only one or two affected?"

"I understand the Fire Witch was with mundanes. She was the only supernatural in the group. The others, I have no idea. The Shifters were with others of their Sleuth, and the Water Witch was with other young Witches. Her cousins, I believe. Yet she was the only one affected."

"If they were targeted, how did it happen? You said the offending parties were mundanes, correct?"

"That's what Shari-Beth said."

"So it's unlikely to be a curse or a spell. All right, I'll see what I can figure out. I'll talk with Peter Brown at the Council too. He deals with Academy issues. I'll see if there have been any other situations like this."

Brendan closed the call, feeling unsettled. These incidents sounded too much like what had happened in Shari-Beth's hometown of Caper's Creek in Wyoming, only there, the Shifter kids overdosed and went into comas from the drugs they were slipped without their knowledge or consent. Shari-Beth's friend Clint had been one of those kids. Another, Sam Johnson, was still in a coma two years later. He seemed to have gotten a higher dose. Those kids had been injected. Could the same thing be happening here?

Brendan turned back to the mirror and called Jason Reilly, former lieutenant with the Caper's Creek police department. His uncle, Jackson Daltry, was the police chief and Alpha of Caper's Creek, a mixed-Pack town. Jason had moved to Valerian's Cove after discovering his fated mate, Betty Gianetti, Tony's mother, living there.

"Hey, Brendan. What's up?" Jason was former military as well as police, just like his uncle and like Tony.

"Shari-Beth brought something to my attention that I think we need to look into," Brendan said. He brought the other man up to speed.

The Wolf was quiet for a moment.

"You're right. This doesn't sound good. I'll check with my uncle and ask him if they've had any more trouble up there. I'll call you back."

Jason ended the call.

Brendan sighed and called Tony.

Tony ran his hands through his hair after listening as Brendan told him what they'd discovered.

"Like we needed anything else right now," he groaned.

"Is Caleb still being a putz?" Brendan asked.

"It's not that, so much. He's actually making an effort and getting better," Tony said. He rubbed his head again. "It's that we've got a lead on Aldo, but what he was doing is completely out of character for him. He would never have done it on his own." Tony filled Brendan in on the sighting of Aldo at the bank robbery in Detroit.

Brendan shook his head.

"So now we've got mind control and drugs. Maybe mind control through drugs. Though I have to say, the circumstances sound different to me."

"I don't know what to think," Tony said. He sighed. "It would be nice if we could live in a peaceful world," he said with a grin.

"You'd be bored, son," Brendan replied with a smile.

"True. Ok, I'll check in with Peter Chizinsky. He's the Shifter liaison at the Council now. You know he's been at the forefront of the efforts to bring the Packs into the current century. I'll see if he's heard anything and get back to you." They said goodnight, and Tony ended the call.

Brendan turned and headed into the kitchen, where Celine was setting a pot of oatmeal to soak in preparation for the morning.

Brendan put his arms around Celine, hugging her and resting his cheek on the top of her head.

"What's wrong, love?" She asked him, hugging him back. She could always tell.

Brendan filled her in, then kissed her, and let her go. Celine stood for a moment, a dishrag twisting in her hands.

"I think we are right to be careful," Celine said after a moment. "It may be coincidence, or it may be something different. If someone is targeting our children again, they will wish they had never been born. Especially with the Alliance now in place. We will rain such retribution down on them as they have never seen."

Brendan found he was a trifle scared himself at the look burning in his wife's eyes.

❦ 19 ❧

Jackson Daltry called Brendan the next day.

"You were right. I called a few friends in law enforcement around the country. It didn't happen here—they would be stupid to try that sort of thing again here so soon after the last time. But there have been incidences in several places around the country of young supernaturals losing their tempers and their hold on their Gifts. All in situations where they were provoked by a group of other kids, usually mundanes."

"So they're targeting all supernaturals now, not just Shifters, this time," Brendan said.

"It seems like it. The method of disbursement is in question. No injection sites on the kids affected, though they probably weren't able to check in time. At least with the Shifters, they would have healed too quickly. It seems that no one has gone into a coma or overdosed this time. Oh, in relation to that. Sam Johnson woke up. He's going to be fine. We're still not sure why Sam reacted so strongly to the drug. The theory is that he was especially sensitive to something in it. They didn't want to test it until he was better. He's officially twenty-one now and has agreed to help once his body fully recovers from the coma."

"Shari-Beth will be glad to hear that. Sam's the one with the boss who's ex-military, right?"

"Yes, Ted's a marine, Supernatural Special Forces Division. He's taken Sam in and given him his job back as soon as he's recovered enough to do the work."

"That's good of him. Sam's lucky to have him."

"Yes, he is. Ted's a good man. Ted is not happy that this seems to be happening again. He's offered to help in whatever way he can. He's reaching out to a few people he knows to see if they've heard anything."

"I appreciate it," Brendan said. He sighed. "I'm going to let the Alliance Council know what's happening. We'll see if anyone else is reporting anything like this."

"Keep me informed, please," Daltry requested.

Brendan agreed and hung up. The more help they had on this, the more supernaturals in authority aware and on their guard, the better it would be.

REBECCA WAS PLEASED WITH THE PROGRESS HER APPRENTICES HAD made in such a short time. It was mid-September, and so far, everything was going well. Simon and Daniel seemed to get along, and Flora was flourishing. Her work was already taking new directions, improving in leaps and bounds. Flora's uncle Lars was due to arrive that afternoon for their first guest teacher experience.

The sun shone down on the grounds of the new studio as Rebecca sat on the patio and ate her lunch. Flora sat on a bench near the cliffs, eating her lunch and working on a design on her tablet. Simon was eating inside while Daniel had gone for a walk. Rebecca had decided to move their work to the new building as soon as it was finished, after all. It made much more sense. They had so much more room here. The studio had been finished weeks ahead of schedule, and it was fabulous.

"Rebecca, there's someone here to see you," Simon said, sticking his head out the door.

Rebecca turned in her chair and saw a Dwarven man standing just behind Simon.

"Rebecca Casey? Lars Ulfrid," he introduced himself.

Rebecca stood and shook the man's hand.

"It's a pleasure to finally meet you in person," she told him.

"It's a pleasure to be here. Our family is grateful to you for giving our Flora a place here. Metalsmithing is all she's ever really been interested in, much to the dismay of her parents, who were hoping she'd go into politics like them." He grinned.

"Flora is extremely talented. I'm hoping I can keep her once her apprenticeship is up," Rebecca told him honestly.

Lars grinned at her.

"We'll see about that." He looked around. Simon was hovering nearby, listening.

"Simon," Rebecca said," "This is Lars Ulfrid, Flora's uncle. He's a Master Armorer. Lars is going to be our first guest teacher. He'll be here for a month. Will you please show him to his room? Then you can go back to your lunch. Lars, Simon will show you where to put your things. Then why don't you come back down? I have something to discuss with you, and you can say hi to Flora," Rebecca pointed out towards the water, where Flora's head was bent over her design.

Lars returned quickly, and Rebecca led him away from the building towards the water.

"That's one of your apprentices, yes?" Lars asked in regards to Simon.

"Yes. He's got some catching up to do, but I think he has talent," Rebecca said.

"He's got something else as well," Lars replied somewhat enigmatically. "That boy is hiding something and is worried about it."

Rebecca looked at the older man in surprise.

"Now," Lars continued. "You said that the Dragon Seer has Seen Flora making armor?"

"Yes," Rebecca sighed. She filled him in on Valerian's Cove's concentration of super-powered children, the Alliance, and everything else that had been happening.

"Lily is the strongest Seer the Dragons have had in centuries. Her granddaughter, Bethie, is even stronger. They're never wrong. Lily says that within a year, you will move here permanently, and you and Flora will make armor here for whatever fight the Goddess seems to be preparing us for. She says that Flora's armor will be the strongest, lightest, most beautiful armor ever made. Flora will become renowned for it. People from all over, all the realms, will search her out. My jewelry will evolve into magical talismans. For now, I was hoping you could share some of your wisdom with us and get Flora moving in the right direction."

Lars was quiet for a moment.

"Our Seers have Seen something coming, too. We as a people use magic less than Witches and the Fae, but we do use it. Our Seers are strong in their Sight, too. They told me to be ready for a change, though they didn't tell me what it would be. I guess this is it."

"Do you have a family you will bring with you if they're right? I can have a house built for you. I was just going to give you the guest room here permanently otherwise, once you come back to stay."

Lars shook his head.

"No, I've never married and have no children. My work has been my life. That's probably why I dote on Flora so much—she's the child of my heart."

"Why don't we talk about it later? Today, let's get you settled in, and introduce you to everyone. We've been invited to dinner at my aunt and uncle's place. You don't want to miss it. My Aunt Celine is an amazing Kitchen Witch."

"Thank you. I would be happy to accept."

They approached Flora, who was sitting facing away from them, deeply involved in her design. It appeared she also had earbuds in, as her head was nodding in time to something only she could hear.

"Flora!" Rebecca called as they got closer. Flora's music must have been pretty loud. Rebecca could hear it as they came up next to her.

"Flora!"

Flora jumped, then looked up at them. She blinked, then jumped to her feet, ripping out her earbuds as she did so. She threw her arms around her uncle, who hugged her back with an enormous smile on his face.

"Uncle Lars! What are you doing here?"

"I'm your guest teacher for the next month, my girl," the older man told her, smiling and hugging her back. He held her at arm's length for a moment, searching her face.

"You look very well, Flora. Being here agrees with you, I think."

"I love it here," Flora responded. "I'm learning so much from Rebecca, and the tool she had made for me to channel Dragon and Mage Fire is amazing! Wait until you try it; you'll love it!"

Lars smiled at her. "Is that a design you're working on? Let's see it," Lars sat down on the bench as Flora handed him the tablet. Rebecca walked a little ways away from them, looking out to sea. A flash towards the cove caught her attention. Light reflected off the scales of a long, iridescent white tail. Sinéad and her guards were in the water.

After a few minutes, Rebecca turned back and caught sight of Daniel heading toward them. She waved at him, directing her third apprentice to join them.

"Lars, this is my apprentice, Daniel ap Ioan of the Fae. Daniel, this is Lars Ulfrid, Flora's uncle. He's a Master Armorer and our first guest teacher. He'll be with us for a month."

Daniel smiled and held out his hand.

"Charmed, Master Ulfrid. It's an honor to make your acquaintance."

After a few minutes of talk, they headed back to the studio. Simon was doodling on his tablet when they walked in. Rebecca took a quick glance as Simon put the tablet away. It looked like a design for one of Simon's sculptures. Nothing covert about it at all. Rebecca wondered what Lars thought Simon was hiding.

Oh, well, she thought to herself. *If it's important, it will all come out eventually.*

CELINE WELCOMED REBECCA AND HER CREW TO DINNER WITH evident joy and grace. The talented Witch truly did enjoy cooking for large parties.

"And my sister Luna portalled in this morning for a visit, so we have plenty of dessert!" Celine told Rebecca with a grin.

Rebecca turned to Lars. "Master Ulfrid, Luna is a famous pastry chef in Paris. You really are in for a treat."

Lars grinned back and rubbed his belly. "I certainly look forward to it!"

The field and patio at the back of the house were filled with people. Sean came over and swept Rebecca into a kiss, bending her backward like a movie hero of old, leaving her laughing breathlessly. Once she straightened up again, Rebecca introduced Lars to everyone.

"Don't worry if you can't remember everyone's names," Celine told the bemused man as she set a platter of veggies and dips on one of the already laden picnic tables. "Please, help yourself to food. We don't stand much on ceremony here. There are appetizers, snacks, and desserts on the tables, along with plates and utensils. My husband Brendan and friends are grilling whatever kind of meat you desire over there," she nodded at several men, who were laughing and joking around as they manned the large grills. Declan staggered back, his hand over his chest as if mortally wounded. He straightened up again, laughing, as he flipped a burger destined for the plate of a very hungry young Carl, Liz's son, who, as a growing Shifter, was starting to eat his family out of hearth and home.

Flora stayed with her uncle while Daniel immediately headed for Siofra and Nathaniel, who were sitting on one of the loveseats by the fire pit. Siofra had a sleeping Dervla on her lap, Nathaniel's arm around them both.

Simon hung back, watching everyone else.

"Simon, come get some food," Rebecca encouraged her apprentice. She led him over to the plates and utensils, grabbing some for herself. Simon followed her and Sean along the tables, choosing from the salads, cheese plates, and veggies piled high on their platters.

"Who are you?" A young voice said suddenly from beside Simon. He glanced down to his left. Two young girls were standing there, looking up at him. His Fire Magic sat up and took notice.

"I'm Simon. I work with Rebecca," he replied.

"You're a Fire Mage, aren't you?" The girl on the right, who had super-curly brown hair, asked. The girl on the left had long wavy red hair. Both young ladies were staring at him.

"Yes, I am. Who are you?"

"I'm Allie Casey-Gianetti, and this is my bestie, Vannie. Rebecca's my cousin. We're Fire Mages, too."

"And Allie's a Pheonyx and a Dragon, too," the other girl, Vannie, piped up.

Simon stared down at the two girls.

"Why haven't you joined our fight practice yet?" Allie asked. "We can use more Mages. We have lots of Shifters, some Witches, and Fae. It would be good to have another Fire Mage to practice with."

"And since you're grown up, you probably know things we don't, and you could help us learn," Vannie said.

"I didn't know fight practice was open to everyone," Simon said.

"Oh, didn't I tell you?" Rebecca exclaimed, appearing beside him again. "I thought I made that clear to all of you. My bad. You're totally welcome to join us. I'll make sure Daniel and Flora know as well. Lars, too." Rebecca headed off towards Daniel, Sean trailing along behind her.

"Well, I picked a good night to come visit!" a voice exclaimed as two tall Aes Sídhe appeared around the corner of the house. Siofra handed Nathaniel the sleeping baby and stood up to hug her brother.

"Ciaran! What are you doing here? We weren't expecting you."

"But now that you're here, we are delighted to see you," Celine declared, swooping in for a hug. She hugged Caoimhe as well, then stepped back. "As you can see, you are just in time for dinner. Which I'm sure Ciaran planned on if I know him."

Ciaran grinned unapologetically. Celine laughed in response.

❧ 20 ❧

There were many, many more realms in the multi-verse than most people knew of. And the veils were slowly thinning, change moving inexorably forward. Realms and possibilities were colliding. And those who could walk the realms were slipping ever more easily through the veils....

Lars decided to keep an eye on Simon. There was just something about the young man that set off warning bells for the old Armorer. On the surface, Simon appeared to be a nice, polite, creative young man, if a bit shy and withdrawn. Still, there was something, and Lars was protective of his niece and her new teacher. He wanted to prevent anything from messing with the wonderful situation Flora had found herself in. Especially since Lars, himself, was apparently going to be living here as well. At least he'd be on hand if anything did go wrong. He found some comfort in that thought.

ALL THREE OF REBECCA'S APPRENTICES JOINED IN FIGHT TRAINING as part of their daily lives. After watching for a few minutes on the first day, Lars joined in as well.

"It's been a while since I've worked on my own training, and I'm getting a little rusty," the Dwarf told Celine with a smile.

"You certainly can't tell he's out of practice!" Celine laughed later as she took a breather to get a glass of water. Lars was truly formidable. Declan was sparring against him as the rest of the group pulled back to watch, forming a circle around the two combatants. Lars was shorter but immensely strong, and he obviously knew how to use the war club he was swinging. Declan had more reach, being taller, but was definitely at a disadvantage.

"He's amazing," Milena said, sitting on the ground next to her grandmother.

"I want to learn to fight like that!" Allie said. She still hadn't met a fighting technique she didn't want to learn. Allie got bored easily. Declan was at his wit's end, coming up with new training techniques to keep her busy and engaged.

Daniel was an elegant fighter if a bit sloppy. But he'd never been in actual combat before. Declan figured he could whip the Aes Sídhe into shape in short order. Flora had been taught basic defensive skills but not truly how to fight. Declan assigned Sean to work with the young woman to bring her more up to speed. After learning that Simon had no fighting skills or training whatsoever, he kept Allie and Vannie busy by having them train the young man under the watchful eyes of Shari-Beth and Joshua.

"Allie, you can't have him start by throwing fireballs!" Shari-Beth exclaimed.

"But he's a Fire Mage. He should know how!"

"I wasn't really taught how to fight, though," Simon said.

"Allie, why don't you and Vannie show Simon what you can do? With your Mage Gifts, please. You can Shift later, Allie," Shari-Beth suggested. Allie and Vannie both grinned, then faced off against each other.

Simon watched as the two young girls started throwing fireballs at each other, then moved to creating weapons out of fire and using them to attack each other.

Simon gasped, then went pale as Allie scored a hit on Vannie's shoulder. Vannie grinned and doubled the efforts of her attacks. Simon glanced over at Emma, who was taking a break and watching too. Though, Emma's eyes may have strayed more towards Shari-Beth than the two combatants.

"This isn't safe! They could kill each other. Where are their parents? Surely they're not ok with this?"

Emma looked at Simon in surprise.

"We've all been practicing together like this for a couple of years now," she informed him. "Don't worry; they won't actually hurt each other. They're shielding, and neither of them is using their full power. Plus, they're best friends. They'd never hurt each other. And their parents are over there." Emma pointed to where Malia and Vannie's mother, Sarah, were sparring with staffs at the center of the practice field. Vannie's grandfather had returned from Ireland with them and was calling out encouragement to his daughter as she fought.

Simon blinked.

Emma gazed at the young man for a moment, then spoke again.

"Simon, Rebecca wasn't kidding when she told you that we were all called together by the Goddess for a reason and that we have some of the strongest-Gifted children in generations here. Allie is uber-strong and really can Shift into two alternate forms. And she's strong in those forms, too. They're not partial Shifts. She's a full-on Dragon and Phoenyx. Her brother, Ian, is a Phoenyx and one of the strongest Techno-Mages we have. The twins will be thirteen this fall. Vannie is an extremely strong Fire Mage. Milena and Mikey are part Dragon, part Phoenyx and part Aes Sídhe. Milena is an Illusionist with a direct connection to the Goddess. Bethie is the strongest Seer the Dragons have ever had, even stronger than her grandmother, Lily, who is stronger than any before her. Our friends in Fairweather Falls, a Sanctuary community on the East Coast, are experiencing extremely strong children, too. They're descended from Starborn and Deravalen demons. We suspect that there's a war coming, though we think we have a few years yet to prepare since most of the kids are still so young. Hopefully."

Simon stared at the young woman. Then he blinked again.

"What are you?" He asked.

"I'm a Swan Maiden. I fight with Shari-Beth, Aiden, and Joshua. Our friends Lucian, Mariah, Anne, and Kelly fight with us, too. We're a team."

"Are the rest of your team Shifters, too?"

"Shari-Beth, Lucian, and Joshua are. Mariah and Anne are part Witch, part Pixie."

Simon stared again, then turned to look back at the people training on the field. Shari-Beth had noticed Simon talking to Emma rather than focusing on the girls' demonstration and had given Allie the nod to Shift. Suddenly, a giant red Dragon snapped out her wings and sent a jet of Fire into the sky. The rest of the Shifter combatants, taking this as their cue, all Shifted as well to practice fighting in their Shifted forms.

"We work together so we can learn each other's strengths and weaknesses and how to support each other in a fight," Emma said. She turned back towards Shari-Beth again. Allie had Shifted to Phoenyx and was harassing Vannie by diving at her while the other girl used a whip of flames to try to knock her friend out of the sky. Vannie's grandfather had drifted over to watch and was now shouting encouragement to his granddaughter while talking to Shari-Beth, who stood beside him.

Simon stared around him, taking in all the fights going on, those resting between sessions, and those stretching and cooling down. Everyone was working together, talking and laughing together. No one looked angry or like they were going to lash out.

"I never expected something like this," Simon said quietly to Emma, who glanced at him quickly before looking back towards the field.

"It's good training, and it's good to know people who will definitely have your back if something goes wrong," Emma said as she stood. Shari-Beth was waving at her.

"Em! Come fight!"

Sean had come over to take over the girls' training. He stopped and said something to them, then headed over to where Simon was sitting.

"Are you ready to start? I promise I'll have the girls go easy on you," the Dragon grinned. He held out his hand to pull Simon to his feet.

"I guess so. I've never done anything like this before. I mean, I'm usually the punching bag, not the fighter."

"We'll fix that. Come on, Si. We'll show you how it's done."

❦

THAT EVENING, AFTER THE APPRENTICES HAD ALL GONE TO BED, Simon sat in his room with his head in his hands. Sean and the girls had worked him hard. He was physically exhausted and sore in muscles he hadn't even known he had. Sean had told him he would probably hurt even more the next day and to ask for a healing potion if he did. Still, Simon found himself enjoying fight practice. It was a revelation to him that these people were willing to train him, that they thought he was worth teaching, worth including in their practice. Sean was pleased with how quickly Simon had understood and carried out his instructions.

"We'll make an excellent fighter out of you, you'll see," the Dragon had told him at the end of the session.

Simon fell backward onto his bed, staring up at the ceiling. His mind was whirling. When his family had found out that Simon had been accepted for this apprenticeship, they had not taken it well. Simon's family valued 'manly' men and thought Simon was soft because he liked to make beautiful things. They didn't understand him; they never had. His father's idea of helping his son was to ridicule him. He said he was teaching him to be strong. To Simon, it seemed that he was constantly being told how worthless he was. His heart broke every time, with a burning feeling in his chest and behind his eyes as if he were on fire, everything he valued about himself being scoured away, leaving nothing but a lump of worthless coal behind. He didn't know how he could be any different than he was. Nothing he ever did seemed good enough to earn his family's love and understanding.

Simon's uncle, Paul, had approached him before Simon left for

Valerian's Cove. Paul was the big success in the family. A Fire Mage like Simon, he had worked his way up and now owned his own car dealership selling high-end cars. He had never paid much attention to his nephew before. Paul had taken Simon out to dinner and quizzed him on his plans. At the end of the meal, Paul had shaken his hand, holding onto it a moment longer than necessary as he looked his nephew dead in the eye.

"I look forward to hearing all about your time with the Casey family, Simon. I'm sure you'll meet many interesting people and see many wonderful things. You'll have lots of stories to tell. I've always heard that the Caseys were some of the strongest Witches around, and now there are Dragons and Phoenyxes, and who knows what else in Valerian's Cove. Give me a call once in a while, and tell me all about it. And if you ever need to talk, you can call me, ok?"

Simon had the feeling that his uncle was fishing for something, but he wasn't completely sure he knew what it was. Uncle Paul was rumored to be into some weird stuff. He had some friends that made the rest of the family look like fuzzy bunnies. Still, Simon had nodded, which Paul took for agreement. Simon figured it wouldn't really matter, as he hardly had any occasion to talk to Uncle Paul. Yet, Uncle Paul had called him once a week since he'd been in Valerian's Cove and expressed great interest in hearing all about the people Simon was meeting.

Simon ran his hands through his hair and let out a breath. He didn't know why Paul was so interested, but he had the feeling (and it had been getting stronger lately) that it wasn't for anything good. Simon liked the people he had met here. They made him feel welcome in a way he had never experienced before. They included him and spoke kindly to him. Any teasing was done in a friendly manner, the same way they treated everyone else, and no one took it seriously. Arguments were rare and never ended in a fistfight or magical duel. At least, not that he'd seen. Simon felt more at home in Valerian's Cove than he ever had with his own family. He had even been thinking about asking Rebecca if he could stay on after the apprenticeship, long enough to start to make a name for himself so he could afford to buy his own place in the town. He felt comfortable here. It felt wrong to pass on stories to Uncle Paul.

The next afternoon at fight practice, Simon approached Sean during a break.

"Can I talk to you for a minute, Sean?"

"Sure. What's up, Si?"

"I'm not sure if it means anything, but I have an uncle who calls me every week to check in on me. Before I came here, I barely ever talked to him, except at family events. When he found out I was moving here for the apprenticeship, he took me out to lunch. I get the feeling he's pumping me for information on the people here. I don't tell him anything important, nothing a visitor to town wouldn't see, but Uncle Paul is the kind of guy you want to be wary of. He doesn't have the best reputation, and he knows some pretty weird people."

"Thank you for telling me, Simon. I appreciate it. For now, keep your conversations with him as general as possible. I'll have someone look into him and see if we can figure out why he's suddenly so interested."

"Thank you, Sean. I just don't feel right talking to him about Valerian's Cove and the people here. I want to stay here after the apprenticeship. I feel more at home here than I ever did with my family. I don't want to be the cause of something bad happening."

Sean clapped him on the shoulder, and they dove back into the training circle for another round.

21

D aniel ap Ioan was known as a dandy in the Aes Sidhe courts. He made pretty things for the ladies, often given as tokens of favor. He never *sold* his creations—his family was well-off. He would never need to work to support himself or a family of his own, should he ever decide to have one. Still, he collected favors himself from the ladies and gentlemen who commissioned his pretties from him. Daniel placed favors due him far, far above money in worth. You never knew when you might need to call one in. What would one owe to the crafter who made the piece that caused one's beloved to fall in love with one in return? Or the perfect engagement and wedding rings? Daniel had some small skill with enchantment and wasn't above adding *encouragement* to select pieces. For those pieces, it was understood that the favors owed in return could be quite substantial when called due. These enchantments bordered on coercion, after all, which was quite illegal. Daniel insisted his spells would only work to stimulate feelings already there—they could not compel someone to do something they wouldn't otherwise do. However, rumors were beginning to flow like small streams throughout the courts that perhaps, perhaps, Daniel ap Ioan's pieces were more than they seemed. In a not-so-good, possibly very bad way.

Daniel had caught wind of the rumors before the rest of his family heard them and decided to take some time in the Earth Realm until the rumors passed. Rebecca's advertisement for apprentices came at the perfect time. Daniel was curious about the people he had heard about at court, these Caseys and their friends. Somehow, they had brought the monarchs of the Courts together to serve on a Council designed to protect all the realms of those on the Council. To be sure, it wasn't like in years past, when the Courts were physically at war with each other. They had been moving toward reconciliation for some time now. Still...still. Actually working together, and with other realms as well? This Daniel had to see to believe. And maybe, there were even greater favors to be had, for the right piece of information given into the right ear.

Daniel showed none of this during his interview with Rebecca for the apprenticeship spot. He could be quite bright and cheerful when he wanted. The Áes Sidhe was careful when around his family, for instance, to only show his good side. He needed plausible deniability should anything ever go wrong. People in high places who would stand up for him and vouch for his character. So far, his playacting had served him well.

DANIEL STOOD ON THE CLIFFS BY THE APPRENTICESHIP HALL, staring out across the ocean. He wasn't really seeing it. His thoughts were turned inwards. He had indeed met many influential people of many races since moving to Valerian's Cove. He could see that they all believed in what they were doing and that the Goddess was the one behind it all. Daniel had no desire to get on the wrong side of the Goddess. If she genuinely still existed and was really paying attention. And it wasn't like he'd learned anything worth passing on, anyway. There wasn't even really any danger that he could see. Daniel, of course, was not a party to the Council's meetings and had no idea of the increase in violence and suspicious disappearances that had been occurring.

He turned and made his way back to his room in the hall. Closing the door behind him, he turned, starting towards his desk. As he spun, he caught sight of an envelope resting on his bed.

The envelope was a creamy, heavy-weight vellum. The seal on the back was generic, just a circle with a sphere inside. The seal used to press the wax had not been carved to fit a particular House.

Reaching out with his magic, Daniel tested the envelope, finding no trace of spells or enchantments beyond the one that ensured that only its intended recipient could read it. He picked it up, breaking the seal and pulling the letter held inside out into the light.

To Daniel ap Ioan, Greetings.

It has been said that you are currently in the Earth Realm, in the same town as those who would bring our Courts together and 'save' the realms. One would find it most interesting to learn of your experiences with these people and of any news of what they are planning.

One knows that you prefer favors to money. Should you agree to send us a message, from time to time, with anything you feel one might find interesting, you will find that you will be enchantingly repaid. As a token of our bargain, you will find that all rumors that may have been swirling about the courts in regard to your integrity and magical skills have been quashed. Apparently, they were nothing more than sour grapes from the mouth of a lord whose darling left him and took his precious gift with them. Not even very well thought out, for if you had used such enchantments on your pieces, undoubtedly, his darling wouldn't have left to begin with! Your family is known to be very strong in their Gifts, after all.

Do let us know if you agree to our terms. It's such a very little thing, after all, to pass on stories? Anyone might do it when talking with their friends. And we are friends, ap Ioan, I hope? If you agree, place your finger on the 'x' below. A way to communicate discreetly will be sent to you.

In friendship,
X.

WELL, THIS WAS SOMETHING MORE LIKE IT. DANIEL GRINNED TO himself. He had his first client. Daniel was absolutely sure he would find something worthy to pass on soon. Daniel touched the tip of his finger to the 'x' on the signature line. The letter glowed, and Daniel hissed, jerking his hand back, then sticking his finger in his mouth. The tip was burned. Daniel watched as the letter caught fire in the air in front of him. As the ash fell, a hard silver shape dropped toward the floor. Daniel caught it, turning it over in his hands. A silver coin, a rose on one side, and a star on the other.

A whisper spoke to him, so quietly he almost missed it.

"When you have something to tell us, hold the coin, and speak clearly. Your words will reach us. Well met, Daniel ap Ioan."

22

Brendan had brought Tony up to speed on the new drug that seemed to make supernaturals lose control of their tempers and their Gifts. Tony told Chief Kenny, who called a meeting of the Town Council and the heads of all the Clans and Shifter Groups who called Valerian's Cove home.

"That's all we know for now," he finished explaining what they had learned to the group before him.

The crowd before him was silent. Shock, outrage, and determination lined the faces in the room.

"I guess Aldo's finally done something good with his life, if only in disappearing," a voice in the back said. There were some snickers around the room.

Tony raised an eyebrow.

"I only meant," the voice began as a woman stood up and faced the Alpha, "that it's because of his disappearance that we are aware of what's going on. I would never want anyone to be so compelled like that, used as cannon fodder. Taken from their home against their will." She shuddered. "You know our history, Tony. Your cousin is not my favorite person. His mistreatment of my Band whenever he was in town was well known. Still, I would never wish this on anyone."

Tony nodded. Rosetta had reason to dislike Aldo and his father, Tony's uncle Caleb. She was Alpha of the Coyote Shifters in Valerian's Cove. Her people had been here before the Wolves arrived, even before Valerian arrived and settled the Cove. Caleb had been jealous of their status in town and treated them unfairly. He had taught the attitude to his older son.

"Is there anything at all we can do to help figure this out?" Mr. Cooke asked. The old Bear was not one to sit idly by while those he loved were in danger.

"At the moment, just be on guard," Chief Kenny replied. "If you see anyone acting strangely or any groups of mundanes try to start trouble, report it at once. Contain the violence, and get the person under attack to safety. Talk to your people. Reach out to others of your people in other towns and areas. Let them know what's happening, and ask them if they've seen anything like this. Any strange behavior at all. Then let us know right away. You can tell Tony, myself, or report directly to the SOC if you are so inclined. Peter Chizinsky will take your calls. The more information we have, the better. Ask your people to watch for Aldo, too. He was last seen in Detroit, robbing a bank, which is way out of character for him. Especially since his new Alpha in LA says that Aldo had been working hard to change and become a useful member of the Pack there. We suspect that some sort of compulsion or control was placed on him. It may or may not have something to do with these attacks on our youth."

The meeting broke up soon after that. Chief Kenny turned to Tony.

"Son, reach out to your commanders in the Army, ok? The Supernatural Special Forces Branch needs to know about this if they don't already. Maybe they can help."

Tony nodded. "I had already planned to. I'll call them in the morning. I'll keep calling until I get someone."

"Thank you. I appreciate it. Have a good night, Tony. Say hi to Malia for me."

CELINE STARTED CALLING EVERYONE SHE KNEW ON THE MIRROR AS soon as Brendan told her about the drugs. She called her friends in the U.S. first, then her family in France.

"If this is happening here, we can assume it will go international soon if it hasn't already," she told her husband as she reached for the mirror.

Celine closed the connection to her mother in Paris, then paused. Their friends in Fairweather Falls were setting up their new branch of the Academy. Fairweather Falls was still a closed sanctuary town. Mundanes were not allowed. But still, young people were resourceful. If this was a drug, and it seemed to be, sooner or later, it would most likely show up in the sanctuary towns too. Better they were told about it now than to be blindsided later. Celine reached for the mirror again and called Nora Sloan in Fairweather Falls.

"Hello, Celine! I was just out in the greenhouse. The new Fae hybrids are doing splendidly out here. Please tell Brendan how grateful I am that he and Siofra are sharing them with me."

"I'm delighted to hear that, Nora. That's not why I called, though."

Nora raised her eyebrows in inquiry.

Celine took a deep breath.

"There seems to be a new drug on the streets, one designed to target supernaturals. So far, there have been cases of Witches and Shifters affected by it. It's popping up randomly in strange places. There always seems to be a group of mundane young people involved. They somehow transmit the drug to their target, then try to start a fight. The drug causes the supernatural or supernaturals targeted to lose their tempers, making it more likely they will respond with magic."

Nora blinked.

"Well, that's not good. Angry teenagers in magic fights with mundanes would definitely cause people to turn against us. Especially if someone gets hurt."

"I know." Celine closed her eyes briefly. "So far, this has only happened in mundane towns and cities. I'm not sure how long it will take to reach the sanctuary towns, or even if it will. But with the new

Academy branch opening soon in your town, I thought I should warn you."

"Thank you. I imagine the Council has already let the Academy know. I'll tell the town. I appreciate your calling, Celine. Thank you." Nora ended the call.

Celine sighed. Then, since she wasn't aware if anyone had told the Guardians yet, she called Susan Montoya of the Guardian Council to give her report.

❦ 23 ❦

The day after the meeting, Tony called his commanding officer from his unit with the Supernatural Division of the Army Rangers.

"O'Shea."

"Tony Gianetti, sir."

"Gianetti! How are you, son?"

"Good, sir. Permission to speak freely, sir? I've come across some information you may need to know."

"Go ahead."

Tony brought him up to speed on the drug and the apparent kidnapping and compulsion of supernaturals. There was silence on the other end of the line.

"We've heard rumours," General O'Shea said after a moment. "We've started keeping track of them. You're saying you know some of the kids this has happened to?"

"My wife's cousins do. And I know of one former Pack member who has disappeared and been caught on camera holding up a bank in a state far away from where he's supposed to be."

"Former Pack member? Are you sure robbing a bank is out of character for him?"

"Very, sir. His current Alpha tells me that Aldo has been making a real effort to be a contributing member of his new Pack, even started dating someone. They were extremely surprised when he disappeared."

"How well did you know him when he was a member of your Pack?"

"He's my cousin, sir."

Silence again.

"If I remember correctly, you were not on good terms with your family, Gianetti."

"No, sir. Aldo and his father left the Pack when I took over as Alpha. My uncle was angry at being replaced. I beat him fair and square, with the whole town as witness. They moved down to LA and joined the Pack there. Aldo's not a bad person, just raised bad."

O'Shea was quiet for another moment.

"Listen, Tony. We're looking into this. Several of our officers broke up a fight in a bar off base a few weeks ago under similar circumstances to the drug you're telling me about. We might have written it off, except one of the soldiers involved is the younger brother of a member of our unit, and he would never, ever touch drugs or alcohol. And that's not an exaggeration. He's quite adamant about it. Horrible family history. Both siblings are completely against drugs and alcohol of all kinds. He doesn't even like going to bars. He was there as the designated driver and, by all witness accounts, was completely sober when he left the bar with his friends. When they left the bar, they were accosted by a bunch of townies, and several minutes later, every supernatural in the group, all Wolves, by the way, were on the verge of Shifting. Witnesses say the townies pursued our boys, following them and harassing them as they left the bar. Our boys tried to ignore them and walk on to their cars, but the townies wouldn't let them."

"What happened, sir?"

"Their sarge was in the bar, and one of the witnesses went and got him. He was able to exert enough control over them to get them safely to base. They were all sent straight to the infirmary and tested for drugs. We reported what we found. I guess the report made its way to the SOC. They let us know what's been going on. We're all looking into this together."

"It's disturbing that they are targeting the armed forces, now. That's more dangerous and a heck of a bigger problem than just targeting young people."

"It is, son. It truly is."

"Sir, I still work for the police department here in Valerian's Cove. I'm also in contact with the SOC, the Alliance Council, and the police department and Alpha in Caper's Creek. Can I report to you when we hear of anything else?"

"Please do. And I'll tell you anything I'm at liberty to pass on, as well. Thank you for calling, Gianetti. Dismissed."

Tony grinned wryly and hung up. O'Shea was career military. He'd probably die in office. He was a good man who truly believed he was doing his best to help his country and his people by staying in his current position. Tony was glad he'd made the call. He stood up and walked down the hall to Chief Kenny's office to report on what O'Shea had told him.

CALEB GIANETTI STOOD UP, STRAIGHTENING HIS SPINE AFTER BEING hunched over under the hood of the car he'd been working on all morning. Will had taken his talk with Mike to heart and gotten Caleb involved in activities around the Pack lands. They had tried carpentry, landscaping and park maintenance, and working in the auto shop. Much to his surprise, Caleb had discovered that he enjoyed learning how to fix a car. It helped keep his mind away from the rage he felt against his nephew for taking his rightful place as Alpha of the Valerian's Cove Pack.

Over time, that rage had begun to fade. Caleb still felt some resentment, but seeing how other Packs were run had slowly opened his eyes. He'd started to realize that his worldview was much narrower and much less accepted than he'd been taught to believe by his father and older brother.

Caleb could admit, now, that the Valerian's Cove Pack was thriving under Tony's leadership. The Pack members were happy; the Pack lands and buildings well-maintained and taken care of. The Pack bank accounts, from what he'd been told, were becoming healthy in a way they hadn't been in generations, if ever. The Pack was growing, too, with Wolves petitioning to join on a regular basis. Tony had repaired the Pack's relationships with the other Supernaturals in Valerian's Cove and was in good standing with the SOC. Caleb had to admit the Pack was a much nicer place to live now. It gave the former Alpha a lot to think about.

Caleb placed his hands against his lower back and bent backward into them, stretching the tight muscles. He leaned sideways, then twisted. Vertebrae cracked and popped.

"Sounds like you need to shift and go for a run," Mitch, one of the other mechanics, said with a grin.

"Maybe so, son. It's been a while," Caleb acknowledged. Caleb had been taught to keep a tight hold on his Wolf, to be the one in charge. To not shift unless it provided some advantage to him. Most Shifters considered their other halves their best friends and let them out often. It was exhilarating in a way that nothing else was.

"We're going for a run after work. You should come with us," Mitch offered.

Caleb thought about it for a moment.

"Maybe I will, son. Maybe I will," Caleb nodded in thanks and bent back under the hood of the car.

☙❧

SHARI-BETH, EMMA, JOSH, LUCIAN, KELLY, MARIAH, AND ANNE were on a small beach just around the bend of the harbor. It was a locals-only type of place. Small, secluded, and frequented by teenagers and people with small children. There was a steep path down to the beach while the cliffs rose up high around it, ringing them in.

The teens had their towels up against the rocks at the base of the cliff, so they could lean against them. Lucian was sneaking longing glances at Kelly whenever he thought no one was looking. Josh was on his back with a hat over his face. It had been a while since he'd shown any signs of being awake. Emma and Shari-Beth sat side-by-side, shoulders touching. Kelly and Mariah were playing a game of cards while

Anne was staring out to sea. Off in the distance, tails flashed as the Sea Fae played in the water. A pod of porpoises had joined them. Anne sighed.

"Go out and play with them," Mariah told her twin. "You know you want to."

"I could never keep up with them," Anne denied.

"Doesn't matter. They'll help you. Go on—it'll be fine," Shari-Beth encouraged. "Come on; I'll race you to the water." She nudged Emma, who got to her feet.

"We'll all race. Come on, sleepy," the Swan Maiden nudged Josh with her foot.

"I'm sleeping. I'll stay here and wait for Aiden," Josh mumbled.

"Whatever," Emma dragged Anne to her feet and pulled her down the beach. Shari-Beth, Kelly, Mariah, and Lucian all jumped up too, and the group rushed for the water, shrieking and laughing. Josh smiled at them and went back to sleep.

Emma dove into the water, then turned, pushing her hair back and shaking the water from her face. Anne had stopped at the water's edge.

"Lucy, go get her!" Emma ordered. Grinning, Lucian turned back towards Anne, who, seeing him heading for her, screamed and turned back up the beach. Lucian caught the reluctant Pixie Witch, carrying her into the waves. When he reached waist height, he tossed her. Anne rose to the surface, spluttering and gasping for air.

"That wasn't fair!"

"Sure it was. Now you're in. Come on, let's swim out."

The little group approached the Sea Fae, who weren't really that far out. The porpoises, seeing a new group of people swimming towards them, retreated a little ways off.

"Hey, guys! Welcome to our world," Jed called, swimming towards them with a flick of his iridescent turquoise tail.

"Anne wants to swim with the dolphins," Mariah told him.

"Sure, no problem." The Sea Fae whistled, and two porpoises approached. They looked him in the eye, then turned to Anne and Mariah. Emma thought they looked like they were laughing.

"Here, come around beside them, and hold on to their dorsal fins,"

Jed instructed. Soon, the twins were streaking through the water, laughing with glee.

Soon everyone had had a go. After a while, the non-Sea Fae tired from treading water and headed back to the beach. They thanked Jed and the porpoises, who cackled and nodded at them before swimming off.

"We'll come in with you," Sinéad told the earthbound teens.

The entire group retreated to the towels. Aiden had joined Josh, the two boys animatedly discussing something as the others approached.

"Hey, guys," Josh broke off and greeted the others.

"Josh, Aiden," Jed nodded. Everyone sat or lay down on a towel or in the sand.

"We were just talking about what we're going to do after school. I can't believe we're seniors already," Aiden exclaimed.

"Ugh, don't mention school!" Lucian groaned. He, Kelly, and the twins were juniors. They still had two years to go. "It feels like we start earlier every year."

"But we get out earlier, too," Mariah told him.

"Yeah, but since we go back earlier, it doesn't make the summer any longer," Lucian griped.

"Why are you talking about after, anyway?" Emma asked. "We all know what the two of you are going to do. Aiden's going into training with the Guardians, and Josh is joining the Supernatural Division in the Army."

The boys grinned. "It's good to have a plan," Josh replied.

"I'm going to France to study Familiar Care with Grandma Marthe, and Emma's coming with me, at least for a while," Shari-Beth said.

"Of course, she is," Mariah grinned.

"What's that supposed to mean?" Emma asked.

The others all laughed. While Shari-Beth and Emma might be a little slow on the uptake, the rest of the group could easily see how the wind was blowing.

"Come on, Em. You guys do everything together. Of course, you're going with her," Jed grinned.

Emma looked at Shari-Beth, who shrugged. "We're best friends."

Everyone grinned.

"Hey, guys. That speed boat is heading straight for that fishing boat out there," one of the Sea Fae, Noah, said suddenly. Everyone spun around to look at the water. Noah and Jed jumped up and ran. Diving into the waves, they transformed, tails shining in the sun. The speed boat rammed straight into the fishing boat, like something out of an action movie. The fishing boat, covered in spells for protection and safe voyages, stayed intact. The fiberglass hull of the speedboat was utterly destroyed. Bodies were thrown—or jumped—from both crafts as they collided. Noah and Jed reached the wreckage quickly, checking on those in the water. There had been a crew of three on the fishing vessel. There were three on the speed boat as well.

"Come on, Jace," Emmett, one of the other Sea Fae, said tersely. They ran for the water to help their friends.

The other teens joined the throng on the beach, watching the scene before them. As the Sea Fae brought the stricken men in, they helped them out of the water, laying them on the beach.

"Someone call Chief Kenny!" Shari-Beth yelled to the other bystanders.

"Done!" A voice called back. Soon rescue vehicles appeared at the top of the cliff, and figures began racing down the path.

Noah and Jace were standing guard over the three men from the speedboat. Two were unconscious. One was staring into space, rocking back and forth.

Jed and Emmett were helping the crew from the fishing boat. Only one of the crew was knocked out. The other two were sitting up, arms over their knees, panting.

"Thank you, boys, for saving us," the captain choked out. "I've never been so scared in my life. I can't believe it—they were heading straight for us! Why didn't they stop or swerve away?"

Everyone looked over at the three passengers from the speed boat.

"I guess we'll have to wait until they wake up to ask them," Jed said slowly. "This one here seems to be in shock, or catatonic, maybe. I don't think he can talk."

The rescue crew reached the group on the beach.

"Thanks, guys. We'll take it from here," one of the healers on the rescue crew said. They started examining the six men, beginning with the two lying unresponsive on the sand. Several police officers and firefighters had followed the healers down to the beach. They loaded the men onto stretchers, and a Witch levitated them up the cliff to the waiting ambulances. Police officers went with the men from the speed boat.

The teens all stared at each other as the crowd dispersed.

"What was that?" Emma asked, looking around. They all turned to stare out at the wreckage of the speed boat, bobbing on the waves as the harbor master and his crew arrived to gather the evidence.

24

Several weeks went by. After the boat crash, things seemed to settle down. There were no more accidents, and no one from Valerian's Cove had any interactions with strange teenagers trying to start fights. The young people all went back to school, groaning about how short the summer had been. Unlike mundane high schools, the seniors and juniors at the Academy had full class loads, including advanced Fight Class. Everyone had to take that.

The Caseys were throwing a party for the Autumn Equinox on September 21. It would, of course, be at the Casey residence. Tom, Rebecca's father, was coming in for the celebration, as were the Caseys from Ireland and France.

"It seems we're getting together for a lot of celebrations lately," Declan, a Casey cousin from Ireland, said as he hugged his U.S. cousins.

"Well, we do love a good party," Malia said, smiling up at him. Declan would oversee the music for the ceremony and party afterward. There would, of course, be live music, with the Caseys and many from the town playing. There would also be recorded music for when the live musicians needed a break.

Celine and her sister, Luna, were handling all of the food. Towns-folk would bring food to share as well—it was just what was done in Valerian's Cove. You never visited empty-handed.

The ceremony was beautiful. The party afterward ran into the late evening, one last musical set being played as the last stragglers made their way to their cars, exhausted children in tow.

Celine kissed Rebecca's cheek before she left for home.

"How are things going with you and Sean, sweetheart?"

Rebecca smiled and shook her head. "They're going great, Aunt Celine. I'm glad I finally decided to give him a chance. He's so easy to spend time with. He always thinks of fun things to do, and I feel completely safe with him."

"That's wonderful, sweetheart. I'm so glad to hear that." Celine hugged her niece as the Dragon in question walked up and held out his hand to his mate.

"Ready to go?"

Celine hugged them both and sent them on their way. She leaned back into Brendan, who had come up behind her.

"They seem to be doing well together," he said into her ear. His breath stirred the curls falling out of her French twist.

"They do. Rebecca is much more happy now. It's wonderful to see. And from all accounts, Sean is doing much better as well."

SEAN PORTALLED THEM HOME, STRAIGHT INTO THE SITTING ROOM OF their beautiful new house. Tonight would be the first night they spent in it. The first night they spent together. It seemed fitting that their first night together was spent in the space that was truly theirs.

The house was white, with two stories. The front door was a bril-liant crimson. Flower boxes hung from the windows. There was a courtyard in front, with two small seating areas on either side of the flagstone patio, surrounded by flowers. In the back, another seating area was bordered by a kitchen garden and an herb garden, followed by empty land sweeping down to the cliffs above the sea. Rebecca had plans for a small orchard to be planted soon. Her family was filled with Earth Witches, after all. Gardens were their business.

Sean looked down at Rebecca, who was smiling up at him, her eyes sparkling. He gently brushed a wisp of hair from her face. "I'm really glad you decided to give us a chance, Bex. I hope I can show you how much you mean to me."

"Now is the right time. I thought, when I met you, that I was too young. And I wasn't sure the Goddess knew what she was doing, bonding me to a practically immortal Dragon. But I didn't want to wait anymore, either. Who am I to question the Goddess?"

Sean lowered his head to kiss his mate, then swung her up into his arms and started up the stairs.

TONY AND MALIA WERE JUST GETTING INTO BED AFTER THE Equinox party when Tony's phone rang. Malia's eyebrows rose in question.

"Gianetti," Tony answered.

"Tony, this is Chief Kenny. I just got a report on Aldo. A John Doe was brought into a hospital in Chicago after a fire in a warehouse. The warehouse contents were completely destroyed. No one there has any idea who the John Doe is. The warehouse belonged to a shipping company. It was filled with clothing made in China, ready for distribution to stores. The owner is insisting the JD must have set the fire. Maybe he was homeless and broke in. Anyway, the JD matches Aldo's description. He's in a medically-induced coma—he was burned badly over seventy-five percent of his body. One of the doctors at the hospital is a Shifter and realized that the JD was too. He called the SOC. They're moving him to an SOC facility as we speak. Can you or Caleb make an ID?"

Tony ran his hand over his face, then through his hair. He sighed. "Yeah, Chief. Is over video enough, or do they want me to go to them?"

"Video is enough for now. If it is Aldo, they'll move him closer to you, if you want, until he wakes up. San Francisco, maybe."

"Wouldn't it be safer to have him in one of the Sanctuary towns? Those haven't been affected yet, right?"

"No, you're right. I'm not sure any of them have an SOC holding facility. I can check."

"Why don't they bring him here? With the Dragons and the Guardians here, this has to be one of the safest places he could be. And the Dragons would be happy to keep an eye on him. They could also get him away immediately if needed."

"We don't have a long-term medical facility here, Tony."

"We can put him in a house on Pack land. Caleb will want to stay with him, anyway. The Pack peacekeepers and the Dragons can watch over the house. We can hire whatever Healers are necessary."

"I think the SOC would rather their Healers be in charge," Chief Kenny said.

"We'll give them housing, too, then. Or Suzette could monitor his condition. Or Marjorie. Marjorie's a senior Healer."

"I don't know if they'll go for it, Tony, but I'll ask. I'll call you back as soon as I know. I'll let you know when they want to do the ID, too."

Tony hung up and stared at Malia.

"How much of that did you get?"

"They found someone that might be Aldo, but he's badly injured, and they don't know where to hold him?"

"Pretty much. If it is Aldo, I'm hoping they bring him here. It will mean added security on Pack lands, though. I'm going to call Declan and give him a heads-up."

◈

Chief Kenny called back an hour later.

"Sorry to wake you, son."

"No worries. I was having a hard time sleeping, anyway. What did they say?"

"They want you to make the ID in the morning, at nine. If it is Aldo, they are willing to move him into your care. They will send an SOC Healer and two guards to supplement the Dragons and Pack so that it's not such a strain on your resources and so they cover all their bases. They think it's a good idea to have him somewhere out of the way. Valerian's Cove is not a Sanctuary town, though, Tony," Chief Kenny pointed out. "Mundanes can come in at will. This has the potential to put the town in danger. I'm of two minds about that. On the one hand, we can be the bait to catch the SOB's that are involved in this. On the other hand, I don't want to put my people in danger."

"I know, Chief. But think about who lives here, for a moment. We have some of the most powerful Beings in the world, in several realms, living here. If we let them know what is happening, you know they will choose to get involved. Aldo may not be well-liked, but he is from Valerian's Cove. They picked the wrong Wolf to try this on. This town stands up for its own."

"You're right; I know it," Chief Kenny sighed. "And I know that many of our townsfolk have wanted to do something about the threat to our children. I'll call another town meeting; I can ask the Witches how hard it would be to close the barriers to the town, to shut it down completely if they had to. We'll come up with a plan."

"Thank you, Chief. I'll be in a little before nine to make the ID. And... I don't think I'll tell Caleb until after I know for sure."

"Probably wise, son. I'll see you in the morning."

Chief Kenny hung up.

Tony turned his head to find Malia watching him.

"We're bringing him here, aren't we?" The Witch asked.

"It looks like it. I hope this works," Tony said. The last thing he wanted was to be responsible for bringing harm to the people of his town.

TONY WALKED INTO THE POLICE STATION AT EIGHT FORTY-FIVE. Chief Kenny looked up from the report on his computer when Tony knocked.

"Thank you for coming, son," the Kodiak Shifter rumbled. He typed on his keyboard for a moment, then motioned for Tony to stand beside him. He turned the screen so that Tony could see better.

"Tony. Thank you for coming," Peter Chizinsky of the SOC said. "I'm sorry to ask you to do this. John Doe's face is severely burned. We've run dentals and come up with nothing, but as a Shifter and one who lived in a reclusive Pack as a child and young adult, that's not surprising. Are you ready for this? If you think it's Aldo, we can do a DNA match between the two of you, or even better, Aldo and his father, who Chief Kenny tells me is staying with you at the moment?"

"Yes, thank you, Peter. Though, I'd rather not bring my uncle into this until I have to. He can be rather... volatile when upset."

"Understood. Here we go, then."

The screen changed to another view. A man lay in a hospital bed, his body covered in a white sheet and blanket. What Tony could see was covered in bandages, except for the right side of his face. The camera moved to a close-up of the uncovered side. The man's eyes were closed.

"That's Aldo," Tony said.

"You're sure, son?" Chief Kenny asked.

Tony nodded.

"Ok, we'll confirm the DNA match and have our Witches make sure there are no illusion or glamour spells or anything else that could fake an ID on him. Once we're clear, I'll have him moved over to your Pack, Tony."

"Thank you, Peter. We'll be ready for him. I'll start getting a house ready today. Please let me know as soon as you have the DNA match confirmed."

"Will do. See you soon."

Peter ended the video.

Tony looked up at Chief Kenny.

"I'm going to start getting a house ready. I'll call Declan and arrange for Guardians to guard the house and Aldo, too. I'm not going to tell Caleb until the DNA match is confirmed."

Chief Kenny laid a hand on Tony's shoulder. "I know this is hard, son. We will get to the bottom of this. The whole town is up in arms about this new threat. We'll work it out."

"I know, sir. Thank you."

Tony saluted Chief Kenny and headed for the Academy. He

decided he'd rather talk to Declan face-to-face. And he didn't want to run into his uncle yet, either. The longer Tony could keep this from Caleb, the better. His uncle was likely to go ballistic when he found out how much Aldo was injured. Caleb would want vengeance on whomever had hurt his son.

❦ 25 ❦

The DNA was a match. SOC Witches (and Seers) confirmed that no illusions or spells were being used to alter the results. It truly was Aldo.

Tony sighed as he got off the phone with Peter Chizinsky. He stood, rapping his knuckles against the solid warm brown wood of his desk for good luck. Then he went to find his uncle.

CALEB WAS IN THE AUTO SHOP, PUTTING A NEW SET OF BRAKES ON AN older sedan. He came out from under the car when Tony called his name.

"What? I'm almost done here. Five more minutes."

"We've found Aldo."

Caleb stared at his nephew. He blinked.

"Well, where is he? Why isn't he here yet?"

"Uncle Caleb, Aldo was badly injured in a fire. He's being kept in an induced coma while he heals. The SOC is bringing him here to recover, but they think that the fire he was in was no accident. They want him protected. The SOC thinks he was supposed to have died in the fire.

Also, when he's able, they want to question him, to find out everything he can remember about what happened."

"But he's coming here? They're bringing him here?"

"Yes. He'll be here later today. I've got a house set aside for him. The Guardians are going to protect the house, Aldo, and you. So there will be a heightened security presence here on Pack lands for a while. The other option was to hide him away in some hidden SOC facility. I thought he would recover better at home."

"Thank you, Tony. You're a good man," Caleb clapped Tony on the shoulder before turning back to the car. Tony blinked. That was the first time his uncle had ever said something nice to him. Maybe the first time Caleb had ever said 'thank you,' and meant it, too. "Let me know when they arrive, ok?" Caleb wiped a dirty rag over his face as he turned back to his work.

⚜

"He actually said 'thank you'? Wow. That's got to be a first," Remy, Tony's cousin, and Caleb's younger son, said at dinner that night. Tony had just finished filling his younger cousin in. Remy was Tony's Third, the head of the Pack's Peacekeepers. Remy's mate, Suzette, was Malia's cousin.

"I know, right? Did you see Aldo this afternoon?"

Remy nodded as he finished chewing. "Yeah, I did. He's in really rough shape. I'm glad he's knocked out. No one deserves to be in that kind of pain."

"Yeah, I know."

"Dad's still sitting with him. I sent over some food earlier and asked the Guardian on duty to make sure he ate. I don't think Dad'll leave Aldo alone until he wakes up."

"That's one of the reasons I gave them a whole house to themselves," Tony replied. "I knew they would need the extra bedroom for Caleb. Though, knowing him, he'll probably sleep on the chair in Aldo's room."

Remy shrugged. "Probably. We all know Aldo was always his

favorite. Whatever. I'm glad Dad'll be there when Aldo wakes up. It will help him to see a familiar face."

"True. I let the Alpha in LA know what was going on, that Aldo had been found but was in a really bad way, and that Uncle Caleb was helping to take care of him, so neither of them would be returning to the LA Pack any time soon. He told me they're welcome back whenever they're ready."

"I wonder if they'll go back when he's all healed," Remy said, his head tilted to one side. "Dad's really starting to seem like a new person. He's voluntarily working and starting to make friends here. The people who knew him before are starting to become more relaxed around him, since he's not acting like a total douche anymore. I wonder if they'll decide to stay."

Tony raised his eyebrows.

"How would you feel about that?" He asked his cousin.

"Ok, I guess. I think I'd like to have a chance to see if we could all actually get along for a change. To see what kind of men Dad and Aldo could be if their heads weren't so far up their nether regions."

Tony grinned. "You know it might take a while. Being back here might bring up old behaviors, old hurts."

"I'll handle it. If they go back to being jackasses, I'll send them back to LA," Remy grinned.

Tony grinned back. "I'll help you," he replied.

26

Milena finished brushing the mane of her Unicorn Familiar, Nimuë, and put the brush away. The stately mare pushed her head against Milena, wuffing softly. It was her way of saying thank you.

"I'm telling you, it's not normal!" Allie was frustrated.

"Allie, it may not be normal, but it's obviously happening whether you like it or not. Get over it," Milena told her cousin.

"No one should find their Fated Mate at twelve years old!"

"Allison Casey-Gianetti, you're jealous, and you know it. Leave Ian and Amie alone. Even our parents are ok with it, though they are keeping a very close eye on them. They'll probably be thirty before they're allowed to complete the Bond."

"How are you not more upset by this?" Allie groused.

"I think it's sweet. Neither of them will ever have to wonder if there's someone out there for them. They already know."

"But what if they want to date other people?"

"Allie, they're *Fated Mates!* They are not going to want to date other people. And why are you complaining, anyway? Your parents met when your mom was five!"

"Yeah, but they didn't get together until three years ago. They were already grown up."

"Uncle Tony knew Aunt Malia was his Fated Mate by the time they were in high school. Maybe even earlier. It was Aunt Malia who took longer to figure it out." Milena turned to her cousin, hands on her hips. "I think you're just jealous because Ian spends more time with Amie than you now. Why that should bother you, I don't know. You spend all of your time with Vannie or training. And you don't see me giving Mikey a hard time for spending all his time with Grandpa Brendan in the greenhouses, do you? Just because they're our twins doesn't mean we own them."

Allie huffed and crossed her arms. She obviously wasn't going to win this argument. And maybe, very deep down inside, she knew her cousin was right.

THINGS WERE QUIET FOR A FEW WEEKS. VALERIAN'S COVE WAS gearing up for their annual town-wide Samhain celebrations on October thirty-first. Mundanes were welcome to participate and usually descended on the town in droves. This year, extra precautions were taken.

"Honestly, I almost canceled everything," Mayor Greta said to Chief Kenny after a particularly frustrating town meeting.

"We have the extra security measures in place. Everyone is on alert. The Witches are putting extra wards around Pack lands. They're making sure that the wards around the town filter anyone out who has harmful intentions. The town's budget depends on the tourist dollars we get from these festivals. I know I don't need to remind you of that."

Greta shook her head. "I know. I think I'll feel much better after it's all over."

"You may be waiting a while. We still don't have a good handle on what's really going on," Chief Kenny replied.

Mayor Greta just shook her head. "Have you heard anything more from the SOC or any of your other contacts?"

"There have been several more incidences of violence involving young people that we've heard of," Chief Kenny said. "Nothing major. They were all diffused fairly easily. Now that our people know what to watch out for, it's going to be harder for that trick to work. There haven't been any more suspicious events like what happened with Aldo, that we're aware of, either. Who knows, maybe whoever is doing this has realized we won't stand for it and has stopped whatever they were doing."

"You don't honestly believe that, do you?"

Chief Kenny smiled wryly, shaking his head. "No, not really. I think they're planning something new. I hope we're ready to handle it when it comes."

REBECCA LOOKED AT HER APPRENTICES WITH A SMILE ON HER FACE. They were already coming along so well. Flora threw herself into her work with exuberance and joy. Her uncle Lars had decided to move his operations to Valerian's Cove early. He enjoyed working with the apprentices, especially with his niece, who really did have an exceptional talent for metalworking.

Daniel was slowly learning to use his Fire Mage Gift in new ways as applied to his jewelry creations. He wasn't yet able to get the same swirling effects that Rebecca did, but it was early days yet. They'd only been at this for a little over a month. There was time. She had the apprentices for three years, after all. If they all decided to stay.

Simon was slowly learning to work with more precious metals. He had never been encouraged in his creativity and was still getting used to the idea that he was allowed to experiment and try new things. Let alone play with so many new things. Here, his creativity was supported. Simon was slowly relaxing and coming out of his shell. A pair of young teenage Fire Mages had a lot to do with that. Allie and Vannie still insisted that Simon practice with them when he joined fight practice.

Sean stood with his arm around Rebecca as she watched her apprentices work. He had stopped by on his way to his afternoon classes at the Academy. He had the middle school kids today. Sean leaned down and kissed the top of her head.

"Everything looks like it's going really well, here."

"It is. It really is. I'm really proud of them."

"Your work is beautiful, too."

"Thank you," she smiled up at him. "I was wondering if maybe the two Deravalan Fire Mages in Fairweather Falls have ever used their Gifts like this. Or if they know of any Deravalan Fire Mages that have. I would really like to see how their Gifts differ from ours."

"Why don't you ask Elizabeth? Maybe we can go for a visit this weekend."

"Maybe I will. Thanks, sweetheart." She lifted up on her toes to kiss him.

Sean kissed her back with feeling. Flora grinned. Daniel and Simon were trying very hard not to smile, too.

"Get a room, you two," Lars joked.

"Uncle Lars!" Flora squealed, thoroughly red-faced.

Rebecca and Sean broke apart, smiling.

"I have to go teach, anyway," Sean said. "I'll see you all later. We'll grill tonight, ok?"

"Sounds good. Have fun teaching impressionable young minds," Lars told him.

Sean grinned wickedly.

"Oh, I will. I have the eighth graders today."

"I thought Allie and her friends practiced with the older kids?"

"Oh, they do. But occasionally, I like to sic them on their classmates, to show the other kids what they can really do. Today is one of those days. I find it makes the other kids work harder to keep up with them."

"Or to prove they are just as good, if not better," Lars joked.

"Well, they try, anyway," Sean grinned. "No one is better for her age than Allie. Though, her little group of friends are all extremely strong. They definitely give the other kids a run for their money."

"Do you have everything ready for the Samhain festival?" Malia asked her foster daughters one evening at dinner about a week before the thirty-first.

"Yep," Anne replied. "We have our tee-shirt booth, which Kelly will run for us. Mariah is doing the sweets again, charming them for different effects and helping Milena and Fionnuala with the story-telling illusions. I'm doing Cloaks and Jokes again. Allie is helping me demonstrate the costumes. Mikey is helping Grandpa Brendan, and Ian is helping run a haunted house with some of his Techno-Mage friends. It's seriously freaky."

Malia smiled. She was glad that the kids were all so enthusiastic about their plans. Anne and Mariah were on their way to becoming serious entrepreneurs. They were already making a considerable amount of money from their creative efforts, especially Mariah. Anne was starting to learn about investing and the business end of owning a business. Between the two of them, they were going to take over the world— if Allie didn't get there first.

"What kinds of things are you planning for the haunted house, Ian?" Malia asked her son.

"You're going to have to come see. We're not telling anyone. But everything we're using, we can use for other stuff, too. Some of it's really cool. We're already applying for patents on it."

The Techno-Mage program at the Academy was growing as more Witches with Phoenyx bloodlines were found. The Techno-Mage program took anyone so Gifted, regardless of age. Ian was getting to work alongside others of many ages and talents. It was extremely good for him. When he wasn't with Amie and Malachai, he worked on projects with the other Techno-Mages. Ian already had several patents to his name, thanks to his work in helping create cell phones and computers that worked on magic so that Witches and other highly magical Beings could use them. They had come a long way in a short time. It was truly amazing to see.

27

Time flew by, the end of October arriving in what seemed the blink of an eye. The rainy season hadn't started yet, though there had been some ominous cloud cover the last few days. Still, it only added to the atmosphere of the season. Plus, Witches. In Valerian's Cove, the weather would be whatever they wanted it to be for the festival.

The day dawned bright and cool, cornflower blue skies studded with fluffy white clouds. The festival opened at ten in the morning. The usual fields had been set aside for parking, with tourists and guests starting to arrive by nine. Officer Jerry Mahoney waited at the gates the Witches had enchanted across the road to the town along with Jason Reilly, former police lieutenant, and Beta in the Caper's Creek Pack. Jason worked part-time as a detective for the Valerian's Cove police department. A young Witch from town, Camilla Rivers, waited with them. Camilla would lift the barriers at ten o'clock sharp and take the first shift ensuring that the extra wards around the town would stay strong and in effect throughout the day.

"I can't believe how many people are already here!" Camilla remarked to Jerry as she watched another car pull into the field on the right. Several more vehicles were pulling in behind it. The first shuttle was waiting, ready to start boarding at nine forty-five.

"The shields look good, Camilla?" Jason checked in.

"All good, sir. Anyone with harmful intentions won't be able to get in. We might have a few disgruntled customers out here, but we'll think of something."

"Could you, I don't know, make it so anyone who's stuck out here gets a stomachache and has to go home? So they don't realize they're being kept out on purpose?"

Camilla cocked her head to the side. "I don't know... it's kind of mean. But it protects our town, and they won't *really* be sick... I can set it so the feeling wears off after a set period of time. Maybe three hours? Long enough so they don't think to come back and try again."

"Better make it twenty-four. The festival runs until midnight. They might come back otherwise," Jason suggested.

"Oh, that's a good idea. Thanks, Mr. Reilly." Camilla thought for a moment, then took out her phone. She made a quick call, then hung up, grinning. "We're good to go. The wards are being tweaked as we speak. I'm excited to see how this plays out. I mean, I don't want people to get sick, obviously, but I don't want anyone coming in who intends harm to our town and its people, either."

Jerry looked at his watch. It was just going on nine forty-five. The shuttles had begun loading the first passengers.

"Here we go, folks. Looks like it's showtime."

<hr />

THE WARDS AND CHARMS AROUND THE TOWN WORKED LIKE, WELL, A charm. For the most part. The festival was a huge success. Visitors flocked to the town. Several went home when they reached the barriers, suddenly feeling ill, but most people entered freely. The Witches, and the Mayor, heaved a sigh of relief.

Around three o'clock that afternoon, down by the harbor, a girl of about sixteen was visiting with her family. She had been with them watching the Sea Fae play in the water, a look of genuine delight on her face. The girl's mother was with her while her father had taken her younger brother to get a treat at The Baker's Delight.

The girl was distracted suddenly by the buzzing of the phone in her pocket. She ignored it at first, intent on watching the beautiful tails of the Sea Folk. She may have been daydreaming about what it would be like to join them. Not that she was that strong of a swimmer, but maybe one of the boys would help her, hold her up? The phone kept ringing. Someone was being persistent.

Sighing, she took the phone out of her pocket and answered it.

"Holly! Why didn't you answer? I've been calling for ages!" Her best friend, Mel, was in fine form. They had been friends since kindergarten. Lately, Holly had been thinking she wasn't so sure she wanted to stay friends. Mel's family had started hanging out with some pretty weird people, people that gave Holly the shivers.

"Did you bring that powder I gave you? Make sure you film what happens on your phone!" Mel told her.

"Mel, I told you. I don't really want to do this. I think it's cruel. And it's such a lovely day here. The town is truly magical. I'm sorry you couldn't come too. You would have loved it here."

"No, I wouldn't. Magic is for kids and freaks. You promised, Holls. You have to do it."

Holly felt a sinking in her gut.

"I didn't promise. You told me to do it and assumed I would."

"Holly, if you don't do this, I'll never speak to you again."

Holly looked at the phone, then stared out over the harbor, her gaze falling on the Sea Fae again. They were playing volleyball in the water, tails flashing in the sun. One of the girls had a purple sparkly Witch's hat on over her curls. Holly wondered how it was staying on in the water. Maybe by magic.

"Mel, I really don't feel right about this. I don't want to do it."

"Fine. Then I'll never speak to you again, and I'll tell everyone what a freak-lover you are. That your whole family are freak lovers. You'll be run out of town. You'll see." Mel hung up.

Holly looked at her mother, who by this time had realized something was wrong and was leaning against the sea wall, arms crossed, as she waited for her daughter to get off the phone.

"Holly? What's wrong? Was that Mel?"

"Yeah. She wants me to do something I don't want to do, and she's threatening to tell everyone I'm a freak-lover and never speak to me again if I don't."

Holly's mother, Dawna, sighed. There had always been something a little off about Mel. She had always just set Dawna's teeth the slightest bit on edge. Her parents weren't any better. They never made any efforts to be friendly, aside from allowing sleepovers and playdates between the girls. Holly had gone on a few trips with Mel's family, and Mel had gone on a few with Holly's. And lately, there had been rumors in town that Mel's family was acting even more strangely than usual. They had been seen with people from out of town a lot lately, telling everyone that they were visiting relatives while withdrawing more and more from the community they lived in. Dawna had thought about asking Holly about it but decided her daughter was smart enough to know when she should say something herself.

"I don't even care if she never speaks to me again. Mel's getting even more weird than usual lately, and not in a good way. The rest of our friends are mad at her. She's been really mean lately, and especially to anyone magical. She was really mean to Samantha the other day, and we've known her all our lives. Mel's never been like that before. She used to love magic and supernaturals as much as I do. I kind of don't want to be friends with her anymore."

"You have excellent instincts, Holly. I've always told you that," Dawna said. She paused, then asked, "What did Mel want you to do?"

"She gave me this white powder. She wanted me to open the bag in a crowded area and let it all out, then film what happened. I just don't feel right about it. She said it would start a riot and it would be funny. I don't think that's funny at all."

"You're right; it's not. It sounds like that's some kind of drug. Which I am sure is illegal. I think we should give it to the police."

Holly looked stricken.

"I don't like Mel anymore, but I don't want to get her in trouble," Holly said.

"Holly, Mel obviously doesn't care about your safety if she asked you to do this. That powder sounds dangerous. There are small children here. Your brother is here. Do you want to place him in danger?"

"I thought maybe we could just throw it away. I was going to anyway."

"Holly, you know we have to turn it in. I bet that's why you haven't thrown it out yet. Come on, let's find the police station. I'll text your Dad to meet us there."

❦

TONY WAS AT THE STATION WHEN DAWNA AND HOLLY WALKED IN. Holly still looked stricken. Dawna looked determined. Her jaw was clenched, and she was breathing quickly, a sure sign that she was upset.

"How can I help you?" Louanne, the receptionist, asked.

"Someone gave my daughter something that I think the police need to know about," Dawna replied. Tony walked over to stand by Louanne's desk.

"I'm Detective Gianetti. How can I help you?"

Dawna looked at Holly.

Holly sighed and took a small bag out of her pocket.

"Someone gave me this. I was supposed to scatter it in a crowded area. It was supposed to start a riot. I don't want anyone to get hurt. I don't know what it is. They wanted me to film what happened."

Tony looked at the young woman before him sternly. Inside, excitement filled him. Had they finally caught a break and gotten a sample of the drug that was being used on young supernaturals?

"Do you know the person who gave you this powder?" Tony asked.

Holly looked at her mother, who nodded at her.

Holly's shoulders were hunched up around her ears. She seemed to shrink before Tony's eyes.

"Hey, it's ok," he told her. "You're doing the right thing by giving me the powder and the information. If that's what I think it is, it's a drug that has been causing a lot of fights and people getting hurt. You're actually protecting people by turning it in. Hopefully, whoever you got it from will be able to tell us where they got it, and we can get this stuff off the streets."

Holly looked up at Tony. He was much bigger than her, bigger than her dad even. But his eyes were soft and kind.

"Are you a supernatural?" Holly whispered.

"Holly!" Dawna exclaimed.

"It's ok, Ma'am," Tony assured her. He turned back to Holly. "I am. I'm a Wolf Shifter. I'm the Alpha of the Pack here in Valerian's Cove. So you see, I really want to protect the people here. And this drug has so far been used to target our young people. We're very protective of our families, especially our children."

Holly nodded once, then handed Tony the small bag.

"It was my friend, Mel. We've been friends forever, but lately, her family has been acting really weird, I mean, weirder than usual. And she said she'd never speak to me again and would tell everyone I was a freak-lover if I didn't do it. I didn't want to. I don't want anyone to get hurt, and I love magicals."

"Thank you for telling me, Holly. I really appreciate it." He looked up at Dawna. "If you don't mind, Ma'am, please give Louanne any information you have about Mel and her family. We'll contact the police in your town and work together on this. This case has been growing nationwide. You've given us a solid step forward in protecting our children and our families, and we are indebted to you."

"You're welcome," Dawna turned to Louanne, giving her all the information she could think of.

The door to the station opened, and Holly's father walked in with his son.

"Dawna? What's wrong? Are you and Holly all right? Why are we at the police station?"

"Holly has just helped us hopefully move forward in solving a nationwide drug case," Tony told the shocked father. The man froze, eyes wide. He looked at Dawna.

"What? What is he talking about? Drugs? It was Mel, wasn't it? What did she do, Holly?"

Dawna finished giving information to Louanne and turned to her husband, putting her hand on his arm. She quickly brought him up to speed.

"Jer, this has gone too far. I've never felt comfortable around Mel and her family; you know that. I gave her a chance because she was just a kid, and I thought maybe we could help her out. But she wanted Holly to start a riot, using drugs, and to film it. People could have been seriously harmed. We could have been harmed. And the people of this town... all the visitors. This has been a lovely day. Such a lovely day. We couldn't let that happen."

"Of course not." He looked at Holly, then pulled her into a hug.

"I'm really proud of you, sweetheart. I know it must have been tough to tell the police about this."

"Mel's going to say things about me. She said she'd never speak to me again."

"Sweetheart, if she wanted you to do this, she's not really your friend. She put you in danger. That's not something a friend would do."

Holly nodded as she clung to her father. He looked over her head at Dawna, and some sort of understanding passed between them. Jer looked up at Tony.

"Sargeant First Class Jeremiah Collins, Supernatural Division, sir. This is my wife, Dawna Myers-Collins, Second Lieutenant, Supernatural Division. We've been sleeper agents for a while. I think it's time for us to come in."

Tony stood to attention, snapping out a salute.

"Major Anthony Gianetti, Supernatural Division, Black Ops. I will report your request to come in to General O'Shea immediately. Please wait here."

Tony turned and hurried to his office. He used O'Shea's private line to reach the General again.

"O'Shea."

"Gianetti again, sir. I have two sleeper agents and their family here asking to come in. Their daughter was handed a sample of the drug we've been hearing about and asked to start a riot. We have the drug and the information of the people responsible."

"Names and ranks."

"Sergeant First Class Jeremiah Collins and his wife, Second Lieutenant Dawna Myers-Collins."

"Request granted. Tell them to stay put; we'll come and get them. A unit will be dispatched to their targets. Good work, Tony. I'll send someone to pick up the drug. Keep it safe until they get there."

"Yes, Sir. Thank you, Sir." Tony hung up and returned to reception.

"General O'Shea has accepted your request to come in and asks that you stay here with us. A unit will be sent to your target, and someone will be sent here to pick up the drug. We have an inn and a B+B here in town, though I'm sure they are full because of the festival. We'll find you somewhere to stay until you're given new orders."

"That's ok; we're staying at the inn, Major," Dawna told him. "We live several hours away, so we thought we'd make a weekend out of it."

"Good. Ok." Tony took a deep breath, then looked at Holly, who was standing a few feet away with her arms crossed, staring at her parents as if she didn't know who they were.

"Holly. I guess you didn't know about any of this, huh?" Tony asked.

Holly shook her head.

Dawna stepped closer to her daughter.

"Sweetheart, we were sent to Crowdensville because of Mel's parents twenty years ago. They're low-level Witches, barely able to perform any spells. They've always been jealous of those with more power and have been in trouble before for... things we won't go into now. I'm sorry you're finding out like this."

"You said Supernatural Division. That means you're supernaturals, that I'm a supernatural. What are we?"

Dawna looked at Jer, who nodded.

"We're Witches, too. We allowed our Gifts to be bound when we went undercover. We had your and your brother's Gifts bound, too. We had to appear as mundane as possible to Mel's family. We never expected you to become friends with Mel, though it did help us keep a closer eye on her family."

"I want my Gifts unbound! You mean I could have had magic my whole life? You *knew* how much I loved anything supernatural!"

"I know, sweetheart. We'll have all of our Gifts unbound as soon as possible, ok?"

Tony cleared his throat. He didn't want Dawna to make a promise to the girl that she wouldn't be able to keep. Who knew what the military's plans were for the family next?

"Can we live here, in Valerian's Cove? Or in another magical town?" Holly asked.

"I don't know, sweetheart," Jeremiah told his daughter. "I don't know what our commanding officers will want us to do next."

A throat cleared behind him. A man had come in and stood at parade rest just inside the door.

"Sir!" Dawna snapped to attention.

"At ease, Collins." He turned to Tony. "Major Kevin Allihies. General O'Shea sent me." Louanne's phone rang. She listened, then handed it to Tony.

"Gianetti."

"O'Shea. Allihies should be in your office. He'll take the drug and take care of the Collins family. They've been under long enough, and it's likely they'll be compromised now. We'll set them up in a magical community that can protect them."

"Sir, they could stay here. Or maybe a Sanctuary town?"

"We'll start with somewhere like Valerian's Cove, then move them if it becomes necessary. Maybe we'll arrange an 'accident' or something, so it's not a surprise when they don't come home. See that they're safe, Major."

"Yes, Sir."

Tony hung up his phone and looked at Holly.

"It looks like you're going to get your wish, Holly. The General says you can stay."

❦ 28 ❧

Holly was ecstatic. Tony told the Collins family to enjoy the rest of the festival.

"Please do give me all of your phones, though. They'll need to be deactivated and wiped so the accident story will stick. We'll get you new ones tomorrow. Also, I'll send the town's real estate agent to your rooms tomorrow. She'll help you find somewhere more permanent to live here. I will also let the Headmistress of the Academy here, Maria Hemenway, know that you will be stopping by tomorrow to register Holly for classes. How old is your son? The Academy starts in sixth grade, now."

"Jesse is ten. He's in fifth grade," Dawna replied.

"Then I will also call Norman Schull, the head of the elementary school. You can register both kids tomorrow. They should start school right away. Maria will make sure that Holly gets the help she needs to catch up to her peers." Tony paused for a moment, then continued. "If it's alright with you, my foster daughters are about the same age as Holly. They're both working at the festival, so I know where they are. I can introduce you. They are half-Witch and half-Pixie. Their names are Mariah and Anne. They're twins. They can introduce Holly around."

Holly turned excitedly to her parents, who smiled and nodded.

"Thank you, sir. That's very kind of you," Jeremiah acknowledged.

"Not at all. For reasons that I will explain in more detail later, we can use more people like you in our town. For now, let's get Holly situated, and I'll show you around. My wife, Malia, owns Wonder, a gift shop here in town. Her sister, Marissa, is a Healer, as is their cousin, Suzette. And their parents own Casey Nurseries and Garden Centers, which is based here in town. They're doing hayrides and stuff at the garden center today. We can go out there, too, if you like. You actually passed it on the way into town. You'll want to meet Brendan Casey, anyway. He's the head of the Alliance Council. Which, since you were undercover, you may not know about, but he will be happy to fill you in on."

"Thank you, sir. We'd be much obliged," Jer replied.

"Oh, and my two middle kids are almost thirteen, but their friend Bethie is just twelve. They have a pretty great group of friends, too. Maybe Jesse can hang with them?"

Dawn smiled. "I think we're going to like it here. I know I'll be very happy to be back in a Supernatural community."

"We are definitely that," Tony replied with a smile. "We have pretty much everyone here—many Fae, Witches, Shifters, Dragons, Pheonyxes, Sea Fae. Valerian's Cove is a really great place to live." He paused for a minute. "If you don't mind me asking, what line of Witches are you both?"

"I'm Earth," Dawna replied. "Jer is Air."

"Excellent. We have fight practice every day after three at the Casey place. I look forward to seeing where your talents lie. All are welcome. Kids, too. Ours have all been training for almost three years now. Be warned; we have some super-powered kids here. Mixed bloodlines that produced Super Gifts. My daughter, Allison, is a Fire Mage, Dragon, Phoenyx, and the Bearer of the Sword of Fire. She's almost thirteen."

Dawna and Jer looked shocked.

"The Sword of Fire is real?" Dawna blinked.

"Yup. I'll tell you the story sometime. For now, let's go enjoy the festival."

Tony led the Collins family out of the station and up the street towards the gate.

"That's my wife's store," Tony pointed at Wonder as they walked by.

"Ooh, we were in there earlier," Holly said excitedly. "There were some really cool things in there. I loved the jewelry. I've never seen anything like it before."

"My wife's cousin, Rebecca, made some of it. She has a studio here in town. She's just taken on her first apprentices."

"How do you get to be an apprentice?" Holly asked.

"You have to be a jewelry designer, preferably a Fire Mage, and be finished with your Academy schooling."

Holly looked interested. "Maybe when I'm done with school. If I'm a Fire Mage, that is."

"You may not have to be—Rebecca developed a tool with our Techno-Mages that allows non-Fire Mages to do the work she does. One of her apprentices is a Dwarven woman."

Holly's eyes grew round again. "That's rad!" she exclaimed.

They were almost to the costume booth near the gate when Tony stopped and hailed a boy and girl coming from the other direction.

"Ian! Come here a minute, please."

"What's up, Dad?"

Tony still felt a huge warmth spread through him when Malia's children called him Dad. They had both started to do so soon after his Bonding ceremony with their mother. Their biological father wasn't in the picture anymore. To everyone's relief.

"This is the Myers-Collins family. They're moving to town. Their son, Jesse, is just a bit younger than Bethie. Would you please show him around and introduce him to everyone?"

"Sure. We're down. Right, Amie?"

Amie nodded.

"Come on, Jesse. We'll find Bethie—if she doesn't find us first. She's a Seer and always knows more than is good for her. She's loads of fun, though. So's her grandmother, Lily."

Ian and Amie led Jesse away, the younger boy asking questions as quickly as he could as they went.

"Ian is my son. We're pretty sure the young lady he's with is his Fated Mate. She's a Phoenyx. Ian is a Techno-Mage. One of the first discovered. Techno-Mages are part-Phoenyx. Brendan Casey's grandmother was a Phoenyx. Ian is one of the Techno-Mages responsible for creating cell phones that Magicals can use."

Dawna and Jer looked suitably impressed.

They arrived at the costume booth. Anne and Allie were both there, Allie being the willing model on which Anne cast her demonstration glamours.

"Hey, Dad!" Allie rushed over and hugged Tony. The young teen currently looked like a biker Demon, with red skin, long black hair, and dressed in black leather. Tony hugged her back.

"Hey, sweetheart. I wanted to introduce you and Anne to some people. Got a minute?"

"Sure! Hey, Anne!"

Anne looked up, her black and turquoise hair swinging. Tony waved her over.

"Anne, Allie, this is the Myers-Collins family. Anne, this is Holly. She's about your age. She'll be registering at the Academy tomorrow. I was hoping that she could hang with you for a while and that you and your friends could introduce her around?"

Anne smiled.

"Sure. No problem. I can call Shari-Beth and have her come to the booth. I'm not due for a break for a while, but Shari and Emma are around here somewhere. The boys, too, I guess. They can introduce Holly around if that's alright?"

Tony looked at Holly's parents, who, seeing the excited look on their daughter's face, nodded.

"Great, thanks, Anne. I appreciate it."

"Of course. Come on, Holly. Let me show you how we do costumes here in Valerian's Cove. Then Shari can take you to my twin, Mariah. She's helping with the illusions for the storytelling circle."

TONY SIGNALED TO NATHANIEL, WHO WAS ONCE AGAIN THE MIND Mage helping with Cloaks and Jokes for the event.

"If you'll excuse me for a moment," he said to the Collins'.

"Hey, Tony. What's up?"

"We have a new family moving to town. The parents were sleeper agents, watching a family that's turned out to be a part of the drug ring we're looking for. They've come in—the daughter of the target family got their daughter involved, and their cover may be blown. Can you read them, as a Mind Mage, and make sure they're who they say they are and that they're clean?"

"Of course. It would be better to let them know what I'm doing, though. More ethical."

"They're career Supernatural Division Special Forces. They agreed to Mind Sweeps as a part of their enlistment in the unit. Which means that if they are rogue, they've been trained to withstand a fairly deep sweep. Which is why I asked you. You're better than that."

Nathaniel nodded. It was true. As a Fae Mind Mage as powerful as he was, he was better than that. He could easily see through any barriers, tricks, or spells the pair may have used to keep out a human Mind Mage.

Tony led Nathaniel over to Jer and Dawna.

"This is my friend, Nathaniel Brooke. He and his family spend most of their time here in Valerian's Cove now. His wife, Siofra, is in business with Brendan Casey, and they are both advisors to the Alliance Council."

"Pleased to meet you, sir," Jer said, shaking Nathaniel's hand. Dawna smiled and shook hands too.

"We're always happy to have new people in Valerian's Cove," Nathaniel said. "You're Witches?"

"That's right. Earth and Air," Dawna said, pointing to herself, then her husband.

"Have you introduced them to Celine yet?" Nathaniel asked.

Tony shook his head. "I was going to take them out to the Casey's in a bit, once the kids have had a chance to make some friends and gotten tired of running around town. Holly is with Anne, and Jesse is with Ian."

"Celine is in town at the moment. I think she's either at The Baker's Delight or Wonder. I'm sure she'd like to meet our newest Air Witch." Nathaniel turned to Jer. "Celine Casey is a talented Air and Kitchen Witch. You haven't lived until you've eaten some of her food. I believe she's the head of the Air Witches in town at the moment." He turned to Dawna. "Brendan, her husband, is probably the strongest Earth Witch in town. His grandson, Mikey, is an Earth Mage, but he's only thirteen. Brendan hasn't taken the leadership role in town—he teaches at the Academy, runs the greenhouses at Casey Nurseries, and is the head of the Alliance Council. I believe Maria Hemenway, the Headmistress of the Academy, is Head of Earth in town."

"We're meeting her tomorrow, I think," Dawna replied. "Thank you for telling me. I'm even more glad to be connecting with her now."

They talked for a few more minutes; then Tony indicated they should be on their way. Nathaniel said goodbye, nodding at Tony as he turned back to the costume booth.

"Let me guess... Fae Mind Mage?" Dawna asked.

Tony grinned and nodded.

"Yes, one of the two strongest they have. You two passed. Congratulations."

Dawna and Jer both grinned back.

"How did you meet him?" Jer asked.

"It's a long story. I'll tell you sometime. Nathaniel and his work partner, Lord Ciaran MacNamara, came to help with a case. Siofra and Brendan started talking plants, and the rest is history. The whole lot of them are here quite a lot. If you join us for fight practice, you'll be meeting a lot of very influential Beings."

Tony led his new friends to Wonder, waving at Malia as he peeked in the door. She raised an eyebrow at him.

"Looking for your Mom!" He called out.

"At the Murphy's!" She called back. He waved and led Jer and Dawna away again.

"I'll introduce you to Malia when things aren't so crazy in the store," he told them.

"She seems to be doing quite an excellent business," Dawna commented.

"Oh, she is. Festivals are crazy for her. They practically carry the store all by themselves."

Tony opened the door to The Baker's Delight, letting a warm, sugary-sweet scented breeze out.

"Oh, I almost went into a sugar coma in here earlier," Jer moaned.

"Well, be prepared, because when Rachel Murphy finds out you're moving here, she'll wheel out the welcome wagon," Tony grinned.

Rachel looked up and smiled from behind the counter. Tony waved. Rachel had three teenagers helping her, and the line was still almost to the door.

Tony looked around and saw a family getting up from a table by the window.

"Jer, go grab us that table. I'll get you something to eat. Any preferences?"

"Chocolate, please. The more, the better."

Tony grinned and moved forward in line. Dawna stayed with him as Jer went to grab the table.

"So, it seems to me that you are the senior Witch, the senior officer, and the pants in the family," Tony said to Dawna. She shrugged.

"We have our dynamic. It works for us. Jer appreciates a strong woman. He's a bit of a sub. It's why he's never cared about moving up in rank so much."

Tony nodded.

"What can you tell me about the family you were watching and their associates?"

Dawna shrugged.

"They were pretty quiet up until this past year. The parents were standoffish. Their daughter, Melissa, was more outgoing than they were. There was always something about her that just didn't feel right to me, though, even though she was a child. She's been friends with Holly since kindergarten. Sometimes, I've thought her family was keeping an eye on us through her, but I have no reason to think that our cover was blown. We've been in that town almost as long as they have. Our story for moving there was to be closer to Jer's family, who live two towns over. He grew up in the area, which is why we were given the assignment, to begin with."

"And lately?"

"There have a been a few new faces in town, and they've all been friends with the Watersons. They keep pretty much to themselves, stay with the Waterson family, and are never around for very long. Melissa's behavior with her friends has been growing increasingly mean and demanding as well. If Holly hadn't decided on her own to break ties with Mel, I would have insisted before too much longer. There is something truly not right about that girl. Maybe from how her parents raised her, maybe something else. I don't know."

"Has Mel been more aggressive over the last year since these new people have been in town?"

"Yes, exactly. And growing more so. She used to be a quiet, almost sly, watchful child. Now she's bossy and demanding."

Tony felt a shiver slip down his back.

"You said her parents were lower-grade Witches, is that right.?"

"Yes, both low Water, I think."

"Dawna, you know that drug is responsible for the all the fights on the news lately between mundanes and supernaturals? Do you think, with your knowledge of the family, that they could have been testing it on Melissa? On their own daughter? And maybe on the parents, too?"

Dawna blinked, then went pale.

"Oh, my gods and little fishes. I feel horrible. I could have helped her. I should have realized. We have to get her out of there. Surely there's some way—they can't be allowed to do that to their own child!"

For a moment, Dawna sounded less like a career soldier and more like a frightened mother.

"I'll mention it to the General. When we pick them up, we'll test all of them for drugs. If Melissa shows evidence, I'll arrange for her care. Would you be willing to take her on, knowing that you had a bad feeling about her even before the drug was introduced to her system?"

"What if she's always been on it or on something like it? What if there's something even worse going on?" Dawna was pale. "I know it would be better to place her with someone she knows. And Holly would understand. They used to be close. I think it would depend on what happens when you take her off the drugs. And I would have to talk to my family first."

Tony nodded.

"Ok. That's fair. I'll let you know what happens. We have to pick the family up and get them tested first. For now, why don't you go sit with Jer? I'll bring your treats in a few minutes."

Dawna made her way through the tables to Jer as Tony moved up to stand before the counter.

"What can I get for you, young man?" Rachel Murphy asked with a grin. She'd known Tony his whole life.

"A slice of your triple chocolate cake, extra whipped cream, a slice of your strawberry shortcake cake, extra whipped cream and chocolate sprinkles, and a dulce de leche cake with extra whipped cream. And three teas, please. Thank you, Rachel."

"Who are your friends?" Rachel asked as she handed the order to one of the teens to put together.

"New arrivals. Sup Special Forces sleeper agents. They're coming in and moving here. The wife's an Earth Witch, and the husband is an Air Witch. They have two children. I sent them off with mine."

Rachel smiled.

"They're in good hands, then. I want to hear all about it later, when this madness dies down."

"I'll be happy to introduce you," Tony promised. He took the tray he was handed. "I'll be right back for the tea."

✿ 29 ✿

Malia sighed as she closed up the shop just after eight. The festival was still going strong outside, but inside Wonder, there was blissful peace. She turned to find her manager, Liz, leaning against the counter, her hands in her hair.

"That was the craziest day we've had yet," Liz sighed. She scrubbed her hands through her long blond locks, then rubbed her face. The two shop assistants, Clairie and Marie, were slumped in the armchairs in the reading nook.

"I think we've sold more today than we have in the last month. Maybe the last two months," Malia stated.

"I think you're right. We'll have to tell Rebecca we're out of her stock again. I hope her apprentices are advanced enough to sell some of their own work soon," Liz said.

Malia nodded.

"She's only had them for a couple of months, so it might be a while. Rebecca's pieces really are best-sellers, though. Even better than the Dragon-made pieces, and I would never have thought that would happen."

Malia leaned against the counter next to Liz. Malia's youngest set of twins was with her sister Marissa at the Casey homestead. Marissa was happy to stay home this time. She had all four babies, hers and Malia's, and her mate Teddy to help. They were going to take the babies over to the garden center for a hay ride and the corn maze, then home for naps. By this time, they should be down for the night. As it was a festival day, and Allie and Milena were working their booths, the older twins were allowed to stay at the festival until it was over, which would be at midnight, after the fireworks over the harbor.

"Food?" Liz suggested.

Malia nodded again.

"Thai?" Liz looked over at Clairie and Marie.

"Yes, please," Marie said. Clairie nodded.

"I was going to hang out with my friends after we closed, but I'm *exhausted*," Clairie all but mumbled. "I never knew working in a store could make you so tired. All the *people!* Did every single Magical within portalling distance, within all the realms, come through here today?"

Malia and Liz grinned.

"We really did appreciate your help today, girls," Malia told the teens. "You'll both be getting hefty bonuses for today, okay? As well as overtime pay."

Both girls perked up at that.

"Really? Thank you, Malia!" Marie exclaimed. Clairie echoed her thanks.

"For now, Liz, if you'll call in an order to Ben Ma, the girls and I will start cleaning up. We'll keep the store closed tomorrow, so we can take a full inventory and reorder. I've already placed the holiday orders for Solstice and Yule, but I think I'll have to double them if I can. The festivals are starting to pick up notice throughout the supernatural world, even the Realms. I really think we are drawing larger crowds with each one. Business is booming, ladies. Even web orders are picking up. I am so grateful that we can all use the computer now!" Malia was very proud of the work that the Techno-Mages had done, especially since her son, Ian, had played a large part in creating the magically-powered tech that even Witches could use.

As Malia and Liz pushed themselves up from where they were

leaning on the counter, Anada, Ben Ma's son, walked by the front window and knocked on the door. He carried a large box tucked against his side with one hand.

Liz opened the door. Anada stepped inside, handing her the box.

"Mom says you need this. You can pay her later. She said that after a day like this, comfort food is best. Everyone's favorites are in there." He grinned around at everyone, waved, then hurried back out again.

"Ben Ma never misses anything, does she?" Liz asked with a grin.

"She always knows. Honestly, I think she's part Seer," Malia replied.

Liz carried the box of food from Thai Star into the back and set it on the table. Malia locked the door again, then she and the girls followed the smell of food into the back room.

❦

REBECCA LOOKED AT HER COUSIN IN SHOCK.

"You sold *all* of my jewelry? All of it? You should have had enough to last through Yule!"

Malia grinned tiredly. They were leaning against the sea wall at the harbor, waiting to watch the fireworks at the end of the festival. Sean had his arm around Rebecca's waist as he rested against the wall on the far side of her. Tony had stopped by to kiss Malia, promising to try to be back to watch the show with her. As the Valerian's Cove police department was still small, it was all hands on deck for the festival, and Tony was on patrol. Chief Kenny had already started the hiring process for new officers, putting out word to other magical towns that they were looking for new hires. Several of Tony's Wolves were applying as well. They were good men, and Tony had given them glowing recommendations. But until they were hired officially, the department was still short-staffed. Chief Kenny, Tony, and Jerry Mahoney were all on duty tonight, with Jason Riley filling in as well. Several Guardians had also been pressed into service.

"We really did," Malia told her incredulous cousin. "Every last piece. Please tell me you'll be able to resupply us soon! Your pieces sell better than anything else in the store."

Rebecca leaned back against Sean, still in shock. She'd never expected her jewelry to sell so well. It was turning her a tidy profit, and keeping her very busy, as well. Between her own work and her apprentices, Rebecca was finding that she had very little time left over for anything else in her days.

"Maybe you need to hire a business manager, Bex," Sean suggested.

"What? Why? I mean, there's not really anything to manage," Rebecca spluttered.

"There has to be a better way to manage your time," her mate replied. "You're starting to look tired all the time. Aren't any of the apprentices far enough along to help with your work?"

"That's not really what they're here for," Rebecca replied. "They're here to learn the skills to improve their own work and start their own businesses. And it's not like I'm selling anywhere else except the garden centers. And those pieces take longer to sell than the ones at Wonder. It's the ones at Wonder that I can't seem to keep in stock."

She looked up at Malia again.

"How are you selling so much so quickly?"

"Your pieces really sell themselves, Bex," Malia said with a shrug.

"We have them up on our website, in their own gallery, like all the other specialty items. They sell well that way. But it's when you can see them in person that they really shine. Really, we should double or triple all stock for festivals. I'm already planning on doubling my holiday orders with all my best vendors, if at all possible."

Rebecca looked out across the harbor.

"I have some pieces that are almost finished. I can get those to you by the end of the week. I have some new designs I want to try out next week. Depending on how those come out, I can probably get you more in a couple of weeks, maybe three. Flora's work is almost ready to sell, I think. Daniel was already selling his back home, but I don't think it's up to the standard of Wonder yet. It would look tacky next to some of those Dragon pieces. And don't you have some of Audriel's silverwork pieces? Daniel can't begin to compete with those yet. He needs to put more heart into his work first." Audriel was a renowned Aes Sídhe silversmith and jewelry maker.

"Ok. Thank you, Bex. Don't exhaust yourself, though. Even a few pieces would be good. Just so we're not completely out of stock. We don't want to lose momentum on your work. If we're out for too long, people might forget about them," Malia said with a grin.

Rebecca smiled back wanly.

"Becca, how long until one of your apprentices could take over teaching?" Sean asked.

"This crew is the first class. I mean, Flora and Daniel could both teach Simon, as he has the most to learn, but there's no one else who can teach them, and they need to learn, too."

"Could you bring in another special instructor for a while?" Malia asked. She, too, had noticed the dark circles under her cousin's eyes. "Would Audriel, say, agree to come teach? Or someone else you admire?"

"I bet I could get some of our Dragon jewelry makers to come teach how they work," Sean offered.

Rebecca considered the idea.

"Thanks, sweetheart. I appreciate it. Let me think about it. Lars is going to be teaching one day a week, but really only Flora is interested in what he has to say as an armorer. Daniel likes being able to conceal weapons within jewelry, so that's keeping him busy for a bit, but Simon seems totally against the idea of anything to do with warfare at all. He wants to focus on the purely ornamental. Maybe another master teacher would be a good idea. I guess I could try it for a little while. Two days a week, so the students have time to work on their pieces in between. With me, that's lessons three days a week, work time two days."

"Isn't there any way your apprentices could help take some of the weight off you?" Malia asked.

"I don't really know how. They're already maintaining the equipment and the workshop. Flora is in charge of ordering supplies. Lars helps her with that. Simon is happy to clean. Daniel helps with correspondence and the gardens out front. He says helping with the gardens recharges his batteries," Rebecca grinned.

"Why don't you put together a list of teachers you'd like to work with, then start at the top, asking one at a time until you find one to work with you?" Sean suggested.

"That's a good idea," Malia agreed. "Eventually, you might even have enough teachers to open a real craft school. Or just focus on different styles of jewelry and metalwork. Simon likes sculpture, right? Maybe get in a Master Metalsmith who focuses on that? Then each student could get a taste of everything and focus on what they like best. Then you wouldn't have to teach so much, and you could hire people to do all the administrative stuff. You already know Flora and Lars will probably stick around. They can teach the armoring classes and the jewelry-as-weapons classes."

Rebecca looked a bit overwhelmed at the idea of growing her workshop into an entire Metalsmith school.

"Maybe you could get some help from the Academy, eventually," Sean suggested. "I'm sure there are students there who would love to learn what you do. Charmed jewelry is a thing, right? That could be a whole other focus. Maybe if you offer a few basic classes at the Academy, your school could be a higher education option for students who want to go into metalsmithing and jewelry after graduating. As such, you could probably get money from the Supernatural Oversight Council for expansion and teachers."

"It's a good thing the piece of land the Dragons gave you is so large," Malia said. "I can see a whole craft village building up around your school."

Rebecca stared at her cousin, eyes wide. She turned and hid her head in Sean's chest.

"What have I started?!?" She moaned.

Malia smiled as Sean patted his mate's back and stroked her hair.

OVER THE NEXT FEW WEEKS, REBECCA FOUND HERSELF WONDERING about the idea of an arts and crafts college attached to the Academy. Maybe not fine arts, like painting and dancing, but the crafts.... It wasn't a bad idea. Imagine having weavers and Stitch Witches nearby who could ask for specific jewelry to accent their own creations. Her students would work directly with them. It would be a great learning experience for everyone. Woodworkers. Metalsmiths. Fabric Artists. Potters and ceramic artists. Sculptors. Rebecca found herself lost in the image of a full-on craft village, where the artists and apprentices lived and worked together.

Malia was right, she thought to herself. *I mean, I went straight into my craft instead of to University after the Academy. I'm sure I'm not the only one who would want to do that. And being a Master Craftsperson is just as acceptable in the supernatural world. It's even becoming more common in the mundane world. Mundanes buy our things, too. And the old apprenticeship model is still valid. It helps foster an excellent work ethic and teaches the business end of the craft from the ground up. Much more helpful than what you learn at a mundane art college, from what I've been told.*

"Why don't you talk to Maria Hemenway and see what she thinks?" Sean suggested one night when he came home to find Rebecca creating a brain map of ideas for the school and village. "If she likes the idea, maybe she'll support you in approaching the council."

So Rebecca found herself in Maria's office one overcast Monday morning in November. The rainy season was in full force, and the ocean out past the cliffs was steel grey and choppy as the rain came down.

"I think this is a wonderful idea, Rebecca!" Headmistress Hemenway exclaimed. "I know that many students go on to mundane art schools because there isn't anything like this anywhere else. And they don't always find what they're looking for at the mundane schools. Especially those who use their Gifts in their art. With your school, they would learn exactly how to do that. You could have full curriculums in each discipline. I will certainly help you present the idea to the Council. This will also bring the different Realms even closer together, as I am sure that there are artists and crafters in each realm that have something to teach in each discipline. This will help us all integrate more seamlessly and gain a greater appreciation for each other's talents and cultures. This is brilliant! And you do have quite a large piece of land already. I'm sure the Council will be pleased that you are not asking them to provide the money for a new site. They will, of course, help with the buildings needed for classes and accommodations."

Maria looked determined. Her jaw was set. Rebecca could tell that the Headmistress was entirely behind this new idea.

"Also," Maria continued," since the Academy is already here, this is a logical place for such a school. And we already have so many Beings from different Realms here. Especially since the Academy has expanded to the University level. Valerian's Cove has become quite the supernatural and magical nexus. It's the perfect place. Eventually, I'm sure other towns will want something similar. Let's put a proposal together and pick a date to present it to Peter Brown."

They chose a date during the first week in December, and Maria called Peter Brown at the SOC on her office mirror.

Peter just shook his head.

"Maria, I know you love education, and I do, too, obviously. But slow down, already! Between your expanding the Valerian's Cove Academy to the University level and the other towns now wanting their own branches of the regular Academy, I'm overwhelmed." He paused. "However, you have a point in how many students we lose to mundane arts colleges, and also in that they get no instruction in how to use their Gifts with their chosen medium." He paused again. "Alright. I'll accept your proposal and bring it before the Council at the next meeting, which is next week, as I'm sure you know."

Maria smiled back at him, a smile full of teeth, like a shark.

Peter sighed.

"It will help that you already have a site and that Rebecca already has a working workshop with apprentices there. Her plans to have visiting teachers come in are sound as well. It might take a while to put this together, as we really are focusing on putting more branches of the Academy where they are most needed at the moment, but I'll make sure this gets approved. I suppose you want to have this up and running for the next school year?"

"Yes, of course," Maria affirmed.

Peter sighed again.

"All right, Maria. For you, I'll do this. But do try not to bring me any more requests for schools for at least a year after this, please? Course curriculum changes and additions I can handle, but whole schools...this is it for a while, ok?"

Maria grinned, then she and Rebecca thanked him and ended the call.

Maria looked at Rebecca with a very satisfied expression on her face.

"Well, my dear. That went very well. Congratulations. The Valerian's Cove School of Magical Crafts is now a reality."

❧ 30 ❧

Rebecca and Sean were leaving for a vacation together the following day. Sean was taking Rebecca to meet his grandparents, then they would see where the wind took them after that. They planned on being back for the Solstice and Yule season with their families in Valerian's Cove.

Shari-Beth sat in her room at home, staring out the window. The school year was almost half over already. She was nearly finished with her time at the Academy. She and Emma would go to her Grandpa Luc in France to learn about Familiar care. Shari-Beth looked forward to it and was glad Emma was going with her. It would be nice to have her best friend from home there too. Still, Shari-Beth felt restless. Something was pricking at the back of her mind, and she didn't quite know what it was.

"Hey, Shari! Grandma Celine says to come down for dinner," Allie called as she ran into the room. Allie had been at fight practice, and her face was still red from exertion. The fiery girl turned and ran back down the stairs.

Shari-Beth had also participated in fight practice before heading upstairs to finish her homework. She was still dressed in her fight clothes. Since Celine fed everyone on practice nights, they ate outside, and most people were still in their workout gear.

Shari-Beth heaved herself to her feet and headed back down for dinner. There was a smaller crowd than usual that evening. Exams were coming up at the Academy, so students were studying, and teachers were grading papers and creating their exams. Declan and Sean were at the Academy. Ralph and another Guardian, Gerald, had run practice that day. Aidan and Kelly were there, out of Shari-Beth's friends' group, but everyone else was elsewhere.

Aiden grabbed a plate of food and plopped down at the picnic table next to Shari-Beth.

"Hey, what's up? You look kind of down." The tiny Sparrow Shifter took a massive bite of his burger.

Kelly sat down on the other side of Shari-Beth.

"You do, you know. What's up?"

"I don't really know. I mean, I'm almost done with school. I'm going to France to study Familiar Care with Grandpa Luc and Grandma Marthe, the two most respected people in the field, and my best friend is going with me. It's going to be awesome. I should be so excited right now. But I feel so... hollow. Like there's something missing, but I don't know what it is."

Kelly looked at her friend, then took a bite of her potato salad. She chewed, then swallowed.

"Shari, you're eighteen. I've never seen you date anyone. Do you think you might be missing out on that?"

Shari-Beth looked surprised.

"I don't think so. I mean, I'm a Shifter. I guess I just figured I hadn't met my mate yet. I haven't really met anyone I was interested in like that."

Kelly raised an eyebrow.

"Really?"

Shari-Beth looked confused.

"I'm sure I would have noticed if I met the guy who was my Fated Mate," Shari-Beth retorted.

Kelly took another bite of food.

"Does it have to be a guy, though?"

Shari-Beth stared at her friend.

"I don't know anyone whose Fated Mate is the same gender or sex they are," Shari-Beth said. "I don't even know if that could happen."

"Why don't you ask Malia what it feels like to meet your Fated Mate?" Aidan suggested.

"But she didn't realize Tony was her mate for years," Shari-Beth protested.

"Malia was afraid she wasn't good enough because she didn't think she was a full Witch," Kelly reminded her friend. "It wasn't that she didn't feel the bond. She just didn't believe in it."

Pretty much everyone in Valerian's Cove knew the story.

"Malia's over there, with Marissa and Suzette," Aidan pointed. "They all have Fated Mates. Go ask them." He took another huge bite of food. For a tiny person, he sure could eat a lot.

"Come on, I'll go with you," Kelly picked up her plate as well as Shari-Beth's and waited for her friend to stand up. The young mundane led the way to where Malia was sitting by the fire pit.

"Hey, Malia," Kelly said. "Hi Marissa, hi Suzette. Shari has a question for you."

Everyone looked at Shari-Beth, who turned red.

"Kelly and Aidan think I should ask you what it feels like to find your Fated Mate," Shari-Beth mumbled.

Malia's eyebrows rose, and Marissa and Suzette grinned.

"For me, it was a strong connection. I always knew when Tony was around. Now, since we're properly bonded, we share thoughts. Before we were, I could feel him. I knew how he was feeling. His energy felt like a warm blanket that I just wanted to curl into and never come out of. I'm not sure if it's the same for Shifters."

"It is," Liz said, coming up behind Malia and joining the conversation. Her kids were off in the field with Malia and Marissa's kids. "With us, it can have aspects of the other senses as well. I can smell Ralph's energy. It smells like home to me. Everything just points to him being Home. I can't really explain it better than that."

"Have any of you ever heard of two people of the same sex being fated mates?" Kelly asked.

Marissa nodded.

"Of course. It's not that unusual. When I was at Healer's College, there were several mated pairs of the same sex there. And several more in the community at large. One of my professors was in a same-sex Fated Mate bond, too. The Goddess knows what she's doing. Just because you share the same sex doesn't mean you're not Fated Mates."

At first, Shari-Beth figured Marissa thought she was attracted to Kelly. Then she noticed how everyone was looking at her like they all knew something she hadn't figured out yet.

"Where's Emma tonight, Shari?" Suzette asked.

"She's at home. She has a big final project to put together for one of her classes. It's due tomorrow."

"Are you looking forward to having Emma go to France with you?"

"Yes, of course. I'm really glad she's going with me. It will be great to have her there, like I've brought a piece of home with me." Shari Beth stopped, caught on her own words.

"Why don't you go think about that for a while, little sister," Marissa told her. Kelly handed Shari her plate, grinned at the others, and headed back to the picnic tables.

Shari-Beth stared at her sisters and cousin for a moment longer, then turned and headed for the tree house down the field.

"Do you think she'll get it, finally?" Suzette asked.

"I hope so," Marissa sighed. "I think we're all pretty sure that Shari and Emma are Fated Mates. I hope they realize it sooner rather than later. One sister in this family taking thirty years to realize what was right in front of her face was bad enough. We don't need another one."

Malia gasped and slapped her twin on the arm. "Hey! I resemble that remark! I got it eventually!"

They all laughed, their voices echoing over the field. Celine, snuggled up with Brendan, smiled as she watched.

JER AND DAWNA AND THEIR CHILDREN WERE SETTLING INTO LIFE IN Valerian's Cove. Dawna had been a police officer in her undercover role, while Jer had taught third grade at the local elementary school. Since they were so short-handed on the Valerian's Cove force, especially with the increase in population that showed no sign of stopping, Chief Kenny had Tony ask the General if they could hire Dawna on as a detective as well. After several weeks of waiting, they received the affirmative, and Dawna became the third detective on the Valerian's Cove police force. As soon as they hired a few more officers, Chief Kenny was planning on promoting Jerry Mahoney too.

"The General said they don't have another mission for us right away since this one isn't technically finished," Dawna told Tony after she was done with her hiring paperwork. "Especially if we end up taking custody of Melissa. Until this drug situation is done with, we're still on duty, but since you all are in the thick of it, the General feels we might as well work directly with you from here."

Jer had been offered a position at the local elementary school as their fourth-grade teacher was ready to retire. It was almost like the same life in a different town. Except now, they could live freely as the magical Beings that they were.

"It's such a relief; you have no idea," Jer told Celine one day at dinner after fight practice. Being military, Jer and Dawna had dived right into training, insisting that their children participate as well. Both children took to it with great enthusiasm. Holly was thrilled with all aspects of her new life, with anything that allowed her to practice her Gifts. Jesse thought it was all great fun. He was turning out to have quite a sense of humor. Sean had to keep a close eye on the boy, as Jesse had a habit of sneaking up behind Bethie in practice and trying to scare her. So far, he hadn't managed it yet.

"I'm a *Seer!*" Bethie exclaimed, thoroughly exasperated, after another of Jesse's attempts to distract her during practice. "I've been practicing using my Gifts in battle situations for almost two years now. You are not going to surprise me! You're just going to get yourself hurt. Please stop!"

Jesse just grinned at her unrepentantly.

Sean sighed and rubbed the back of his head.

"Jesse, Bethie's right. This isn't a game. This is serious fight practice. We're here because the Goddess has gathered us together for some reason and needs us to train. We need to be the best fighting force that we can. If you don't leave Bethie alone and stop trying to scare her, I will make sure you practice with another group. There are practice groups at the Academy as well—you can easily join one of them."

Jesse sobered up immediately.

"I want to stay here, sir," he replied.

"Then you need to show me that you can take practice seriously."

Jesse nodded.

⚜

By the week before Solstice, the Myers-Collins family had settled into their new routine. Holly turned out to be a strong Earth Witch, even stronger than her mother. Her testing showed that she would most likely be at least a level three once she'd grown into her Gifts and been properly trained. Just below Earth Mage. She was ecstatic with the news and thrilled with all her classes at the Academy. She had fit right into Mariah and Anne's group of friends and was often with the twins at Malia's house on Pack lands.

On December twentieth, the day before Solstice, Dawna received a call from Major Allihies.

"Lieutenant Collins. General O'Shea has released Melissa Waterson into your custody. I'll bring her to Valerian's Cove this afternoon. Be ready to receive her at thirteen hundred."

"Yes, sir. Thank you, sir." Dawna hung up, then sighed. The schools were already on holiday break. Holly was with Mariah and Anne, and Jesse was with some friends from school. Jer was out in the garden, playing his flute, his preferred form of relaxation. Dawna stepped out onto the back porch. They had been able to rent a sweet cottage two streets up on the right arm of the harbor, above the inn. The owners had decided to take a year and travel, as their son had graduated from the Academy and was taking a gap year before settling into University studies. They had been happy to rent the home to the Collins family, fully furnished. The house had three bedrooms and a small office, in addition to a small garden that looked over the harbor. Dawna had been delighted to agree to maintain the herb and flower gardens already planted. As an Earth Witch, she was delighted to have a small patch of ground to take care of. That was her favorite form of relaxation and solace. It brought her closer to nature and the Goddess.

"Jer," Dawna called as she stepped out onto the porch.

Jer lowered his flute and looked up at his wife.

"Mel will be here at one. Major Allihies is bringing her."

Now Jer sighed.

"I guess that means they found drugs in her system."

"Or there was another reason her parents could no longer look after her. They could have sent the whole family into protective custody," Dawna answered.

Jer shrugged.

"We'd better tell Holly and Jesse before Mel gets here. Do you think the office is big enough for a bedroom, or will she move in with Holly?"

"I think we'd better ask Holly what she wants," Dawna replied. "She was ready to drop Mel as a friend. It might be better to start Mel in the office and see how it goes."

Jer nodded and stood. They went into the house to get the room set up. Thankfully, there was already a daybed in there, as it had been used as a secondary guest room by the original owners. They would only have to remove the large desk and a few boxes.

They moved the boxes into the linen closet and the desk into the living room against one wall. Then Dawna called Holly. The whole family had gotten the special cell phones that ran on magic after having their Gifts unbound.

"Hey, Mom, what's up?" Holly answered.

"Mel is coming this afternoon. She'll be here at one. Do you want to be here when she arrives?"

Holly was silent for a moment. Just as Dawna was getting impatient at the delay, Holly spoke again.

"Is it all right if I'm not? I'll be home for dinner. I'm still not sure how I feel about Mel anymore. I know she was probably drugged, herself, and we used to be really good friends. But I really don't like how she changed. And I'm having a really good time with my friends right now."

Dawna could hear what sounded like a crowd of young voices talking and laughing in the background.

"That's ok, sweetheart. Where are you right now?"

"We're on Pack lands. At Mariah and Anne's house. Kelly and Lucian are here too. Josh, Shari-Beth, and Emma are coming over later."

"Ok, sweetheart. Be home by six for dinner, please. That should give Mel some time to settle in."

"Thanks, Mom." Holly hung up.

"Holly not coming home to meet Mel?" Jer asked from behind Dawna.

Dawna turned and faced her mate.

"No. She's still not sure how she feels about Mel, and she's having a good time with her friends. I am not going to push her to be friends with Mel again. Even if it makes things awkward at home for a while. We still don't know for sure what was going on in Mel's life, why she changed the way she did. And I've always felt weird about her, even when she was a little girl. Holly will be home for dinner. We'll just see how it goes then."

31

Holly ended the call and stared down at her phone for a moment.

"What did your Mom want?" Anne asked her.

Holly looked up at her new friends.

"Mel is moving in with us this afternoon. Mom wanted to know if I wanted to be there when she arrived."

"That's the girl whose family your parents were supposed to spy on, right?" Lucian asked.

Holly nodded.

"Mel was my best friend since kindergarten. But she started changing, getting really mean, and I decided I didn't want to be friends with her anymore. Especially after she gave me that stupid powder and wanted me to use it to start a fight."

Malia had come out onto the patio where the teens were lounging and heard the rest of Holly's words.

"Holly, I'm not sure how much your parents have told you, but there is some suspicion that Mel's parents, or the people who visited them, were testing the drugs on Mel. She may not have had any say in the matter. It's possible she wasn't in total control of her behavior."

Holly looked shocked, her face pale.

"But my mom said she's never trusted Mel, even when she was a little girl. I used to be mad that Mom never liked her. It made me want to be friends with Mel just to piss her off—my mom, I mean. It wasn't fair that she didn't like my friend. Do you think they were using drugs on a child? Mel was only five when I met her."

"I don't think we know yet, sweetheart," Malia answered. She put her hand on Holly's shoulder and squeezed. "Until we know the whole story, give your friend the benefit of the doubt, ok? She may have been doing the best she could in a horrible situation."

Holly nodded, looking down at the ground.

"And we'll help you," Kelly said. "If she really is mean and tries anything, we've got you. We'll help you handle her." Kelly could be very intense sometimes. Holly looked around at her new friends and realized all of them were nodding.

"Thanks, guys," Holly whispered.

❦

MAJOR ALLIHIES HAD CALLED TONY, TOO, BEFORE BRINGING MEL to town. Tony had spoken to Chief Kenny. After dropping Mel off with Dawna and Jer, Major Allihies stopped by the police station.

"It's a really messed up situation," Kevin Allihies told Tony and Chief Kenny. "Apparently, the Watersons fell in with these people when Melissa was around two. They agreed to allow the drugs to be tested on their whole family, including Melissa and any other children they might have. They were told the drugs were to enhance Gifts. Mrs. Waterson had several miscarriages, though no other children after Melissa. The SOC doctors suspect the drug had something to do with that."

"Were the Watersons able to give you any names or information about the people they worked for?" Chief Kenny asked.

"It seems like they only knew a few people and that the names they were given were false. Also, it is beginning to look like this group is very well organized—almost like a terrorist group. In cells, so that no one knows everyone. Even if one cell were taken out, the others could continue to function."

Tony sighed.

"Well, that's not good."

Allihies shook his head.

"It's frustrating, is what it is. Every time we get a piece of information that lets us move forward on figuring this whole thing out, we end up getting blocked. It's like they have Seers of their own and can clean things up before we get there. As it was, we had to have our Mind Mages go through the Watersons' minds to learn what we did from them. A lot had been wiped. We think there was more than a wonder drug being tested going on, but we're not sure what. Mrs. Waterson had flashes of something else in her mind, of being terrified of something, but the memories were covered over and buried."

"And Mr. Waterson?" Chief Kenny asked.

"He's practically comatose," Allihies answered. "Whatever was done to him before we got to them almost killed him. It looks like he was given a strong dose of the drug so that he would fight us when we arrived. We would have fought back and possibly taken out the whole family. That would have cleaned things up nicely for them. But it looks like the dose they gave him was too strong. It almost killed him instead of making him stronger."

It being the holiday season, the town of Valerian's Cove was in festival mode again. There was a town-wide Solstice festival on the twenty-first. People came from all over to be there. The Witches enchanted the town to resemble a winter wonderland, including snow everywhere that wouldn't melt, an ice skating rink, and sleigh rides in the field outside the town.

Malia had managed to replenish her stock, and Wonder was once again doing a thriving business. The Solstice Festival was set to end at six, so families could go home and celebrate the longest night together. The festival would end with a bonfire in the field where the sleigh rides were being held.

Brendan Casey had invited their friends, the Sloans, from Fairweather Falls, a Sanctuary Town in Maine, to visit for the festival. Nora

Sloan was an Earth Mage and the sole source on the East Coast for many of the plants that Brendan and Siofra had developed through their Fae—Earth hybrid breeding program. Nora's daughter, Elizabeth, had children roughly the same age as Malia's children, as did Elizabeth's sister, Lucy. They were going to spend the day in Valerian's Cove before taking the Dragon portal back to Fairweather Falls for their own celebrations.

The Sloans arrived with a few friends at ten o'clock that morning. Malia had left Liz to mind the shop for a bit so she could meet the Sloans at the portal.

"Hey, Lizzie Grace!" Malia hugged Elizabeth as she came through the portal. The Sloans and the Caseys had grown quite close.

Elizabeth hugged Malia back, then drew a tall, blond-haired man forward to join her.

"Malia, this is my Fated Mate, Shane Truesdale, Fire Mage and teacher at our new Academy."

"It's very nice to meet you!" Malia said. "Congratulations, Lizzie Grace! That's awesome!"

Elizabeth then reached out to a young girl of about sixteen, who was hanging back with Elizabeth's children, Joshua and Maddie.

"This is my new foster daughter, Joey. And these two gentlemen are her uncle and grandfather, Solan and Andor. They are Deravalen Fire Mages and will teach those with Deravalen Gifts at our Academy."

Malia looked up at the two tall men in front of her. Both men had red flecks in their eyes but otherwise looked utterly human, like any other Witch.

"It's nice to meet you, gentlemen, and you, Joey. You look about the same age as my foster daughters, Mariah and Anne. I know Josh is the same age as they are. They're working their booths at the moment, but I'm sure they would be happy to meet you and show you around the festival. Anne is at the entrance to town with the costume booth. They're not doing to have the jokes part this time, but they thought people might still want to dress up. Josh, do you know where that is? It's right past the Sweet Delight." Josh nodded and led his sisters away.

Malia looked up at the two Deravalens. "I don't suppose you gentlemen know of any Deravalen metalsmiths, do you? My cousin

Rebecca is looking to add teachers to her workshop so her apprentices can learn more ways of working metals. She works primarily on jewelry, but her co-teacher Lars is a Dwarven Armourer."

Andor raised an eyebrow.

"I do know someone. And they would appreciate being able to leave Deraval. I can give you their name for your cousin."

"That would be great! Why don't I show you around town before you go see my parents? They're working at the garden center today—they have sleigh rides and hot chocolate and mulled cider, and donuts, and other stuff, there as well. I think my mother is supervising wreath making. But let me show you around town first?"

Elizabeth agreed, and Malia led them away. Elizabeth's sister, Lucy, followed with her family. Nora and her husband, Elliot, decided to go straight to the garden center. Malia asked questions about Deraval as they went, in between pointing out various shops and introducing them to her friends as they moved through the crowds.

Outside of Wonder, they ran into Kelly, Holly, and Melissa. Andor and Solan both stared at Melissa for a moment before looking at each other in seeming confusion. Melissa looked pale and seemed tired. There were deep circles under her eyes, which were slightly bloodshot. The veins in her skin were slightly more visible than they should have been.

After the girls had moved on, Andor turned to Malia.

"Has that girl been sick, Malia? She doesn't look well."

Malia sighed.

"Melissa just arrived yesterday. Her family was caught up in this drug mess that's causing so much trouble lately. The doctors suspect that Melissa was being used as a test subject for the drug from a very young age. A family that has known her for most of her life says her behavior has gradually changed, becoming increasingly mean and angry over the years. Though, the mother says there's always been something wrong with the girl, as far as she could see. Still, Melissa was her daughter's best friend, so they took her in when her parents were brought in for questioning."

Andor looked at Solan. Then he turned back to Malia.

"We haven't been in this Realm for very long. What drug trouble is this?"

"There's a new drug being used on supernaturals to cause fights with mundanes. It seems like whoever's behind it is targeting our young people and our off-duty military. A group of mundanes approaches them, somehow inoculates them with the drug, then starts a fight. Gifts and Shifts happen out where anyone can see them. It could be a real problem and cause a lot of trouble for the supernatural population if it becomes more widespread."

"What effects does the drug have?" Solan asked.

"It seems to lower inhibitions and increase anger and rage," Malia replied. "My mate is the Alpha of the Valerian's Cove Wolf Shifters, as well as a police detective and retired military. He's in the middle of trying to figure it all out. Plus, his cousin was kidnapped and forced to rob a bank under the influence of the drug or something like it. There's been a lot going on."

"Malia," Solan said slowly. "I would like to speak to your mate about this drug, please. I may know what's going on."

Malia and Elizabeth looked at him in surprise.

"There is a drug on Deraval that is fed to our military before battle. It has similar effects. It sounds like someone has somehow gotten hold of it and brought it here. I'm not sure what long-term effects it would have on the people in this Realm. That it affects those here at all bothers me greatly. That it is even here bothers me even more. It is supposedly strictly regulated by the Dervalan military. I feel it is my duty to look into this and to bring it to the attention of the authorities on Deraval. They need to know that it's being smuggled out of the Realm."

"You don't suppose they would do it on purpose, to cause chaos so they could come here and take over, do you?" Malia asked.

Andor shook his head.

"No. The current government is sick of war. They have already decided that a mass move to Earth would not be advantageous. But that isn't to say that everyone agrees with them. If this is our drug, they need to know about it. Also, I wonder how it is being made here.

The plants that go into it can only be grown on Deraval and are very strictly controlled."

"Someone must have gotten ahold of some seeds or of something like it," Elizabeth said.

"They would have to know the formula, though, and that is also a closely guarded secret."

"Is it possible it's something else, something similar?" Malia asked.

"It's the drug from Deraval," Lucy's daughter, Louisa, declared. She was staring straight ahead, her eyes unfocused. "Someone on the Deravalen Council is not happy with how things are being run. He wants to take over other Realms. He wants to be in charge. But he's being bossed around by someone else. I don't think he knows it, though. He gave the seeds for the plants and the recipe for the drug to someone here, someone he trusts. Someone who is half-Deravalen... oh. It's his nephew. His brother's child with an Earth Water Witch." Louisa gasped and shook her head, blinking rapidly. "I'm not going to watch the rest of that. It's not nice." She clung to her mother, rubbing her head against Lucy's side.

"Louisa is the next Oracle," Lucy told Malia quietly. "The current Oracle has already come from Themis to train her."

"She's been working with Bethie and Lily, right?" Malia said. Lucy nodded.

"Let's find Lily. Louisa could probably use some time with her after this."

"I'm already here," Lily said as she walked up behind Elizabeth. Bethie trailed along behind her grandmother. "I saw that Louisa needed me. I know you were planning to stop by while you were here, Lucy, but if you don't mind, Bethie and I will take Louisa now. You can pick her up again before you leave."

Lucy nodded, then hugged Louisa, who went willingly to Lily. Lily hugged the girl, too, then led her away, Bethie holding on to Louisa's hand as they walked.

"I think I would like to speak with your mate, Malia, and then I should probably return to Deraval and report to the Council," Andor stated. "Solan, stay in this Realm. If you learn anything more before I come back, let me know straight away."

32

Tony sighed and hung up the phone. He had reported Andor's thoughts to General O'Shea, who had taken the information and promised to handle it himself.

"Since Andor and Solan came through the Veil, we've been in talks with the Deravalen Council," O'Shea had told Tony. "I'll give Andor a few hours, then check in with them myself."

Tony had to be content with that for the time being. He stopped into Chief Kenny's office to share the latest developments.

"Well, it's in the hands of the Councils, now, then," Chief Kenny sighed. "We'll keep an eye on everything here and report anything new we find. It was lucky that Elizabeth thought to bring Andor and Solan to the Festival."

"And that they happened to run into Melissa, or we might never have known what was going on," Tony added.

"True. It would take someone from Deraval to recognize the signs of its use and the withdrawal from it," Chief Kenny agreed. "What did Andor do on Deraval, do you know?"

Tony shook his head. "I just know that he is the new Deravalen Fire Mage teacher at the Fairweather Falls Academy."

"It might be useful to know. Maybe suggest to Brendan that he invite Andor to join the Alliance Council once we know a little more about him?"

"I think that's already in the works. Though, I don't know how we're going to learn more about him, seeing as how he and Solan are our primary contacts with Deraval. And we have only their Council's word on his integrity, but we don't have a long-term relationship with them, either. We can only take them at their word and watch him ourselves."

"I'm sure Brendan will have Nathaniel or Ciaran check both Andor and Solan out," Chief Kenny said with conviction.

"You're probably right," Tony agreed.

REBECCA AND SEAN RETURNED FROM THEIR HONEYMOON JUST IN time for the Festival. Rebecca had managed to restock her jewelry at Wonder before she left. Even so, they still ran out on the third day of the Festival.

"I really think you need to raise your prices and make your stuff more exclusive," Malia told her younger cousin as they watched Malia's middle set of twins and their friends take advantage of the skating rink on the third night of the Festival.

Rebecca shook her head. "I'm still having a hard time believing it's all selling so well. I mean, before your shop, I only sold through the garden centers. And a little bit online. But even that wasn't nearly as much as I'm selling now."

"Well, you're the hot new thing, now," Malia assured her. "And the sales don't seem to be showing any sign of slowing. I keep getting inquiries for more. I've started keeping a notebook of serious inquiries for you. There are some for custom pieces, as well. You could charge a fortune for those. I was going to give you the notebook or email you the list at the end of the Festival."

"That would be great, thanks, Lia. I guess maybe send me any new ones once a week, so I can get back to them quickly? That's better than making them wait, right?"

"Right. Still, you don't have to take every commission. Pace yourself. You have apprentices to teach and a new school to get set up. Don't overshoot. Are you sure none of your apprentices can help you make new stuff?"

"None of them really work in my style. Though, I guess they could be helping me with some of the stuff, like setting the stones and putting the clasps on and stuff. Final polishes. I mean, that's how they'll learn, right? Yes, I want them to develop their own styles using my techniques, but the best way to learn my techniques is to work on some of my pieces with me, not just watch me do it."

Malia nodded. "Maybe you could sell those pieces for slightly less and include a special tag saying which apprentice helped make it? That might help them start building names for themselves so that when they do start putting their own things out there, they already have a market for them."

"That's an awesome idea. Thanks, Malia. I think they've gotten the basics down enough to start helping. I just have to be willing to let them."

SHARI-BETH AND HER FRIENDS WERE AT THE ICE RINK, TOO. THEY had spent some time chasing the younger Caseys and their friends around, and were now collapsed by the booth the Murphys had set up selling hot chocolate with flavored whipped cream. And sprinkles. Mollie was taking a turn at the booth, and kept the teens well supplied.

Shari-Beth took a sip of her chocolate with peppermint whipped cream and peppermint stick sprinkles and sighed with bliss. It was a glorious evening. Even Aidan was with them, having been forcibly kicked out of the practice field by Declan and Sean.

"Go have fun, be a kid, Aidan. You're friends are starting to complain that they never see you anymore. You need a break. Even Guardian trainees get breaks every so often—especially when there are Festivals involved. Shari-Beth will come drag you away herself if you don't get out of here. She might even threaten not to feed you any of Celine's food if you don't hang out with them tonight."

Aiden had swallowed nervously, and hurried to put his gear away and get changed. No one in their right minds did anything to jeopardize their supply of Celine's cooking. And Celine's sister, Luna, was in town for the Festival, so there were her cakes and pastries to think about, too.

So Aiden had skated with them, and was happily collapsed at Kelly's feet sipping his own hot chocolate with mocha whipped cream and chocolate sprinkles.

Kelly was leaning into Lucian, who sat next to her. Mariah and Anne were still on the ice with Holly and Melissa. Melissa was starting to show some signs of enjoying herself. Shari-Beth had even caught her laughing once this evening, as she was swung around by Josh Merrit on the ice. Josh, having grown up in the much colder climate of Caper's Creek before settling in Valerian's Cove with his father, Ralph, was completely comfortable on the ice. So was Shari-Beth, as she had grown up in Caper's Creek as well. Mariah had been there for a little while, but not long enough to be completely comfortable on a pair of skates. Still, she and her twin were enjoying shuffling along the edges of the rink with their friends. Josh took them out in turns, swinging them over the ice till it felt like they were flying. He always returned them safely to the side of the rink when they were done.

Kelly's brother, Christopher, had been away working on a project in Marin, but had made it home the day before. He was determined to spend the holiday season with his sister, the last remaining member of his family. Chris was an architect, who, through working with Malia and Marissa on their homes, had been welcomed into the paranormal community even though he and his sister were completely mundane. Chris was apprenticing with one of the Fae architects to learn more eco-friendly design techniques and loving every minute of it. He worked almost exclusively for paranormals, now, though he and his mentor had plans for Chris to teach what he learned to other mundane architects eventually when he started his own firm.

Chris smiled as he approached the teens lounging by the skating rink.

"Have you guys given up already?" He asked with a grin.

"We're just taking a break," Emma grinned back. She was sitting at the other end of the bench from Shari-Beth, on the other side of Lucian.

"Get some hot chocolate, Chris! It's really good," Kelly told her brother. Chris grinned back at her, before making his way over to the booth.

"Here you go, Chris. Saw you heading this way," Mollie winked at him. Her fiancé, Nils, was helping his grandfather, Mr. Cooke, at their booth nearby. The Bear Shifters were supplying hot food to the crowds enjoying the winter wonderland put on by the Witches.

Mollie handed Chris a cup, then waited while he tasted it. Winter-green whipped cream, with white chocolate sprinkles.

"Oh, wow, Mollie. This is excellent. Thank you!" Chris exclaimed.

Mollie grinned. "Glad you like it." She looked over at the teens and smiled. "It looks like Lucian's crush finally paid off. Kelly looks very comfortable over there."

Chris glanced over at his sister. He smiled in return. "Moving here was the best thing we ever did," Chris told the Brownie. "Kelly had a really hard time after our parents died. Since coming here, she's really come into herself. She's happy, healthy, and I love her friends. I know Lucian came from a difficult background, but he's a really nice guy now, and I know he'll take care of Kelly and protect her when she needs it."

"You do realize that the Goddess has a habit of encouraging Fated Mate pairs around here, right?" Mollie asked.

Christopher looked at Mollie in surprise.

"I thought that was a paranormal thing? Can mundanes have Fated Mates?"

"Yes, they can. Especially if the mate is a paranormal. It's rare, but not completely unusual for a paranormal to have a mundane Fated Mate."

Christopher looked back at the teens again. Kelly really did look comfortable leaning against the young Wolf Shifter. Lucian's arm was around her now, her head resting on his shoulder.

"I guess it wouldn't be such a bad thing. I wouldn't have to worry about her getting her heart broken. If he is her Fated Mate, she'll always be a protected part of the Pack. She'll have more family than she'll know what to do with, and they'll always look out for her."

"She already is, and already does," Mollie replied. "We've adopted both of you, you know. You belong to Valerian's Cove, now, and we always take care of our own."

Chris blinked, his eyes tearing up suddenly. It had been a hard couple of years, after his parents passed on, before he and Kelly had found their way to Valerian's Cove. He had known that Kelly was fitting in well here, but he travelled from job to job, even into Faery, now that he was apprenticed to a Fae Architect. He hadn't realized that he had been unofficially adopted as well.

"Thank you, Mollie. That means a lot to me. You have no idea."

"No problem. Just, you know, realize that we *will* treat you like family. Nosey grandmas, matchmaking aunties and all. In fact, I know there are several mothers who are working on plans to make you take notice of their daughters...."

Chris looked at Mollie in some alarm.

Mollie laughed.

"Don't worry. The daughters won't go for it. If they are interested in you, they'll ask you out themselves. We just have some very long-lived folks around here, who remember other times, when it was their duty to find suitable matches for their children."

"I'll count myself warned, then," Christopher replied with a grin. He waved goodbye, then headed back over to the teens.

Lucian looked up at him as he approached. There was a wariness in the young man's eyes, but he kept his arm around Chris' sister. Kelly was completely oblivious. She was watching the people on the ice with a smile on her face. Chris realized he had hardly ever seen her so relaxed and happy. He decided that once this job was finished, he was going to be working from home, or on nearby jobs, a lot more.

Chris cocked his head at Lucian. Lucian stared back for a moment, then nodded, slowly. Chris grinned at him and gave him a thumbs-up. Lucian looked surprised, then a smile spread slowly across his face. He turned his head gently so he could lay a soft kiss on Kelly's hair.

Chris smiled, then looked at the rest of the teens. He saw Shari-Beth watching Lucian and Kelly, then shift her gaze to Emma, sitting on the end of the bench. There was such a look of confusion and longing there, that Chris felt his own heart ache in response. He sat on the other end of the bench, next to Shari-Beth.

"Someone told me that the Goddess has a habit of interfering in people's love lives here. That she's made a lot of Fated Mate pairs in Valerian's Cove. I think Kelly might be Lucian's Fated Mate, even though she's a mundane. Look how comfortable she is with him. She's never been that way with anyone before. Completely relaxed and trusting. She knows he'll have her back, no matter what. She feels safe with him. And he obviously adores her. Your sisters have Fated Mates, too, right? And someone said that your nephew, Ian, has one already, even though they're only thirteen? How do you suppose you recognize a Fated Mate? Is there a special feeling, or something?"

Shari-Beth was still watching Emma. "It's like that. Being completely comfortable with them. You want to be with them all the time. You know you're completely safe with them. They're your best friend, and you can't imagine being with anyone else."

"It must be hard to not know if your Fated Mate feels the same way, or if they don't recognize what they're feeling."

"It's confusing." Shari-Beth turned to face Chris. "I mean, most Fated Mate pairs are opposite sex. But Marissa says she knows a lot who aren't."

"Shari, one thing I know from watching your family since we've been in Valerian's Cove. They are going to love you no matter what. No matter who your mate is, or what gender they are. Your family will love them because you do. And they already know and love Emma. I think your family has probably known she was your Fated Mate longer than you have. They are a very smart family, you know." Chris smiled down at the Falcon Shifter.

Shari-Beth took a deep breath.

"Yeah, you're right." She stood up, and went to throw her cup in the compost can.

"Let's go back out, you lot!" Shari-Beth called to her friends. As they all stood up, walking unsteadily on their skates, Shari-Beth stopped by Emma and took her hand. Emma looked surprised, then, as she gazed up at her friend, a smile slowly spread across her face. She reached down and kissed Shari-Beth's cheek, then grinned at her, pulling her back towards the ice.

"Finally!" Malia walked up beside Chris, Rebecca and Mariellen McCormack in tow. "I don't know what you said to her, Chris, but thank you. We've been hoping that would happen soon."

They stood and watched the teens for a few more minutes, then Malia looped an arm through Chris' and one through Mariellen's.

"I want Thai food. Let's go see Ben Ma."

33

Aldo was recovering, slowly. The healers had worked on him daily, so he was healing, physically, much more quickly than a mundane burn victim would. There would be much less scarring, as well. Mentally, Aldo was a mess.

"Come on, son. Come outside. It will do you good to see the sun. And you can run for a bit in the woods. You haven't Shifted in a long time. Your wolf needs to come out," Caleb begged.

Aldo shook his head. While there was not much scarring left, after the healers were finished with him, there was still a smoothness, a pink color to his skin, that hadn't been there before, and no matter what the healers had done, they hadn't been able to save Aldo's left eye. The lid was permanently fused shut, the eye behind it removed when it was determined that it was too far gone to heal.

"No one wants to see me, Dad. I can see the sun from in here."

"That would require going near a window, son," Caleb replied, sarcastically. He sighed. "Son, everyone knows what happened. No one blames you for what you did under the influence of whoever had you. And no one cares that you don't look quite the same anymore. Most people think you're incredibly brave and strong to have survived.

There have been others who haven't survived much less horrific things happening to them. Come on, son. I never knew you were so precious about your looks. Come to dinner with the Pack. Please, son."

Aldo shook his head. He was sitting in an armchair in the living room of the house Tony had set aside for his use. The curtains were drawn, cloaking the room in shadow. The house felt musty, the energy stagnant.

Caleb sighed and left the house. He went looking for his younger son, Remy. Caleb had always thought of Remy as weak. Remy had always been more like his mother, Tracie-Marie. Caring, sensitive to the needs of others. Quick to cry if upset. Caleb had seen it as his job to toughen the boy up, especially after Tracie-Marie died. Contrary to what everyone believed about him, Caleb had actually loved Tracie-Marie, as much as he was able. When she died, he was crushed. The light that she had woken in him was extinguished for good. Caleb had fallen even further under the thumb of his older brother, Clive, a hard man groomed in his ways by their father before him. Remy, so like Tracie-Marie in appearance, had been salt in the wound caused by her death. Caleb had taken out his anguish over her death on his younger son, even when he tried desperately not to. His brother, the sadistic bastard, had encouraged this behavior, enjoying seeing how far he could push his younger, and weaker, sibling.

Remy had been, if not completely welcoming, at least tolerant of Caleb since his return to the Valerian's Cove Pack. Caleb had the feeling that Remy was waiting to see if his father would return to his old ways and start treating everyone around him badly. Caleb was making a herculean effort not to, and it was starting to pay off. The Pack was slowly coming to accept him, to relax around him. Caleb knew that this could change in an instant if he slipped up, and knew that his nephew, the Alpha, would ship him right back to LA if Caleb put so much as a toe out of line. So Caleb made the effort, and behaved himself. To his own surprise, Caleb had grudgingly admitted to himself that Tony was an excellent Alpha, and the Pack was thriving under his leadership. The members were happy, healthy, and a real community, now. And it was growing, more Wolves petitioning to join every week. The Valerian's Cove Pack had become one that Caleb could see himself actually enjoying living in, if he were allowed to stay.

It would all depend on what Aldo wanted to do when he was fully recovered from his ordeal. If Aldo wanted to go back to LA, Caleb would go with him. They could still visit Valerian's Cove whenever they wanted to. Maybe Remy could visit them in LA.

Caleb found Remy in his office in the Pack Community Hall. Remy looked up when Caleb knocked on the door frame.

"Dad," Remy said, getting to his feet.

"Sit down, son. I'm not here to start a fight," Caleb replied. He stood in front of Remy's desk, unconsciously twisting his hat in his hands in front of him.

"What can I do for you, Dad?" Remy asked.

"I was hoping... I was hoping that you would come talk some sense into your brother, son," Caleb blurted out. "He refuses to leave the house. He's well enough to walk, and he needs to Shift, but he thinks no one will want to see him like he is now. You know he lost an eye, and his skin is still a little shiny on one side. I never would have thought he cared so much about what other people thought of him, but there you go."

Remy stared at his father for a moment.

"What makes you think Aldo would want to see me, or would listen to anything I have to say?" Remy asked.

Caleb shook his head.

"I just figured, you know, maybe, if you went to see him, maybe he would make the effort, for you," Caleb said quietly.

Remy blinked.

"Why would he do that? Dad, you know Aldo and I have never gotten a long all that well. He was too much like you, and I wasn't."

Caleb sank into one of the chairs in front of Remy's desk.

"Remy, I know I was a terrible father to you, to both of you. And I know I trained Aldo to treat you the way that Clive was taught to treat me by our father, and for that, I'm sorry. I know now that it was wrong. But I have to tell you, Aldo always stood up for you as much as he could, even if it meant catching a beating for it, from me or your

Uncle Clive. Especially after your mother died. Aldo loves you, as much as he is able. I think, if you asked him to come out of the house, he would do it for you."

A dark shadow had passed over Remy's face at the mention of Tracie-Marie's death.

"About that, Dad. Mom's death. You know that most of the Pack think you killed her, right?"

Caleb stared at his son, completely blind-sided.

"What? Why would they think that? Tracie-Marie was the one light in my life. The only one who could make me try to be a better person, a better man. I know I should have tried harder, only I was too afraid of my brother, so I maybe didn't treat her as well as I could have, but I *never* would have killed her! Never!"

Remy blinked again at his father's insistence.

"Dad, you know that fall shouldn't have killed her, right? I mean, nothing about her death makes sense."

"I always thought your uncle killed her, or at least, had one of his enforcers do it," Caleb said softly. "I was thinking of taking Tracie-Marie and you boys and leaving the Pack, starting over somewhere else. Your uncle was starting to make moves on Tracie-Marie, and she didn't feel safe here anymore. When she died, the light went out of my life, and I was in a dark place for a long time. I thought your uncle had her killed to keep me here, to keep me in line. Though I don't know how he found out we were going to leave. We didn't tell anyone, not that I know of, anyway."

Remy's eyes were wide.

"Why didn't you leave when Uncle Clive died?" Remy asked his father.

"By then, I had pretty much given up. I thought it was safer for you boys if I became what your uncle wanted me to be. Before he died, he told me he wanted the Pack to stay in the family, which meant if anything ever happened to him, I had to be Alpha. So I fought the challengers, and I won. Gianettis are some of the strongest Wolves, after all." Clive smiled wryly at his son.

"Dad, I know we haven't talked much since you've been home, but did anyone introduce you to Lexi, Jamie, Frankie and Liz and their kids? The Wolves from Canada?"

"I met 'em. Why?"

"Jamie is Mom's sister. Lexi, Frankie and Liz are my cousins. They came down here seeking sanctuary from a Pack even worse than ours. They found Tony, and he and the SOC lead the effort to clean up the Packs, largely because of what they found when they investigated the Pack our family came from. Mom's real name wasn't Tracie-Marie. It was Thérèse Marie Trudeau."

Now Caleb stared at his son.

"Tracie-Marie had family? She told me they were all dead."

"She was running from an arranged marriage with an abusive man who probably would have beaten her to death. She didn't want anyone to find her."

"And she ran right to me. I wouldn't have ever beat her to death, but I was no prince, either," Caleb shook his head, and sighed.

"Listen, son. I would like to meet Jamie and her family again, properly, if that's ok with them. Maybe you could come see Aldo, then we could meet with Jamie afterwards?"

Remy watched his father for a moment, searching his face for something. Apparently, he found it. He placed his hands on the top of his desk and stood.

"Ok, Dad. Let's go see Aldo."

☙❧

ALDO WAS STILL IN THE SAME CHAIR HE'D BEEN IN WHEN CALEB HAD left the house. He was staring at the flickering flames in the fireplace, lost in thought.

Remy looked around, noticing how dark the room was. He moved to the windows and threw open the curtains. Aldo started out of his reverie.

"Come on, Al. Get up." Remy stalked over to his brother and pulled him out of the chair. "Really, your face doesn't look so bad. I've heard some of the Pack talking about how strong you must be to have survived. They see your scars as badges of courage. And they could have been a lot worse, you know. We have very good healers here."

"If they were any worse, I'd be dead," Aldo replied gruffly.

"See? So you're already doing better than you thought. Come outside. This house needs to be aired out. It's musty. And your Wolf needs to run."

Aldo shook his head.

"Running is a Pack thing. No one will want to run with me. I'm better off staying here."

"I'll run with you, son," Caleb offered. "The guys from the shop will run with us too. And Remy, right, son?" Caleb looked at his younger son, hope in his eyes.

Remy nodded.

"Come on, Al. We'll all run together. When Tony gets back from town, he'll run with you, too. You'll see. It's not nearly as bad as you think it is."

Remy dragged his brother towards the door. Aldo, though larger than Remy, was still weak from his recovery and not having moved much in a long time. He tried to resist, but Remy just kept a strong grip on his brother's arm and pulled him outside.

Aldo blinked in the bright sunlight. Caleb, perhaps fearing that if given the chance, Aldo would run right back inside, Shifted, and howled, calling all who were available to come run with their injured Pack-mate. Answering howls rang from around Pack lands. Soon, the street in front of their house was filled with people and wolves.

"Come on, brother," Remy said, softly. Aldo, tears in his eyes, gazed at his younger brother. Remy was tall and strong. He had a good mate. He was Third in the Pack. He had a good life. He had no reason to help Aldo after how Aldo had treated him when they were younger, yet Aldo saw only compassion in his brother's eyes. He lurched forward, and Remy caught him in a full-on hug. After a moment, Remy stepped back.

"Shift," he told Aldo.

And Aldo did.

LATER THAT EVENING, REMY STOPPED BY TONY AND MALIA'S HOUSE to report on how the day had gone. He was still feeling like his world had shifted after his talk with his father.

"Wow," Malia said, as she handed Remy a mug of tea.

"Right?" Remy exclaimed. "I mean, I can't even... I had no idea that Aldo was protecting me when we were kids. I only saw him being mean to me. And I had no idea how Dad really felt about Mom. He was sure good at hiding it."

"My father had a lot to answer for," Tony said in a low voice.

"And you brought healing to the Pack," Malia told him. "You have made amends for all he did, by being the Alpha that this Pack needs to grow and to thrive now. Don't get caught up in the past. You're alive and well. So is your mom. And your relationship with your uncle and cousins is healing. Right, Remy?"

Remy nodded.

"Totally. You giving me the opportunity to change, to be your Third, and showing me how a good man, a good person, a good *wolf*, behaves, have changed everything for me. I have a Fated Mate, a family I love. I respect my Alpha, and have the respect of the Pack. And now, maybe, a chance to heal my relationship with my father and my brother. I didn't think that would ever happen. So, thank you, Tony. None of this would have happened without you. You stopped the chain of dysfunction in our family. We all should be thanking you." Remy slapped Tony on the shoulder, then pulled him into a hug.

"How did it go when Caleb met Jamie again?" Malia asked. Malia had been at Wonder with Liz.

"It went... well, I think. Now that we know my dad didn't kill my mom, that he truly loved her as much as he was able, and that he was planning to leave with her to protect her, I think it will bring healing for Jamie, too. When I left, they were sitting on the patio behind the Hall, drinking tea and telling stories about mom. Dad thought her family was dead, so he's enjoying hearing stories about when she was little. I think this is healing for him, too."

"Were your parents mates, after all, do you think?" Malia asked.

Remy shook his head.

"I don't know. I don't think so. I think Dad would have left sooner if they were. He wouldn't have been able to tolerate how some of the others treated her. But I do believe, now, that he loved her."

"Maybe your dad will find his mate someday," Tony said.

"If he does, he has a much better chance of her staying with him, now, since he's becoming so much nicer," Malia joked.

Remy and Tony grinned back in reply.

34

Holly rolled over in bed and sighed with bliss. Christmas was over, there were still two weeks left of the winter vacation, and she was a *Witch!* Holly still felt a surge of excitement each morning when she woke and realized she could still do magic. Her lessons at the Academy were fascinating. Holly had taken to them like a duck to water—she absolutely loved using her Gifts! It had been determined that Holly was an Earth Witch with an affinity for metals, though she could also work with plants in potions as well. She was learning how to draw metals from the earth, how to shape them with her Gift, and what she might be able to do with her Gifts after school. She could go into mining, into industry, into art...and all using her magic! She went to school with people from all sorts of different races, from four different realms, and she had met people from a fifth! Her friends were all magical too, even Mel, though Mel's Gifts seemed to be very weak.

At the thought of Mel, Holly felt her mood drop, and she sighed. Holly still wasn't sure she liked the idea of Mel living with them. Mel had gone very quiet since she had been removed from her parents' care. Finding out her whole life was a lie was probably part of it, like Holly's parents said, but, well... Holly was starting to see what her mother had meant about there being something wrong with Mel, something watching and sly. Sometimes the feeling was so strong Holly wondered how she'd never seen it before. Maybe she just hadn't wanted to.

Thoroughly awake now, Holly pushed back the covers and sat up, stretching as she sat on the edge of her bed. She could hear Jesse talking loudly about something in the kitchen, and her parents' voices more quietly replying. She didn't hear Mel. Maybe the other girl was still asleep.

Holly made her way down to the kitchen, yawning as she stepped into the room.

"Good morning, sweetheart!" Her Dad smiled at her, as her mother put a plate of eggs and bacon on the table in front of her. There were cinnamon buns and fruit salad on the table as well.

Holly's parents seemed much happier now that they didn't have to hide their true natures from their children. Not that they hadn't been happy before; they had, only now that they didn't need to hide, Holly realized that there had been something missing in their relationships with each other and their children before. Dawna's food even tasted better, and Jer had taken to playing tricks on his kids with his Air magic. He seemed much more light-hearted and playful since they had moved to Valerian's Cove.

Holly thanked her mom and dug into her breakfast.

"What do you have planned for the day, Holls?" Dawna asked her daughter.

Holly swallowed before answering.

"I'm not sure yet. I was thinking that I might hang out with Mariah and Anne, or maybe Lauren, that new girl in my Earth Studies class? She said her grandmother might be willing to teach us more about plants today."

"Is Mel going with you?" Jer asked.

Holly shrugged.

"I haven't talked to her about it. I mean, it's not like we have to do everything together, right? Mel needs to make other friends, too."

Mel stumbled into the room, wiping sleep from her eyes.

"Thanks, Holls. Love you, too." She sat down as Dawna placed a plate of delicious food in front of her.

Holly looked uncomfortable, her face going slightly pink.

"Whatever. It's fine," Mel said. She played with the food on her plate. "Maybe I'll go down to the harbor and take a walk out on the cliffs. I hear there's a good place to sit up there. You can see out over the whole ocean."

Jer glanced at Dawna over the girls' heads.

"I haven't heard you talking about the other kids your age much, Mel. Have you made any new friends?" Dawna asked.

Mel shrugged.

"The other kids are ok, I guess. They've all been at this magic stuff a lot longer than I have. They can all use their Gifts really well. I'm, like, the weakest in town. I mean, I'm barely a Witch at all."

"You are a Witch, though, Mel," Jer replied. "It doesn't matter how strong your Gift is. And the Healers at the SOC have told me that they are fairly sure that you're stronger than you think. That having your Gifts suppressed for so long, combined with the drugs you were on, messed with your Gifts, but that with time, they'll heal."

"I guess," Mel shrugged, going back to her food.

Holly looked at Mel.

"If you want, you can hang with me today, Mel."

"It's fine," Mel replied. "I kind of want to explore on my own, anyway. If that's ok?" She looked up at Jer and Dawna.

They shared a glance, then looked back at the teen before them.

"I think it's fine," Dawna replied. "Please check in with me every so often, though. Valerian's Cove is safe, but it's not a Sanctuary town. Anyone can come in. If you get scared, or feel something strange, or someone bothers you, call Jer or me right away, ok?"

Mel nodded, her mouth full of eggs.

"Ok, then. Jesse is going to his friend Evan's house for the day, so it looks like you all will be out of the house today. Finally! Some peace and space to ourselves!" Jer grinned and winked at Dawna.

Holly rolled her eyes. Jesse groaned, and even Mel smiled; just a quirk of her lips, but it was there.

AFTER THE KIDS HAD ALL LEFT THE HOUSE, JER LOOKED OVER AT Dawna. "I want to check in with Tony to see if there is any news about Mel's parents. They've been in custody for almost two months now. The SOC must have learned something from them. I want to know what will be done with them, too, and if Melissa will be able to see them if she wants to. So far, she hasn't said anything, at least not to me, but she might. They are her parents, and she must have questions for them about everything."

Dawna nodded. "I agree. I was thinking the same thing myself. Afterwards, let's go to The Baker's Delight for a treat. I want chocolate."

They made their way to the police station. Louanne smiled when she saw them enter the building.

"Hey, newcomers! How are you settling in?"

"Hi, Louanne. We're doing great. Everyone has been so kind and welcoming," Dawna replied with an answering smile.

"Tony's not here today," Louanne said, "But Detective Reilly is in. He's kind of a part-time detective. He's mostly retired. I don't know if you've met him yet, Dawna? He's the former Beta to the Caper's Creek Pack, and also Supernatural Division Special Forces. His uncle is the Alpha in Caper's Creek. He's been in on the drug investigations from the beginning, or the beginning as we know it, anyway. He's been keeping up with everything, so I'm sure he'll be able to fill you in. You want me to ask him to come out?"

"I'm here, Louanne," Jason Reilly interjected as he stepped out of his office. He nodded to Dawna and Jer, coming over to shake their hands.

"Jason Reilly, Sergeant First Class, Supernatural Division, Black Ops. Nice to meet you. Come into my office, and I'll tell you what we know so far."

Jason led them into his office, indicating they were to be seated. He took his own seat behind his desk.

"So, you've had Melissa for almost two weeks, now, is that right?"

They nodded.

"Have you noticed anything out of the ordinary, any traites that might indicate that Melissa is not one hundred percent Witch?"

Jer and Dawna blinked.

"Nooo, why would you think that?" Jer asked slowly.

"While testing all three Watersons for drugs, their blood was typed and registered in case of any further activity on their part in less than savory occurrences, should they ever get out of custody. Melissa's blood type is not a match for either of her parents, and there are some markers that show that she may not be entirely of this realm."

Jer and Dawna blinked again.

"Say what now?" Dawna exclaimed.

"I guess this is a surprise to you, too," Jason said with a smile.

"But she looks just like them," Jer replied, shaking his head.

"It appears that is an amazing coincidence. We ran Melissa's DNA, and came up with a partial match to a missing person from almost twenty years ago, a Brianna McKenna from Galway, in Ireland. She went missing while on a gap year between secondary school and university. Her parents have been searching for her ever since. They've never given up hope that Brianna would be found. They had no idea that Brianna had had a child."

"It sounds like you've spoken to them?" Dawna asked.

"General O'Shea had Allihies talk to them. They very much want to meet Melissa. They're ready to Dragon portal here immediately as soon as given permission to do so."

"If Melissa is this girl's daughter, they realize that she doesn't know, right? That she's been with the Watersons since she was tiny? I mean, when we got there, she was two, and we were told that she was six months old when the Watersons moved to Crowdensville," Dawna said.

"I know. I think they are just happy to get a piece of their daughter back, even if Mel never knew her real mother."

"She doesn't know she's adopted," Jer said.

"Are you absolutely sure of that?" Jason asked.

Jer nodded.

"Mel's mother has this long, drawn-out birth story that she tells when she wants to embarrass Melissa in front of her friends. Holly told us about it, and we've heard it ourselves over the years. Have the Watersons said anything about this? Because I never would have guessed she was adopted from talking to them."

Jason shook his head.

"Once the blood tests were back, and believe me, they were re-done to confirm the findings, the Watersons were asked about it. Turns out, both of them truly believe that Melissa is their daughter. It looks like at some point a Mind Mage had a hand in their heads and messed with their memories. The SOC Mind Mages found quite a lot of tampering in the Watersons' minds. In Melissa's, as well, I'm sorry to say. It was decided to let most of it be, in Melissa's case. The things she witnessed were not the sort of things that a sixteen-year-old should have to worry about, or have in her head. The Mind Mages were able to ensure that those memories were very well hidden away."

"What if the blocks on them fail?" Dawna asked in concern. "She could end up with horrible nightmares, even psychosis."

"If the blocks ever fail, or Melissa decides that she wants to know more, the situation will be revisited, and perhaps the memories will be restored to her, under the care of a Mind Mage and a Mind Healer. Melissa is aware that there are memories she probably doesn't want to know about. For now, she has agreed that they stay buried. The advocate assigned to her agreed as well."

Dawna and Jer stared at each other for a moment.

"But she doesn't know about the adoption thing, yet?"

"She hasn't been told yet," Jason replied. "It was figured that she had enough to deal with, including settling into her new life with new Gifts. But her grandparents are becoming very insistent. As you can imagine."

Dawna looked at Jer again.

"Let us talk to her about it tonight, ok? If she wants to meet them, maybe we can set something up for after the new year? She's off school until January seventh. Then she'll be having to get used to being in a magical school, and learning to use her Gifts," Jer said.

"Has there been any luck tracing her birth father?" Dawna asked. Her intuition was firing on all cylinders.

Jason shook his head.

"He's not in any database, either supernatural or mundane, in this realm," Jason replied.

"Has anyone checked Themis and Deraval?" Jer asked.

"Nothing on Themis. Nor with the Dragons nor the Phoenyxes. Nor the Fae. We're still in talks with Deraval on a bunch of things, since that relationship is still fairly new, but a request has been made to run her DNA there. Their system is a bit different than ours, so it might take a while. Hopefully, we'll know soon. Also, if there is a match there, and they find her father, he may want custody of her. If that happens, we'll have to decide what is in Melissa's best interest at that time."

"For her sake, if he is found, I hope he's a good man," Jer said in a low voice.

" So do we all," Jason replied. "What with her birth mother still missing, though, and Melissa being adopted so young, I have a feeling this may not turn out the way we'd like it to."

35

Dawna and Jer stepped out of the police station, holding hands. As they started to cross the street, Jer dropped his wife's hand and placed his arm around her shoulders instead.

"It's going to be ok, you know that, right?"

Dawna looked at him, her eyes haunted.

"How is it ever going to be alright? That poor girl, and we never knew. I should have been nicer to her. I should have realized there was something going on. No five-year-old is that sly unless there is something terrible going on at home."

"You did your best under the circumstances as you knew them. We both did. All we can do now is to move forward. Telling Melissa and letting her decide what she wants to do is the next step, right now."

"Telling me what?" Mel asked from behind them. She had been in Wonder, asking Malia about a job, when she saw the Collins' in front of her. She had heard only the last part, about telling her something, and of course, she wanted to know what they were talking about.

Jer and Dawna turned around in surprise.

"Mel. We didn't know you were there," Jer exclaimed.

"What is it you want to tell me?" Melissa asked again.

Dawna looked at Jer. Then she reached out and put her arm around Melissa.

"It's not that we want to tell you something, sweetheart. It's that we just had some news from the council. I'm not really sure how you're going to take it." She looked into Melissa's eyes.

"We were heading over to The Baker's Delight for a treat," Jer said. He put his arm around the other side of Mel and drew both women across the street towards the bakery. Warm, sugary-sweet smells of cinnamon and chocolate were wafting out from the open doorway as another customer left the shop.

The three ordered, then found an empty booth to sit in. Dawna sat next to Mel, while Jer sat across from them. He laced his hands together on top of the table, looking at Mel. Dawna kept her arm around the girl, watching her nervously.

"So? What is it? Has something happened to my parents?" Melissa demanded.

"Mel," Jer replied slowly. "There's really no easy way to say this. You know how the Healers took blood samples from you when they were testing you for drugs?"

Mel nodded.

"Well, they took them from your parents, too. It turns out that the Watersons aren't really your birth parents. It looks like you were adopted, pretty soon after you were born."

Mel stared at Jer, then turned quickly to look at Dawna.

"That's not true, is it? That can't be true. My mother has that whole story about my birth, and everything. I've heard it thousands of times."

"The Mind Mages for the Supernatural Oversight Council and the military say that the Waterson's memories were tampered with, so that they would believe that you were their daughter. Mrs. Waterson had several miscarriages before you came a long. It seems that they were already part of this drug group, and had agreed to be tested on. They were under the impression that it would make their Gifts stronger, which is the one thing they would have given anything to have happen. It seems that the drug trials rendered Mrs. Waterson infertile. That birth story is a complete fabrication, an implanted memory, placed there by an extremely talented Mind Mage."

Melissa had gone completely white. Dawna had the fleeting thought that Melissa looked rather like Snow White at that moment, with her pale skin, blue eyes, and dark hair.

"Then, who are my parents? I mean, the Watersons were in with bad people. Was I stolen? Because it sure doesn't sound like I was adopted legally. Are my parents searching for me? Do they know I'm alive?"

Jer looked at Mel again for a moment before speaking.

"Your blood is a partial match for a young woman who went missing from Galway, Ireland, almost twenty years ago, when she was not much older than you. Her name was Brianna McKenna. Brianna is still listed as missing. Her parents are still alive—they are higher-level Water Witches. They've never stopped looking for their daughter, and they are desperate to meet you."

Melissa blinked. She sat for a moment, processing this new information.

"What about my father?"

"We don't know, sweetheart," Dawna said softly. "There are no DNA matches for him in any of the known realms so far. The only one we are still waiting for confirmation from is Deraval. The SOC hopes to have word from them soon."

"Deraval is that new Demon realm, right?" Melissa asked.

"'Demon' is not really the right word, but yes," Jer replied. "Deraval is what many people would call a 'Demon' realm. It's climate is much different from ours, much hotter and more harsh. But like any realm, not everyone is good or bad, there. And the terms 'good' and 'bad' are relative, anyway, because of different cultural ideas and norms."

"And Deraval might make sense as your father's home realm, since it's been discovered that the drug used on you and your parents has its origins in Deraval," Dawna added.

Mel stared at Dawna for a moment, then turned her head to stare out the window. She was sitting next to the window, with Dawna on the outside of the booth.

"My mother's parents want to meet me?"

"Yes, sweetheart," Jer replied. "If you want to meet them, we will support you through it. It will only happen if you want it to. No one is going to force a meeting on you, at least, not right now."

Mel turned to Dawna.

"Would you please let me out? I want to think about this by myself for a while."

Dawna nodded and stood up from her seat.

Mel turned back to them before leaving the shop.

"Thank you for telling me. I never felt connected to the Watersons, for some reason, and now I know why. So, thank you." She turned again and left the shop, heading for the harbor.

Dawna sat back down and stared at Jer.

"Should we follow her, do you think?"

Jer shook his head.

"No, not yet. She's safe enough. I think we should give her time to process. We'll check on her in a little bit."

Rachel Murphy stepped up to the table, holding a new pot of tea.

"It looks to me like you could both use another cuppa," the Brownie said gently.

"Thank you, Mrs. Murphy," Dawna said softly.

"Call me Rachel, everyone does," Rachel replied. "Now, I couldn't help overhearing some of your conversation. Melissa has a rather carrying voice when she's upset," Rachel smiled at them. "I don't know if you are aware, but Mariah and Anne have a similar story. Their parents were killed in front of them, then Anne was kidnapped. Their memories were meddled with. Their grandfather was behind it all." She paused for a moment. "What I'm saying is, there are people here who know what Melissa is going through. Maybe it would be a good idea to have them check on her?"

"Did the twins' family ever find them?" Dawna asked.

"By coincidence, yes. It turns out that they really are related to the Caseys, and to Pixie royalty as well. Their mother was the daughter of a Casey Witch and a Beaulieu Pixie. She was spelled to fall in love with an unscrupulous Earth Witch, who arranged for the death of her family and took her back to the States. It all came out when Mariah found her way here a year or so ago."

Dawna looked at Jer.

"Maybe we should ask the twins to talk to her."

Jer nodded.

"Good. I'll call Mariah for you. She often helps out here at the bakery. She's the one who puts the charms on our special charmed line of baked goods. It's Pixie magic. Also, when Melissa is ready, Marissa Casey-Thorndike is a Mind Healer, and the Caseys are friends with four of the top Mind Healers in the Fae Realm. They will all be willing to help you, and to help young Melissa. All you have to do is ask."

Dawna reached out and took Rachel's hand. She gazed up at the other woman intently.

"Thank you, Rachel. You have no idea how much this helps."

"Oh, I do, dear. Trust me, I do. Now, let me go call Mariah, and I'll send her after Mel. Don't worry. It will all be all right."

Rachel bustled off behind the counter, leaving the teapot on the table between them.

MARIAH AND ANNE HAD BEEN AT HOME, PLAYING WITH THE BABIES and trying decide what to do with the rest of their day. Holly had decided to go visit Lauren's grandmother to learn more about her Gifts, and the twins' other usual cronies were busy doing other things. Mariah put down the wooden block she held to answer the phone when it rang in her pocket.

"Mariah, it's Rachel. Listen, Melissa Waterson has just had her whole world crushed, again, and she needs you and Anne. It turns out she was adopted, not legally, and her parents weren't really her parents. Also, her birth mother has been missing for almost twenty years, and there is no blood-trace of her father in any known realm so far. They are waiting to hear back from Deraval. No one has any hopes of her father being a good man, at this point. I'm not even sure I'd want to find him alive. Anyway, will you go find her? She headed down towards the harbor after she found out."

Mariah agreed, and ended the call.

"Come on, Anne. Rescue mission," she said to her twin. Calling out to Malia, they rushed out the door.

"What's going on?" Anne asked as Mariah paused to bring her Pixie wings into being. Anne brought hers out as well. Their wings glittered and shone, like a dragonfly's, their colors matching the streaks in each girl's hair.

"Follow me. I'll fill you in as we go."

❦

THE TWINS FOUND MEL DOWN BY THE HARBOR, LEANING ON THE sea wall. A fishing boat was coming back in followed by a dolphin leaping along in the wake of the boat. The fishermen would toss him a fish every now and again. Since the Sea Fae had set up a home in Valerian's Cove, the local sea creatures had been much more frequent visitors.

Mariah landed a few feet behind Melissa and tucked her wings away again. Anne followed. They moved up to either side of her, leaning on the wall themselves.

"Hey, Mel. We heard that you got some really shocking news this morning," Anne said gently.

Mel glanced at her, quickly, then turned back out to the harbor.

"Did you know that we had a similar thing happen to us?" Mariah asked. She told Melissa the story of how she and Anne came to live in Valerian's Cove.

"At least you got some justice—you know who did it to you, and he's dead now," Mel said.

"It wasn't justice, really, since he killed himself rather than face the consequences of his actions," Anne replied. "But yeah, at least we know. I think the SOC will figure out who did this to you, too. And we heard that you have a family who wants to meet you. For us, that's been the most amazing thing. Our family thought our mother had died in the fire with her parents and sister. They didn't know she was alive, or that we existed. But since we all found each other, they've all been around a lot. We go to France to see our family there, and they come here, and here we live with our cousins, the Caseys. Our lives are so much better now than they ever were before. You have no idea how much better."

"How do you know all this already?" Melissa exclaimed. "I only just found out myself."

"Mrs. Murphy," Mariah said. "She heard everything at The Baker's Delight, and told Mr. and Mrs. Meyers-Collins about us. She called us to come see if we could help you through this, since we have a similar background."

"I bet neither of you were drugged for your whole lives, though," Mel grumbled.

"No, but our Pixie sides were bound, until we came here. A Fae figured out what was going on and tested us for Pixie Gifts. Now we can do extra cool things, like fly, and change size. And charm things so much more easily than a Witch can. And we have our Witch Gifts as well. It's so cool being doubly Gifted!" Anne grinned.

"Yeah, we can get in so much more trouble!" Mariah grinned too.

"They think my father might be Deravalen. There are no teachers for Deravalen Gifts here. If Deravalens have Gifts. And if I have them. Which, I mean, I've never noticed any strange Gifts. But then, I thought I was mundane, so...."

"Now you know you're a Water Witch, right? You'll get training in those Gifts when school starts again. And the new Academy in Fairweather Falls has a couple of Deravalen teachers. They were here for the Festival—Andor and Solan. They're friends with our friends in Fairweather Falls. If you have Deravalen Gifts, you might have to go to school there, but you'll love Elizabeth and her family, and she'll take care of you, even if you stay in the dorms. And her foster daughter, Joey, is half-Deravalen. She's a Deravalen Fire Mage, a Fire Witch, and a Starborn, too. And she's your age. She's just sixteen, like you. Andor is her grandfather, and Solan is her uncle. They didn't know about her, either, until Solan went looking for his brother, who had vanished on a mission in the Earth realm. So even if you are part Deravalen, you're not the only one. They actually think there are a lot of people who have Deravalen blood, which is why the new Academy there is building a Deravalen curriculum as well as a Starborn one. They'll be the center for those two trainings in this country. Other Academies around the world are going to have curriculums like them as well."

"My mother's family apparently is from Ireland. I wonder if I'll have to move there," Mel said.

"I don't think anyone will make you if you don't want to," Anne replied. "We were given the choice of where we wanted to live. We go back and forth for holidays and on long weekends, sometimes. Dragon portals mean that it's much easier since we don't have to spend time flying in planes. Since you were raised here, I bet they'd let you stay if you wanted to, as long as they got to visit, sometimes."

"If you want them to, and they're good people," Mariah added.

Anne nodded.

Mel looked at Anne, then at Mariah.

"Thanks, guys. I really appreciate you talking to me about all this. I just feel all lost and confused. Like, nothing I though I knew is real, so, where does that leave me? And I know the Meyers-Collins' took me in, but I haven't been that nice to Holly lately, and I'm sure they don't want to keep me any longer than they have to. So I don't really have a home anymore. I don't know where I'm going to go, or what's going to happen to me. It's like a great gaping hole I'm on the edge of falling into, and I don't know what to do."

Both twins put an arm around Melissa, hugging her close.

"It will all work out. And the Meyers-Collins family seems really nice. I'm sure they'll keep you for as long as you want to stay with them. For now, you're safe, and you have friends here. Ok?" Mariah said.

Mel nodded, and leaned into Mariah, tears streaming down her face.

36

Louisa trained with her tutor from Themis during the week, and every other weekend they both went to Valerian's Cove to work with Lily, Bethie, Sinéad, Fionnuala and Milena. Since it was the holidays, they had been a bit off schedule. Now, the holidays were over, and regular meetings were back in session.

Mel had decided to meet her mother's parents. They were coming to Valerian's Cove via Dragon portal today. At the same time, Louisa and the other Seers and Oracle would be working together to deepen their Gifts and their ability to work together.

Mel waited nervously by the portal in Valerian's Cove. Malia, Dawna, Tony, Jer and Major Allihies were there. The General had sent the Major to find out anything he could from Brianna's parents about their daughter and where she might have gone, and who with. Even the tiniest detail. Finding out about Mel's past had become mission number one.

The Deravalen Council had done their own search with Mel's DNA, and come back with surprising news. Melissa's father was the nephew of one of the Council members, a man who had been sent to the Earth realm on many missions for the Council. No one had any idea that he had had a child in the Earth realm. Given Louisa's vision, witnessed by Andor and Solan, who were both highly respected on Deraval, in which she had seen that the drug causing so many problems on Earth had come from Deraval through the nephew of a Council member, inquiries had been made. The Council on Deraval had discovered that the rogue Council member had been supplying the drug to the Earth realm for years. He had also supplied it's formula and the base ingredients. His nephew had been handling private missions for the Council member while in the Earth realm on Council business. And those missions were of a more...nefarious nature.

The nephew, who was half Earth Water Mage, was missing. No one had seen him for at least six Earth months. It seemed that he had not returned from the last mission to Earth that his uncle had sent him on.

The uncle, however, was where he was supposed to be. He did not enjoy his interrogation at all. Deravalen Mind Mages were not gentle with traitors. Those subjected to their Gifts were usually left a hysterical, crazy mess. The Council member was no different, once they had wrung every last drop of information from his weakened mind.

"It seems that the traitor was... encouraged... in his plans by an outside force," Dorann, the Head of the Council, told the SOC and the Alliance Council. "It was subtle. We're not even sure if he was aware that many of his prejudices and plans were not his own. There was a murky black smudge over many of his memories. It seems that he was corrupted at a young age, with the control growing ever more deep and complete as the association continued through the years."

"So, has someone else on Deraval been working to cause a war with Earth?" Lady Caoimhe asked.

Dorann hesitated for a moment.

"We don't think the person behind this was actually from Deraval," He said, slowly. "The Mind Magic used wasn't ours. It feels different. It took our Mages longer to break. They said they hadn't seen anything like it before."

"Which means it's not Starborn, either," Malcolm Starborn stated. "As I am sure that you train your Mind Mages in our techniques as we do in yours."

Dorann nodded in agreement.

"So someone else is pulling the strings," Peter Chizinsky of the SOC surmised.

"This... isn't the first time we've seen this," Brendan Casey said slowly. "Remember, we all felt that there was someone else feeding into Faith's delusions, when she went after my daughter's mate, Theodore? And again, with the old men who tried to steal the Sword of Fire?"

"Is it possible it could be the same person?" Malcolm Beaudry of the Seelie Fae asked.

Everyone looked around at each other.

"I mean, I suppose so," Brendan replied. "But, it would have to be someone incredibly old. And they would have to have knowledge of all the Realms, and an incredibly good Seer or Oracle of their own."

"Or a stable of them," Lady Caoimhe said slowly.

Everyone looked at her in surprise.

"Well, think about it," she said, exasperated. "We have our own little Seers Council developing here. They all know they are stronger and more accurate when they work together. Surely they're not the first ones to figure that out. If this character is old enough and canny enough to plan all of this out, to put all this in place, all these strings, attached to so many realms, surely they're smart enough to pick up strong Seers and Oracles when they find them and use them."

"Strings. Attached to so many people, in so many realms," Brendan said under his voice.

"Like a spider, in a very tangled web," Lady Caoimhe, who sat next to him, replied.

⚜

"WELL, THAT WOULD EXPLAIN WHY SOME THINGS WERE BEING blocked," Lily replied when they suggested the idea of a rogue Seer's Council to her. She thought for a moment. "It's strange, though. Seers are usually extremely well protected, because there are so few of us. I mean, one or two might go missing or die suddenly, but not enough of us to make a group like ours, not without someone catching on."

"Could memories have been changed, so that no one remembered they were missing? Maybe even that they existed to begin with?"

"I suppose it's possible," Lily said. "Either that, or he's somehow found a way to breed his own Seers. Which, as the trait doesn't breed true in every generation, would be an extremely long-range plan, and risky, as he couldn't guarantee he would get any, even from a line of strong Seer blood."

"And what would happen to those who didn't turn out to be Seers?"

⚙️

So now, Louisa was with the Seer's Council, and Mel was waiting nervously for her first meeting with her grandparents.

The portal flashed as they stepped through. The McKennas were a striking couple. Daniel McKenna was a tall man, and it was from him that Mel got her looks. He had dark hair and brilliant blue eyes. Eimear McKenna had the rare fire-red hair and green eyes that most people thought of when they thought "Irish."

Both were strong in their magic. Daniel, a strong Water Witch, and Eimear, a Water Mage.

They stopped just outside the portal, staring at Melissa.

"Jesus, Mary, and Joseph, she looks just like Brianna!" Eimear exclaimed.

"Why don't we all step away from the portal, and we can get better acquainted," Tony suggested. He led them a little ways away to the clearing where the storytelling was held on festival days. There were enough stumps and benches for everyone to find a seat.

"Melissa, I'm your grandfather, Daniel McKenna, and this is my wife, and Fated Mate, your grandmother, Eimear O'Callahan-McKenna."

"Hi," Melissa said, her voice shaking a bit. Her hands were clenched in her lap.

Eimear brushed her hand across her eyes as she stared at her new granddaughter.

"You look just like your mother. Who, obviously, looks just like her Daddy," Eimear smiled tremulously.

"I don't remember ever seeing her," Melissa said, softly.

"Eh, we know that, sweetheart," Daniel replied. "We brought you some photos to look at, so you could see her, our Brianna."

Daniel took an old photo album out of the satchel on the ground next to him. "We haven't gotten around to digitizing them all yet, but here you go." He handed the album over to Mel.

Mel opened the cover and stared at the face of a baby that looked identical to the pictures she'd seen of herself as a child. She looked slowly through the pages, seeing Brianna with her parents, her sister, her friends. After a moment, Eimear moved to sit next to her, and began pointing out various people and naming them for her.

"That's your aunty Roisín, Brianna's twin. She wanted to come to meet you, but we thought maybe for the first time, it should be just us, so you didn't get overwhelmed. But you've got loads of family waiting to meet you, love, whenever you're ready. Rosie has two sets of twins, two girls and two boys. The girls are about your age and the boys two years younger."

Mel looked around at everyone.

"How come I don't have a twin?" She asked. "Don't Witches always come in pairs?"

"Not always, it seems," Malia answered. "It seems when bloodlines from other Realms or races mixes in, it's not a sure thing. Apparently, Starborn and Deravalen births are usually single, and since you're part Deravalen, you may not have a twin. No one else with your DNA turned up in the search. Though, it's possible that it never got into any of the systems. We don't know enough about your past, yet, Mel. You may have a twin that we haven't found yet."

Mel paled as this occurred to her for the first time.

"I might have a twin?" She whispered.

"Let's not worry about that right now, though," Malia continued. "We're hoping that as we dig deeper into your past, we'll find out more. If we find your father, we should find out if you have a twin or not."

Mel nodded, somewhat in shock. She turned the page in the album again.

"Who is this?" She asked suddenly. She was looking at a photo of Brianna, around her age, maybe a little older. She was standing next to a tall young man with brown hair and a grin on his face. He had his arm around her, and Brianna was laughing. She looked to be having the time of her life.

"That's Eddie, the boy she was spending time with on her gap year before she vanished. She was all set to go to Brazil with her best friend, Aoife, when they met Eddie and his friend George. They all got along so well. We met the boys, and they seemed lovely. They were very good to the girls, and treated them well. They decided they'd all travel together, as it would be more fun. They made it to Brazil, and had a ball there, from all accounts. They were supposed to go to Australia next, which is where the boys were from. But they never made it there. We were never able to find the boys' parents, so we don't know if they ever made it home. Aoife and Brianna never did."

"Was Aoife a Water Witch, too?" Tony asked.

"No, Fire," Eimear answered. "Both girls were highly Gifted, just below Mage level."

"I would like to have any information that you may have on these boys, and on Aoife as well," Major Allihies requested.

"Of course," Daniel replied. "It's not much, but I'll tell you everything I can."

"Would you object to a Mind Mage examining your memories, just to make sure we get everything?"

"Not at all. We'll do anything that might help us find out what happened to the girls," Eimear answered. "Aoife's parents will as well. They've been helping us search, all these years. Not one of us has ever given up hope."

"I had a thought," Malia said, suddenly. "What if they didn't grab Seers, but people with strong Seer Gifts in their family lines?" She turned suddenly to the McKennas. "Do either of your families have Seer Gifts?"

"Mine does," Eimear replied. "We're part Sea Fae, and can trace back to the Seer two before the current one."

Malia blinked.

"You're related to Maeve and Sinéad?"

"The current Seer's daughters? Yes, cousins, I believe. We haven't seen them since they were children, though."

Malia looked at Tony.

We'd have to ask them if it was ok. They're here to protect Sinéad. We can't go telling everyone they're here. Tony sent mind-to-mind.

But most people know there are Sea Fae here now, Malia answered.

Suddenly, Sinéad, Maeve, and their entourage walked out of the trees.

Eimear jumped up and ran to them.

"Maeve! Look how you've grown! You look just like your mammy, sure you do!"

Maeve hugged her cousin, then looked around the clearing.

"It's ok. Sinéad saw this coming. Eimear, we're trying to keep it quiet that Sinéad is here. We're hiding her in plain sight, as it were."

"Oh, of course. We won't tell anyone, will we love?" She turned to her mate.

"Of course not, Maeve. Come, sit down, the lot of ye."

The Sea Fae joined the group.

"Now, Sinéad and the other Seers have a few things to say," Maeve stated.

Sinéad cleared her throat.

"So, it seems that there is one person or group controlling everything, like the Alliance Council thought. There was a... kind of break... in the blocking we've been coming up against. We were able to catch a glimpse of a few things. So, there have been a lot of people that went missing over the years, that were picked up, targeted, for their bloodlines. Strong Gifts, Seer bloodlines. They've been kept, trained, and bred to build an impressively large force, all loyal to this spider in the middle of the web. Only, it seems like there are a few tears in the web. We're getting fractured visions of people trying to break free. And we don't think it's going to be too much longer before things come to a head."

"How much longer?" Malia asked, sharply.

"Two years at the very most. I'd be surprised if it took that long," Maeve answered.

Malia looked sharply at Tony.

"Could this be the reason the Goddess has been gathering us all together? The kids are still too young!"

"I don't know if it is the only reason, but I think it's a large part of it," Sinéad answered softly. She looked at Malia, smiling gently.

"What? What did you see?"

"I can't tell you everything. Some things have to play themselves out. I'm sorry, Malia. I would if I could. The Goddess won't let me, not until the right time."

Malia frowned, feeling extremely frustrated and afraid for her children. For all the children involved. They were still so young.

"Why don't we all go into town and get something to eat." Major Allihies suggested. "Daniel and Eimear, you can spend some time with Melissa, and tomorrow we can have a Mind Mage look through your memories. We'll see what we can find. Melissa, when you've had enough, tell us. We understand that this is hard for you. Ok?"

Mel nodded.

"Right, let's go, everyone."

🎜 37 🎜

Eimear and Daniel couldn't provide much more information than they already had, even with Ciaran MacNamara and Nathaniel Brooke searching diligently through their minds. However, they did get a very clear picture of the two lads, Eddie and George. Tony immediately sent it to Peters Chizinsky and Brown at the SOC and to General O'Shea.

An hour later, General O'Shea called back.

"O'Shea here. Listen, Gianetti. Those boys in that picture you sent me, we found them. One of them, George Heraldson, was a Fire Mage from Sidney, Australia. He went missing around the same time as the girls. His history up to that time is easily and thoroughly documented. He excelled in his Gift, and in all his studies at the local Academy. He comes from a strong family of Witches, with a Fae ancestor thrown in about three generations ago. That ancestor, and their mate, are still living. The whole family is being pulled in for questioning." The General paused. "Eddie Garza is another kettle of fish." O'Shea took a deep breath. "Eddie Garza was born to Melanie Garza, a Water Witch. She was just below Mage level in power. Ms. Garza lived in the Queensland area of Australia. Eddie's father, who went by the name of Paul McCormack when she knew him, came seemingly out of nowhere. He was a traveling musician, or so he said. When he started dating Melanie, he stayed in town. He started a business teaching guitar and played gigs on the side. Paul would occasionally pick up a touring gig with some band or other. Melanie, who was a teacher at the Academy, usually did not go with him, though she would occasionally go to shows when she could. When Eddie was thirteen, Paul and Eddie were supposedly killed in a car accident coming home from soccer practice one night. The driver of a delivery van fell asleep at the wheel and hit them head on. Their car spun out and went down a cliff. It burned. There were two bodies in the car, which were identified by dental records as Eddie and Paul."

O'Shea paused again and took a breath.

"Melanie lost it, went completely off the deep end, after the accident. She claimed that she had been kept under compulsion for years, that Paul was a demon, and her son was still alive. She claimed that Paul had taken her son and gone home to whatever realm he was from. Remember, this was before the Veil started to thin, and the idea of other realms being accessible was largely thought to be fantasy. As we know, it was possible, if the person crossing had the power. And it has only gotten easier since. Anyway, Melanie was inconsolable. She filed reports with the local SOC representative, and made a general nuisance of herself. Finally, he had her powers bound and Melanie was sent to the local Witch's Sanitarium to be kept under guard. She was deemed to have become a danger to herself and others. She couldn't let it go."

"Is Melanie still alive?" Tony asked.

"Yes, she is. She's been medicated for a long time, Tony. We may not be able to get anything from her, but the SOC is sending agents to bring her in, and then Lady Niamh O'Shaughnessy and Lady Caroline Ember will be having a go at healing her mind, and harvesting her memories. I believe the SOC is also going to be looking into the representative that ignored her stories and had her committed to begin with. As an SOC rep, he would have known that Realm crossings were possible, and he should have looked into her story before having her placed in the sanitarium. All reports there say that while she is medicated, Melanie is a model patient, if somewhat depressed and morose. If the medication wears off for any reason, she goes insane, and still insists on her claims being true."

"And now we get to tell her they are. I hope this is validating for her. I hope she can heal her life after this," Tony said.

"I do too, son. What this means, though, is that Melanie is most likely Melissa's grandmother on the Witch side. If Melanie is able to be healed, she will probably want to meet her granddaughter. Please prepare Melissa and her other grandparents for that possibility."

"I will, sir. Thank you for the information. Please let us know how it goes."

"I will. Please tell Allihies to be expecting my call. He will remain point of contact and mission head for the Valerian's Cove part of this mess."

"Yes, sir."

General O'Shea ended the call. Tony looked up at Chief Kenny, who had wandered into Tony's office in the middle of the conversation. Chief Kenny raised an eyebrow. Tony filled him in.

"Well. It seems like a lot of old wrongs are coming to light. I hope they can be laid to rest, and those involved healed."

"Me too, sir. Me, too."

۞

Mel's Irish grandparents stayed in Valerian's Cove.

"We'll stay until this is all sorted out," Eimear declared staunchly. "We're not leaving our girl to go through this alone. And, we want to meet Melanie. I feel so sorry for the poor woman. I hope we can help her heal."

Lady Niamh and Lady Caroline, Fae Mind Mages in the Unseelie Court who sometimes worked with the Council, spent several weeks with Melanie. There were almost forty years of trauma to be healed, after all. Finally, Melanie was deemed well enough to travel. She wanted to meet Melissa. DNA tests, both magical and mundane, had concluded that Melissa was definitely her granddaughter. Which rather proved her story that Eddie had not died in the car accident. With Louisa's visions, and Sinéad's, they were able to figure out at least a part of the story. Paul must have been Deravalen Councilman Shor's brother. He had traveled to the Earth realm, and chosen Melanie to bear his child. Most likely because of her strong Gift as an Water Witch.

"It looks like she was part of this whole breeding program," Malia commented.

"But then why didn't he kidnap her? Why, when all the others went missing? Including his son's choice, Brianna?" Liz asked. They were discussing the mystery during a slow time at Wonder. It was late morning, and their afternoon helpers wouldn't be in for another couple of hours, yet.

"I don't know. Maybe she would have been too missed? Maybe there wasn't an easy way to grab her?"

"Or maybe," Liz said slowly, "Maybe they wanted someone who was raised in this realm, and could more easily pass, like a sleeper agent."

"Like Jer and Dawna were sleeper agents?"

"Yes, exactly. Only, for the bad guys."

Tony ran this idea by Major Allihies, who ran it by General O'Shea.

"That's something to be considered. There may be more like him, if that's so. We'll start looking into sudden deaths of teenagers and at least one of their parents together. Tell Malia and her friend thank you."

"But how would no one have noticed, when he came back?" Liz asked the following day. She had been turning the whole thing over in her mind. It was fast becoming an obsession to figure it out.

Malia leaned a hip on the counter by the pay terminal.

"You know, you're right. He can't have been using his own last name, and must have been using forged documents."

Tony entered the store right at that very convenient moment, and both women turned to him.

"What? Do I have something on my face?"

"Was Eddie Garza using his own name when he stalked Brianna?"

"No, actually. He was using a different last name, and forged documents. He was identified through Mel's DNA and old photo records. George was using his own name. Remember, he disappeared around the same time as Brianna and Aoife. It's possible that he was unaware of who and what Eddie really was. George may be as much of a victim as the girls in this whole mess."

"There's a lot more going on here than we are aware of, yet, isn't there," Malia stated woodenly.

Tony hugged her, pulling her tight against him. He knew she was worried for their children, and feeling the pain of all those children lost, those that might never be found.

"I think there is, sweetheart. It seems like they deliberately chose certain people for certain things. Some had children that were allowed to grow up here, some were taken elsewhere. Some were used as test subjects, like Mel. And there is probably a lot we still don't know. You're right about that."

"I hope we get it all figured out, and this is all over soon," Malia mumbled against his chest. Her voice hitched as if she were crying.

"I do, too, sweetheart," Tony said, as he looked over her head at Liz, whose own eyes were filled with tears. Behind the tears, an angry fire burned.

❧ 38 ❧

Melanie arrived in Valerian's Cove on a Wednesday afternoon. She arrived just after lunchtime, while Melissa was still in school.

"We'll bring her straight to you after school gets out, Melanie," Major Allihies told her. "Until then, would you like to get settled into the inn? Or, if you're feeling up for it, Eimear and Daniel McKenna would very much like to meet you."

Melanie was still wan and pale after her ordeal. Having forty years of compulsion, memories, and drugs sorted through and rearranged in her mind had been grueling. Remembering her life with Paul had been no walk in the park, either. When the compulsion had lifted, presumably when he had left the Earth realm, her true memories of her time with him had returned. They were not pretty.

"I would like to meet the McKennas, please, Major," Melanie said softly.

So Major Allihies arranged for the McKennas to meet them in the lounge at the inn.

Melanie waited restlessly for the McKennas to come down from their room. Eimear swept into the lounge, her hands held out to

Melanie. When she reached her, she pulled the stunned woman into a tight embrace.

"I'm so sorry for all you've gone through, sweetheart. No one should ever have to lose a child, and no one should ever have to endure the things you've gone through. You're with family now, though, and we'll see this through together."

Melanie relaxed into the other woman's hold, sobbing. After a long moment, she stepped back, wiping her eyes. Daniel handed her a box of tissues. She took a handful, then handed the box to Eimear, whose eyes were also damp.

"I was going to apologize to you," Melanie said with a hitch in her voice. "I mean, it's my son that kidnapped your daughter. This is all my fault. If I had been able to get someone to listen to my story, to believe me... I guess I just didn't try hard enough."

Major Kevin Allihies cleared his throat.

"Actually, Ms. Garza, someone did believe your story. That's why you were committed to begin with. It seems that the SOC operative that you spoke to after your son's accident was somehow working with Paul. He covered everything up, and is the one responsible for your being sent to the sanitarium. We've since discovered that he vanished soon after, himself. None of this is your fault, at all. It never was. You are as much a victim as anyone else in this whole mess."

Melanie broke down in tears again. Eimear pulled her onto one of the two green brocade sofas in the room, and put her arms around the other woman. She held on until Melanie's sobs began to fade.

Dawna and Jer picked Mel up from school. Malia and Marissa were waiting for them at the inn, along with the McKennas, Major Allihies, and a very nervous Melanie. Melanie stood up as Melissa entered the room. She reached out towards Mel, then drew her hand back.

Dawna led Mel up to her new grandmother.

"Mel, this is Melanie Garza, your father's mother. Ms. Garza, this is Melissa. She goes by Mel."

Melanie smiled, a tiny little smile. Her lips trembled as her eyes filled with tears again.

"I do, too," she whispered.

Mel smiled her own tiny little smile back.

Melanie reached out again, this time brushing a lock of hair away from Mel's face. Mel's hair was the same color as her grandmother's.

"You have your father's eyes," she said. "You get them from my mother." She turned to Eimear and Daniel.

"She looks just like our Brianna," Eimear said, gently. "Brianna had blue eyes, too."

Melanie smiled. "My mother always said her blue eyes came from an Irish pirate that was sent to the colonies and ended up married there. He was killed in a fight when she was young."

Melanie turned back to Melissa.

"I am so very glad to meet you, sweetheart," she said gently.

Mel reached up, and placed her hand over her grandmother's, which had come to rest on her cheek.

Eimear stood and drew them both into a hug. Daniel followed, holding all three women close. Mel held onto her grandmothers in the center. Her adoptive parents had never been good at showing love or affection. Sometimes, she had felt starved for the kind of all-encompassing hug she was receiving now. True loving touch. She hadn't realized how much, until she'd met Eimear. And now, Melanie.

Marissa cleared her throat and stood up.

"I think this is going very well, given the circumstances. Major, I'll be at the clinic until six tonight, if you need me. Otherwise, you can reach me at home. I think you can do without a Mind Healer right now. I am happy to work with everyone as needed, of course. Right now, just let them be together."

"Thank you for coming, Healer Casey-Thorndike. I will reach out when we need you." He nodded to Malia, who had accompanied her sister. Malia would report back to Tony on how the meeting had gone. The Caseys left the inn, and the new family inside.

Major Allihies cleared his own throat.

"Mr. McKenna."

Daniel looked over at him, his arms still around his family.

"I'll leave you to get to know each other. Lieutenant, I trust you will take Mel home when it's time, and look after her."

"Of course, Major."

"Then I'll talk more with you tomorrow." Kevin Allihies looked back at the family, still huddled in their multi-armed hug, as he left.

Eventually, Eimear, Melanie and Melissa sat on the sofa, Mel in the middle.

"I'm sure you have so many questions," Melanie said to Mel. Mel nodded.

"It's like, I don't even know where to begin. Grandma Eimear showed me photos of my mom—that's how we found you, actually. There was a photo of her with my dad. Before they left Ireland together. Somehow, the SOC used the photo and my blood to figure it out."

"I'm so glad they did, sweetheart," Melanie replied. "I can tell you what your father was like as a boy, up until the accident. I can tell you what I remember of your grandfather. I can tell you about my family. I have a sister, though we're not very close, even though we're twins. My parents died young, unfortunately. We're still not completely sure what happened. My sister and I drifted apart after that. We had such very different personalities and interests. But she has children, so you have more family in Australia and England, too."

Dawna looked up sharply when Melanie mentioned not being aware of how her parents died.

"Melanie, excuse me. What do you mean, you weren't sure how your parents died?"

"They passed when my sister and I were eighteen. We'd just finished secondary school. My sister wanted to be a Healer—she could tell when there was something wrong with a person's blood. So she went to the Healer's College in England. I wanted to be a teacher, and to stay near the water I loved at home. So I attended the Australian Paranormal University, and came home to teach. My parents always encouraged us to follow our dreams." She paused and took a breath.

"Anyway, just after we finished secondary school, they were on a boat researching something off the coast a few miles—they were both marine biologists, studying paranormal sea life—when there was a freak storm. The boat was lost with all hands. Even with two Water Mages and several other highly talented Water Witches on board. It never made sense to us, but we found the...." Melanie's voice petered out as she stared at Dawna in growing horror.

"Oh my gods. This has happened before, hasn't it. My parents... they might not be dead."

"There are striking similarities to your son's story, Ms. Garza," Daniel commented gently.

"But I know both my parents were Witches. I know it."

"You said that there were other highly-talented Witches on board. And that they were *all* lost?" Dawna clarified.

Melanie nodded. "The boat was found drifting at sea, showing damage from what looked like a major storm. One had been reported off the coast the night before. The Coast Guard still doesn't know what to make of it, to this day. We get rogue storms, but to lose all hands, with no trace...."

"No bodies were ever found?"

Melanie shook her head.

Dawna turned to her mate. "Jer, get Major Allihies back here. We need the names and families of everyone on that boat."

Jer jumped to his feet and left the room, taking his phone out of his pocked as he walked.

Melanie stared into space, her mind completely overwhelmed.

"Melanie," Daniel McKenna said, gently. "I think, maybe, that you should rest. You and Melissa will have a lifetime to reconnect. We can try again tomorrow. As soon as Major Allihies has had a chance to look into your parents' deaths, I think you should call your sister. Ok? You need her, I think."

"We were closer, when we were younger," Melanie whispered. "We've just, I don't know, drifted apart, somehow. I'm not very good about staying in touch."

"But you know how to reach her?" Eimear asked.

Melanie nodded.

"Good. Let's do that, then. We'll give her a call as soon as we know something."

MAJOR ALLIHIES ENDED THE CONVERSATION WITH JER AND TURNED to Chief Kenny.

"Sir, I need to call the General. Another piece of information has come to light."

Chief Kenny nodded and led the Major to his office. Then the Kodiak left the Major alone. He went back out to reception and looked at Louanne.

"What's up, Chief?"

"Lou, I think you'd better get the Alliance Council on the line. Things are speeding up. I'm no Seer, but I have a feeling something big is coming. Sooner than we'd like. Also, call Tony, and warn him to be on guard."

"What do you want me to tell the Alliance Council?"

"Tell them to talk to their Seers. Tell them to search their records in all their realms for all missing and suddenly suspiciously dead people over the last several hundred years, if they aren't already doing it. And tell them to be ready."

GENERAL O'SHEA SIGHED WHEN MAJOR ALLIHIES FINISHED HIS report.

"Son, I'm going to tell you, I'm not surprised to hear what you're telling me. We've started to turn up stories of such things on all continents in the Earth realm. We're waiting to hear back from the others. We're also working with the Deravalen Council to find all people of Deravalen descent on Earth. Their Mages have come up with a way of tracking their blood, and their magic. They've just begun. The suspicion is that we're going to find a lot more than we, or they, were aware of."

"So, you think there were other rogue Deravalens on Earth, breeding with highly talented Witches, for whatever this plan is?"

"We're pretty sure of it. It would be illogical to leave it up to one man, especially since we've seen that Paul stayed with his family for thirteen years. One man could hardly breed an army, as much as he may have tried."

"But he was on tour a lot, according to Ms. Garza. He could have had other families, too."

"You're right, and it's being looked into. If he did, though, he hid them very well. Like we told young Melissa, we didn't find her DNA anywhere else. Which means they were kept out of all systems, or the records were altered."

"Do you think that the other children were used as test subjects, like Melissa, or turned into agents, like Eddie?"

"Probably both, Major. We need to be prepared for whatever we find. And if we do find more young people, like Melissa, we'll have to be prepared to help them heal and to educate them in their Deravalen Gifts. That new Academy in Fairweather Falls had better be prepared."

"Sir, about that. Will Melissa need to transfer to Fairweather Falls? She's only just gotten used to being in school in a magical Academy here."

"She will be required to transfer, yes. The Fairweather Falls Academy is the center for Deravalen training at this time. But I think we can wait until the end of the current school year. Give her a little time to settle, to get used to all the new family and Gifts that've been thrown at her recently."

"Thank you, sir. I appreciate the concern being shown for her well-being."

"Are you getting soft on me, Major? You sound like you care for the girl."

Major Allihies blushed.

"Um, I think her grandmother, Melanie, is my Fated Mate, sir."

"Well, congratulations, son. And take it slow. That family has been through a whole hell of a lot, and it's not over yet."

39

The Seers were on high alert. The Alliance Council and the SOC were searching for, and finding, other Deravalen descendants. Mel was getting to know her new family. And Rebecca's business was expanding more rapidly than she had ever expected. Lily had spoken to Rebecca one day after fight practice, and told her it was time for Flora to start focusing on armor. And for Rebecca to start charming her jewelry as protection amulets.

"But I haven't even met Sarah yet, that High Magic Mage you told me about," Rebecca protested. "Don't I need her to create the talismans?"

"She'll be here soon. You start working on your designs," Lily instructed.

So, Rebecca did. Around Bealtaine, in May, Malia called Rebecca in the middle of the morning. Rebecca, who had been in the middle of trying to work out an incredibly frustrating design, was glad of the interruption.

"What's up, Malia?"

"Bex, come down to the police station, would you, please? Now?"

Rebecca waved her hand at Lars and the Deravalen metalsmith that Andor had found to help her teach. She had also contracted with a

Fae, a Dragon, and a Phoenyx. They would start in the new school year, after the summer. Lars nodded at her, so she dropped her pencil, put her sketches away, and headed for the door.

"I'm coming now. How important is it? Do I need to find a Dragon to teleport me?"

As she stepped out of the door, a young dragon Guard greeted her.

"Lily sent me," he said. "I'm to take you into town now."

"Never mind, Malia. Lily sent me a Dragon. I'll be there in a minute."

The young Guard took them right outside the police station.

"I'll wait here for you, your Highness," he said, standing at parade rest.

Rebecca still had trouble with the idea that technically, since she and Sean were mated, she was now a princess of the Fire Mountain Dragon Clan. Usually, she managed to tuck that knowledge away and forget about it.

Rebecca strode into the reception area, where Louanne smiled up at her from behind the desk.

"They're in the conference room, Bex. Go right in."

"Thanks, Louanne," Rebecca waved as she hurried past.

At the door of the conference room, she paused, taking in the large group of people sitting at the table. Chief Kenny, Tony, Major Allihies, who had managed to stay attached to Valerian's Cove as their representative to the SDSF branch and the SOC, Malia, Dawna and Jer, and, sitting next to Malia, a young woman about her own age, with long, straight brown hair pulled into a braid over her left shoulder. She looked up as Rebecca stood there, her gaze locking on Rebecca's own. What felt like a lightning bolt passed between them.

"Sarah," Rebecca breathed.

STAY IN TOUCH!

Want to stay in touch? Join my newsletter for updates on new books and other fun stuff from me! There will be no spam-just news about upcoming releases, sales and promotions, freebies and some fun facts about the worlds and characters in my books.

THANK YOU!

Thank you for reading *Tangled Webs*! This was Book Five in the Valerian's Cove series. The Caseys will return shortly.

If you liked the book, please leave a review. As an indie author, good reviews help ratings, which in turn helps sales. So they are really important! Also, I enjoy hearing from readers who have read my creations. Honest opinions help me to know what I can do better to improve my storytelling. Please let me know what you liked most! If there is a character that you would like to see developed further or even given their own story, please let me know. Thank You!

ACKNOWLEDGMENTS

To all of my friends and family who have supported me thus far in my author journey, thank you. I love you.

Also, I would like to thank my mother, Teren de Cossy, for reading and editing for me! I really appreciate it!

Thank you!

ABOUT THE AUTHOR

H.C. de Cossy (Hetty Cate) writes paranormal fiction. She lives on the Pacific Coast with her son and two cats. Hetty Cate has family all over the place. She loves to travel, paint, dance, and sing. She occasionally makes her own clothing, chocolate and costumes. She has always felt close to fairies, nature and the paranormal world.

www.hettycate.com

ALSO BY H.C. DE COSSY

PARANORMAL FAMILY MYSTERY

The Valerian's Cove Series

Waken the Witch

Broken Bonds

The Sword of Fire

Alliances

Tangled Webs

The Sola Blake Trilogy

Hidden Witch

Spirit Walker

Fate Weaver

The Fairweather Falls Series

Herbs and Homecomings

Potions and Possibilities (Forthcoming)

www.ingramcontent.com/pod-product-compliance
Lightning Source LLC
Chambersburg PA
CBHW070849250626
47159CB00003B/1002